AN INHUMAN
WORD

MICHAEL SPINNEY

For Kate, Rebecca and James with love.

CONTENTS

ACKNOWLEDGMENTS

With deep appreciation and heartfelt thanks to those who shone a light where I was in the dark: David Moore, Ted Espir, Tim Hennessey, Steve Nesbitt, Dr Paul Jeffrey, Lieutenant General Sir Mark Mans, Jude Collins, Jeremy Spinney, Edward Stanton, and also to my wife, Caroline whose proofreading endeavour was Herculean! Jenny Munro as my critical reader issued challenges that helped me to focus.

Alexis Kandra has allowed me to use her wonderful picture of Leda and the Swan for the cover and I am profoundly grateful.

Why not see Helen
as the sun saw her with no Homeric shadow,
swinging her plastic sandals on the beach alone
as fresh as the sea wind.

Derek Walcott – *Omeros*

India and Pakistan

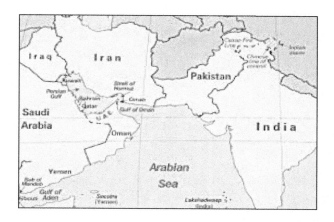

East and West Punjab

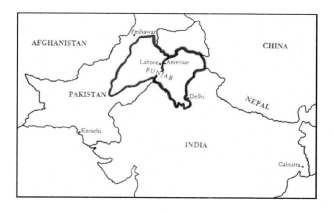

For anyone interested in the classical influence upon this story
there is an account at the end of the novel.

PROLOGUE

Troy, Greece, 1184 BC

Bobbing effortlessly and serenely in the middle of the lake the swan unfolded its great wings and with Herculean thrust drove forward explosively. With that one movement it released such colossal energy that it was lifted clear of the surface and its wingbeats caused currents and eddies in the water below as it lumbered forward. Stepping across the ripples it gained speed and breaking the earth's hold became airborne. Ascending, it triangulated, orientating its course in preparation for the long-awaited journey.

It circled and for the last time looked down upon the ruined landscape. As it gained height, and the perspective flattened, the battlefields below diminished, although there was no disguising the devastation of a land mired in the blood of recurring destruction, a riven terrain soaked in tragedy. The swan perceived the indifference of the men walking below, immune to the suffering they had caused and inured to the grief, misery and woe that accompanied their war. Pools of vermilion blood stretched behind them across a decade all the way from Troy to Sparta.

Dusk was approaching, as the great bird made one last circuit over the breached walls where a beautiful, tousled, flaxen-haired woman stared upwards to meet its gaze, the face that had launched a thousand ships.

The swan made a compass adjustment and aligned its heading, looking now towards the heavens where a black universe filled with points of cold light would guide it unerringly on a journey, a passage that would be hard and long. But, unlike the voyages of men, its course would not be charted by ambition, greed and revenge.

Making a final turn the mighty bird looked down for the last time and noted the pain and despair etched on the face of the mortal goddess who had brought ruin upon her world. Was it possible human history would be influenced by her tragic story, or only inevitable that human nature and human misery would always walk side by side, hand in hand?

Much, much later the swan began its spiral descent above a Norfolk marsh, where, looking down upon the brittle, cold, silvery mere, it observed another strikingly beautiful flaxen-haired woman approaching a small hut perched on the coastline. The woman looked up and, momentarily, their eyes locked before, with a minimum of fuss, the cob made its landing deploying its webbed feet to lose speed and folding its great wings. It alighted gently beside the pen patiently awaiting its return.

ACT ONE

Punjab, India, 1947

The nine-year-old, Zuraib, ducked into the tall, white, frond-waving maiden grass that grew thickly beside the school wall and prayed that the boys chasing him, armed with machetes and murderous intent, would pass by. He knew his life depended upon remaining concealed from his pursuers who were consumed by a blood lust that would only be assuaged when they had hacked him, or some other unfortunate son of Islam, to death.

Random acts of violence had been erupting in isolated pockets around the city for weeks, but mere brutality had now escalated into something more organised and systematic. Zuraib neither understood the reasons why or the fear and hatred that was the cause, he had been on his way to meet his older sister from school when they spotted and cornered him.

They surrounded him, and their intent was to cause him grievous harm. He could see hatred in their expression, malevolence that was simultaneously hot and cold, full of loathing and merciless. He looked into the eyes of the leader and knew he had to make the first move and so, without signalling his intention, swung his school bag at the youth's head while extracting a knife he kept hidden in his belt. Relying upon momentum and surprise he capitalised upon his advantage with a crippling stab to the boy's stomach, noting the increased resistance as the sharp blade perforated the abdominal wall.

Immediately he reversed direction, plucking his knife from the wounded assailant, while delivering a vicious kick to the kneecap of the boy on his right that resulted in a bellow of pain and fury.

Without waiting he ran into the third and pushed him to the ground, setting off as fast as he was able.

Unnoticed within the dense brush of bush Zuraib crouched perfectly still, nerves stretched as tight as elastic, and listened until the disgruntled voices began to recede, at which point he eased aside some of the long bamboo-like stalks and risked a look over the wall of his sister's school where, in his worst imaginings, he could never have conceived such a sight as that which faced him. Fifteen or twenty of the older Muslim schoolgirls had been rounded up and forced into the school playground where they were stripped naked.

As Zuraib watched, the men were seized by a sexual frenzy and fell upon the girls, irrespective of age. They were indiscriminate in their brutality and yet the fortitude of the young women was extraordinary for they did not scream or shout, a lack of response that seemed to goad the men to greater depravity. Then the girls were ordered onto their knees and butchered without mercy; in a matter of minutes what had been a children's playground had become a charnel field littered with mutilated bodies. Shocked beyond comprehension, Zuraib looked at the carnage before him in a state of stupefied horror and, incredulous, could only stare until mind and body began to function again as one, when his only thought was to run for the safety of home.

Ducking and weaving through alleys and passages Zuraib managed to avoid marauding packs of noisy, homicidal men as he bolted for the only protection he knew, that of his parents. He scuttled through backyards and gardens of the houses in his neighbourhood until he reached what he believed would be sanctuary.

His father, a learned man, trusted and respected in the community, was a teacher at the University where he lectured on trust law and economics. His mother devoted her life to her family and the local community as a support visitor to those most in need. Together they had always worked hard to ensure Zuraib and his sister grew up in a happy home and there had been much rejoicing recently when they shared the news that they were expecting another child.

As Zuraib approached the door at the rear of the house his nervousness turned into foreboding for it had been ripped from its hinges. He entered timorously and tiptoed through the cooking area towards the comfortable room where the family spent most of their evenings. It was at the base of the stairs that he found his father's body spread-eagled; his throat slashed and open, gaping like some ghastly maw, a pool of blood congealing on the floor beside his lifeless corpse. Flies were already gorging. There was worse to come. His mother was laid out neatly on the rug inside the front room as if asleep but with breasts laid bare, below which her abdomen had been opened from ribs to pelvis and the foetus she was carrying removed. Placed side by side, mother and child were still joined by a white umbilical cord.

Zuraib's mind could not cope with the horror and he crept upstairs and into bed where he curled up and fell into a disturbed sleep, unconscious to a world too painful to inhabit.

When he awoke, light was streaming through the window and, with complete clarity, he recalled the events he had witnessed. He tried not to open his mind to the images of horror, but they forced themselves upon him grievously. At first he could not bring himself to stir but then he heard movement below and knew looters were in the building. Once again immediate action was required. An agile boy who had often left the house through the bedroom window, he dropped onto the roof of an annexe and lowered himself into an adjacent passageway from where he was instantly absorbed into the labyrinth of alleys and channels that intersected the closely built houses. He knew his only course of action was to escape the city and travel to the new country of Pakistan where his uncle lived. Following a very imprecise route he set off for the railway station hoping that he would be unremarkable in the crowds now moving through the city, knowing that if caught his *khitan* would prove his death warrant.

The station was awash with humanity so dense that he wondered if he would ever make it to where trains departed for Lahore. By dint of perseverance and progress at knee height he managed to wriggle through a forest of legs until he emerged near platform 14 from where he remembered his family had departed when they last made the journey. No one paid any attention to a child on his own.

He had expected to see a mass of people hanging like a swarm of bees from the train but was faced with a very different scene for the coaches were deserted. When he stole closer, he understood why; viscous blood was dripping through the planks of the carriages forming large puddles beneath. This train was not going anywhere. Unable to face the sight of any more slaughter he slipped away.

Zuraib had no idea where to go or what to do, so he just allowed himself to be swept up in the torrent of people flowing out of the city. Without making any conscious decision he was drawn into an apparently endless stream of humanity, and like everyone else around him he kept walking. Within hours he was numb, exhausted, tortuously thirsty, disorientated and utterly confused. It seemed as if he had placed one foot in front of another for as long as he could remember and he stumbled, in great danger of being trodden underfoot by the insensible mass behind. At just the moment he would have fallen he was unexpectedly grasped from above and deposited in the back of a bullock cart where there was a stoppered skin of water from which he drank before squirrelling himself between some large baskets and falling asleep.

Hours passed and then days, all in mindless succession. The only thing of which he could be sure was that he was still alive, while those he loved were not. Occasionally he was passed a piece of maize bread and a little water to drink from a calabash gourd.

With each successive day the cart was surrounded by a deeper and deeper throng of humanity swelling like a vast migratory confluence that he could not know stretched for fifty miles. As it flowed the interminably long caravan sometimes parted, like a river around rocks, as those too heavily burdened shed the weight of their possessions. He watched one woman, who no longer had the strength to support her infant, place it beside the road before she was carried on and away.

In the end his journey concluded at a refugee camp in Pakistan where Zuraib gave thanks to Allah for his salvation. Having been plucked at random from inevitable death during the long march he was handed over to workers at a camp near Lahore where, by another miracle, he was interviewed by someone who knew of his relative. Uncle and nephew were united, and his father's brother solemnly undertook to ensure that his newly adopted son would receive every possible advantage of education and social advancement.

*

It took many, many months before the night horrors and tremors that haunted Zuraib began to fade. His sleep was always disrupted, and he would wake early, which was when he would slip out of the house undetected.

He loved the hours following dawn when the air was fresh and the light flawless; the dewy grass tickling his feet through his sandals. He was free to roam in any direction that took his fancy, and on some mornings he went into the city where he watched the early risers preparing for the day.

Hot, flat loaves prepared by the bakers and charred at the edges gave off tantalising, crisp whiffs and the fragrance of caramelising onions always provoked his hunger. The sweet aroma of samosas and chaats drew him to the women cooking, and if he was lucky, he might just be offered a fresh, hot, tangy, soft, stuffed and doughy, mirchi bajji, newly fried.

That early in the morning market traders were preparing their stalls, some setting out tables of vegetables of all colours, sizes and shapes, and others opening sacks of spices, the musk of which hung in the air like smoke.

He watched, fascinated, as chicken sellers reached into large woven baskets plucking out birds that looked around angrily before a cleaver removed their head, iron ringing out against hard wood. Rivulets of metallic-smelling blood emptied into runnels between the butchers' legs and rapidly eviscerated offal was chucked into one bucket while plucked feathers were deposited in another. The carcasses were strung on strings for sale and it always seemed to him that the discarded heads looked at him accusingly, like those of the girls at the school.

Sometimes he would deliberately set out to provoke his own fear by exploring the network of alleyways and paths that criss-crossed the town where peril lurked in dark passages, especially down by the muddy and sulphurous river. He learned to be invisible and to flit between buildings.

On other days he would leave town and head out into the forest beyond the city where wide branched trees offered cool shade and the river ran fast in spring bringing meltwater down from far away mountains. When he stripped and leaped into the water the cold would take his breath away.

On one occasion climbing back onto the bank Zuraib saw a large banded krait resting on his clothes where he had left them to warm on the rocks. The boy waited and watched the snake with its distinctive yellow and maroon vertical stripes. After a while it turned and looked at him dismissively before slipping away, slithering slowly into a stygian black crack in the rock. The thought of the terror it would unleash in the underworld made him shudder.

Unable to shake this image Zuraib became convinced the krait had issued him a challenge, and so one morning he cut a forked stick and waited patiently by the rocks knowing the snake would return to bask. When it emerged it looked around languidly, its black pronged tongue flicking across dry lips. In its unblinking stare the boy saw utter contempt. He watched knowing not to make any sudden movement until, gradually, it grew soporific in the sun, which was when he struck, trapping its neck in the V of the stick. The reptile writhed unleashing a strength that surprised the boy who struggled to hold it down knowing the cost of failure. It managed a half turn to look up at him, baring its fangs tipped with glistening poison, which was when he struck with the kukri slicing its head from its body. The loathsome length thrashed convulsively on the ground, and in that moment Zuraib was overwhelmed by an atavistic sense of elation, revenge and conquest at his triumph.

Zuraib was a solitary, introspective boy fascinated by how the creatures of the forest killed. He observed numerous predators and their methods, and in the end concluded the most fascinating were the patient wolf spiders who constructed large, elaborate webs across bushes in the forest; a lattice beautiful and glistening like filigree. Fashioned from steel-strong silk, pliable but tensile, they spun and repaired their webs, endlessly weaving snares perfect in geometry and measurement. Zuraib learned that a web is flexible and intricate, and its effectiveness lies in a design that combines complexity with elasticity. When satisfied with its construction the spider waits silently until its victim becomes hopelessly trapped and then it kills with deadly efficiency.

If he were ever to hatch a plot, he would weave a beautifully convoluted web in which to enmesh his prey. He would be patient and then when the time was right, he would strike with the speed of a snake. He would be cunning and pitiless.

*

As he matured, he wanted to learn about the events that had resulted in the murderous violence in which his family had been caught and he sought understanding from his uncle.

The old man explained that hostility had been building for months as the separation of an ancient continent into two countries approached, one for Muslims and the other for Hindus and Sikhs. In June 1947 the British announced the end of their rule, the Raj, but then they brought forward their departure date without attempting to negotiate a peaceful agreement between the ethnic groups. This resulted in violence that spiralled out across the continent.

"At midnight on the 14 August 1947," his uncle told him. "The British Raj was replaced by two self-governing countries, India for the Hindus and Sikhs and the new country of Pakistan for the Muslims. It was this that led to the displacement of millions of people and resulted in the genocide and overwhelming refugee crisis in which you were caught."

Fascinated by the history of his nation Zuraib read voraciously:

"The ethnic violence that followed Partition broke down established relationships as communities and neighbourhoods embarked upon ferocious purges that initiated mass migration in both directions; the newly-formed governments were completely unequipped to deal with a refugee crisis of such magnitude. Estimates of deaths later exceeded two million as religious nationalism rapidly turned to retributive genocide… for centuries India was a liberal, cosmopolitan, tolerant country where all religions lived prosperously in a generally progressive society, but after 1947 the divisions between the peoples of the new two-nation state, were so damaged by Partition that hostility and suspicion became a permanent rupture, nowhere more so than in the wealthy region of Punjab which was separated into east and west. The British were responsible for a crime against humanity for which they have never atoned."

As time passed the years of accumulated hurt, loss, pain and hatred found a focus within Zuraib, that consolidated around a single purpose, revenge. Revenge for his father, mother, sister and the unborn child his mother carried, but also revenge for his religion, his nation and his people.

When the time came for Zuraib to leave school he was drafted into the army where he flourished and hoped for the day when he would have the opportunity to live up to his name, the name Zuraib being derived from one of the Prophet's companions, Zuraib ibn Naqeer ibn Sumair; Zuraib denoting a 'fierce attacker', a noun formed from the verb 'to strike'.

*

Zuraib studied hard and was considered an outstanding student, although more of an academic than fighting soldier, and it was for his strategic and tactical capability that his name came to the attention of the intelligence services. After receiving his Commission, he served as a logistics officer and was gradually introduced to more covert activities. At a relatively young age he was selected to attend the Command and Staff College where he excelled and was rapidly promoted to rank of Colonel. He did not serve on the frontline in the war with India of 1965 but saw action in 1971, which was when it first became clear to him that if he were to accomplish his self-imposed mission it would not be as a conventional soldier.

In 1973 Zuraib Gush ceased to exist and Zuraib Nasir (one who strikes for victory) came into being, almost always referred to in closed circles as *The Colonel*.

ACT TWO

England, 1991

The dining room at Sandringham, the British Royal Family's Norfolk retreat, combines elegance and grandeur with an unpretentiousness that belies its status. The intricately embossed, plastered ceiling contributes to a sense of refinement, as does the detailed mural from a collection of Spanish tapestries presented to the Prince of Wales in 1876 by Alphonso XII of Spain.

When the winter evenings close in and dusk descends, the curtains are drawn, and the long drapes bestow an intimacy to a room where tall doors stand like sentinels. The bay window harbours a small, exquisite circular table inlaid with intricate marquetry on top of which on this evening has been placed a vase of long-stemmed gladioli, casa lilies, alstroemeria and scented freesias that convey colour and vibrancy to a room that might otherwise seem stiff and formal. The atmosphere this particular winter's evening is one of warm, comfortable seclusion rather than pomp.

Dividing the room along its length is a long, highly polished, mahogany table capable of seating eighteen, although tonight it is laid for twelve. As might be expected the silver cutlery and Waterford lead crystal glass has been placed with exact, glittering precision and military alignment, an ensemble that catches and reflects the light from small lamps that stand to attention.

An atmosphere of conviviality and welcome contentment is enhanced by a crackling log fire that creates dancing shadows and a soft luminescence. It is perfect for those in the afterglow of a day's shooting.

That morning the bleached, denim-blue, wintry sky had held a suggestion of snow although, as it transpired, the weather proved ideal for the shoot. As they walked along muddy paths and tracks frozen glassy puddles cracked and splintered behind them and galvanized metal gates, decorated with a tracery of silvery fern-shaped patterns and welded shut by the cold, snapped open with pistol-shot reverberations. Stiff, dark, decomposing leaves formed stylised William Morris designs along the fringe of the woods and as the morning progressed a watery sun offered a little warmth and the overnight frost made wispy mist retreat into the woods, although in the lee of any shadows the ground remained as hard as concrete when they made their way to their pegs.

On her wedding day Leda had been given by her husband a 'Royal Deluxe' 12 bore shotgun fashioned with exquisite care and craftsmanship by Holland & Holland. It was a work of art that she adored and cradling it in her arm that cold and bracing morning she felt energised.

Leda was an excellent shot, her reactions being instinctive and well-practised. She combined speed with composure and so gained extra moments that ensured accuracy. In the morning she had picked out the partridge unerringly as they were driven over the trees, and during the afternoon beat she was just as proficient locking on to the devilishly elusive teal as they bobbed over the hedgerows weaving ahead and above her. Once she had fixed upon the trajectory of a bird her poise, balance and fluidity of movement usually resulted in a hit.

The day had been enjoyable and now, on this evening, in this room and in this company, she felt relaxed as she settled into the comfortable chair at the far end of the Prince's table indulging herself in the warmth of the fire and comfort of his hospitality.

She took a few moments to study her fellow guests, most compelling of which was the man sitting opposite smiling and engaging her in conversation. She knew of Lord Peter Baird by reputation, although they had never met. He had inherited his title at a young age and was reputedly very successful. She was sure she would enjoy the dinner.

When his attention was drawn by another guest, she observed him critically. Physically he was striking and displayed a sharp intelligence that revealed a wicked wit. There was about him a charm, a magnetism; charisma that he was now directing across the table at her. At a couple of inches over six foot he projected self-belief and she had heard it said that he exercised power and influence. Her impression was of a man who knew what he wanted from life and probably made sure he got it; as a woman she could tell he was interested in her.

His hair was cut short and his movements were neat, a man with a tidy and methodical mind she concluded. His tortoiseshell glasses and intense mien contributed to the impression of an academic; all in all, a striking character in control of events and a man about whom there was strength and an air of mystery.

He was amusing Margaret the Countess of Frome, seated on his left, who was clearly enamoured. Dressed in an evening gown she was every inch the image of a Dowager and when she talked it was in a thin reedy voice.

"People talk about you Peter, you are referred to as, what is the word? Oh yes 'enigmatic'. There is much speculation amongst the gals as to your marital status and no one seems to know what the initial C stands for in your name."

He had half turned towards the elderly lady listening to her with the same intensity he would afford a young and attractive female. It was clear that she was responding to him as a woman, albeit one old enough to be his grandmother.

"Well Countess there is no great secret. I am unmarried. My father was an ornithologist and academic of repute who made his reputation studying the social habits and lifecycles of swans. They are fascinating birds. Did you know for instance that swans mate for life, as I hope to when I meet the right woman, and it is said that when one swan dies the surviving partner perishes of a broken heart. The ancient Greeks believed that swans sing a beautiful song just before they die, their swansong."

"Oh my," twittered the old girl, "just imagine."

"In recognition of the reverence my father had for these graceful and sophisticated creatures he named me Peter Cygnus (which is Latin for swan), and there you have the explanation."

As Leda listened to his warm baritone, she noted that there was a refined sensitivity to his movements which were precise and displayed economy of expression.

His emerald green eyes sparkled with amusement, although not condescension, as he chatted with the Countess who was now espousing trenchant views that reflected her bigotry rather than, as she assumed, intellectual acuity. Leda tuned in to the sound of his mellifluous voice and was reminded obliquely of her cello, the velvety bass notes, deep and resonant with mellowness.

There was a slight lull in the conversation, and he transferred his attention back across the table, looking at Leda with an expression of such intense, piercing scrutiny that momentarily she felt herself redden and her pulse increase.

The general conversation turned from the killing of fowl to its conservation, the apex of the north Norfolk coast being devoted to both in equal measure. The day had begun with Peter having drawn a stand to the left of Leda's and when they broke for morning coffee, he congratulated her upon her skill as a huntress. Later he had teasingly referred to her as Diana and now as they dined, she suspected that he was embarking upon a different quest, one that began with oblique parries. He employed argument as his weapon of choice and probed to see how effectively she could construct an opinion and defend her point of view. She enjoyed these exchanges and subtly deflected his flirtatious arrows. She was pleased that she had him on the defensive once or twice but was taken by surprise when he suddenly changed tack and challenged her to join him the following morning, "To observe rather than shoot the wildlife that visits the shores of England in winter."

Her immediate reaction was to refuse as ornithology had never held any interest for her. "As far as I'm concerned," she said. "Birds are for sport and the pot. I match my skill with a beautifully fashioned, perfectly weighted gun, against the meticulously evolved dexterity of an elusive opponent." However, when he repeated his offer, she understood that he was issuing a challenge and she was not going to back down or concede an easy victory.

The Duchess wrestled back his attention and Leda glanced across at her husband, David Strachan, who appeared effete and ineffectual by comparison with this man who was bringing to bear upon her the full force of his masculinity and who was dancing a courtship ritual from the other side of the table.

David was a rising star in political circles, already a junior minister in a popular government; an academic whose intellectual brilliance as an economist contrasted with his ill-disposed ability to form close emotional relationships. An alumnus of Winchester College, and like so many thinkers Leda had known, probably at the mild end of the autistic spectrum; a brilliant academic who scored poorly in respect of sensitivity or empathy.

Tall, roman nosed, impeccably dressed, aristocratically suave and socially well-connected David lived in London during the week affecting an interest in her well-being, but more devoted to his work and epicurean lifestyle than her happiness. They had married because, on balance, it had seemed sensible and she, being pragmatic, recognised that marriage to him would offer her the lifestyle and security she sought; she had never experienced high passion and navigated her life according to the topography of expediency. As yet they were childless and while David looked after her with gentleness and generosity, it was without emotional attachment or intensity for theirs was in effect a marriage of convenience that suited them both.

Rather loftily David addressed Peter down the table. "I gather you read History at Balliol and I happen to know that you influence events, so tell me, given that we live in such interesting times, what do you conclude from your study of the past." There was a pause in the conversation around the table as the other guests tuned in.

"What do we learn from history?" Peter seemed to roll the question around, like a cat with a ball of wool, before replying. "Well, my conclusion is that human history is not linear, it is cyclic. Over time the human condition improves but not its humanity, at least not commensurately. Be it a society that is religious or secular, liberal or totalitarian the sands that underpin human behaviour are an unstable bedrock which means, and it is an unsavoury conclusion, when conflict erupts it is usually man's inhumanity that surfaces rather than his enlightened conduct; the first law of evolution being the survival of the fittest. In my experience history teaches that greed, ambition, intolerance, selfishness, prejudice, perversion and personal aggrandisement are at the root of most human struggles. It is these weaknesses that sanction and perpetuate the ceaseless corruption and exploitation we find in all societies and debases our ideal of what being human should be. With each revolution of the wheel honesty, integrity and civilised values are the victims. The Greek philosophers were the first to explore human nature and they created a society founded on progressive principles, but human weakness - envy, avarice and hatred - led to their destruction almost as they had predicted. So, it was then and has been ever since."

"That's a depressing conclusion. If human nature repeatedly undermines civilised behaviour, then the concept of social evolution is a chimera?" David challenged.

"It's only depressing if you are a pessimist, and despite what I have said I am not, for humans have a capacity for kindness, courage and even altruism, but, crucially, they need protection from the forces that grow from the weakness of their own natures, which is partly what we mean by 'civilisation'. But, as I say, the wheel revolves."

"And what of technology, man's creation?"

"Well, certainly technological evolution progresses rapidly, but only because it doesn't replicate its mistakes, which is my point."

As Leda listened to this exchange, she concluded that her

husband was pecking away at the other end of the table, completely unaware of what was taking place between this man and herself. David was far too wrapped up in his own opinions; the cock was crowing while the fox circled.

The evening concluded congenially. Leda agreed to accompany Peter early the next morning to a hide on the marshes near Blakeney, not far from Holkham Hall where the party were due to lunch.

As she slipped into bed and turned out the light and, accompanied by the trumpeting of her husband's breathing, she thought of Peter's penetrating green eyes which had held her gaze as hypnotically as a snake when they wished each other goodnight.

Leda

Leda awoke as the day began, and as she peeked through the curtains at the sunrise she was greeted by a perfect icy, crisp morning heralding another joyful, rosy dawn. The formal gardens were illuminated by the opalescent light slanting in from the east, bringing its geometric proportion into sharp relief. Hoar frost sparkled across the lawns and when she looked up, she revelled in the big sky, the vast expanse of powder blue that is such a feature of Norfolk. She felt buoyant and energised.

As she lay in her hot bath, she was aware of her body responding to an unconscious sense of anticipation and she took particular care choosing her clothes, seeking to combine warmth with allure. She decided upon a close-fitting cashmere pullover over a high collared shirt with a silk camisole below. To highlight her femininity, she went with a tailored woollen skirt, wide belt and hacking jacket. Medium denier stockings were held in place by a suspender belt, an anachronism in which she revelled, while her Dubarry 'Galway' slim fit boots seemed a sensible choice.

She was the first guest down to breakfast where the curtains were open allowing the low, early morning sunlight to flood the dining room in wide shafts that changed the mood from the intimacy of the previous evening into one of energy. She felt an eagerness for the outdoors and the day ahead.

She was soon joined by Peter who was neatly dressed, sporting a tie embossed with white swans woven into a burgundy silk background. He greeted her jovially.

The discreet house staff had filled the silver entrée dishes on the sideboard and a liveried young man popped in and out offering fresh tea and coffee and various shades of toast. She opted for kedgeree while Peter helped himself to sausages and devilled kidneys. "Just the meal to set me up for a cold morning," he exclaimed. Over breakfast he was jocular and attentive, amusing her with details of the various peccadilloes of some high-profile personalities; she was astonished at how well informed he was and entertained by his scurrilous indiscretions.

Peter's gleaming Bentley Continental awaited them on the drive. She was surprised by the level of security that attended him but did not know he had left strict instructions the close protection team were to remain at a distance.

The benign sky was accompanied by a bitingly cold east wind, a bitter but invigorating morning. Leda had left her husband asleep knowing he would awake to a filthy hangover, the product of too much wine, port and brandy, compounded by a fat Churchill cigar. He would not emerge for some time.

They purred across the countryside along the narrow roads that crisscross north-west Norfolk, a cosy and relaxing drive. Over the weathered hedgerows she saw gently undulating fields with their dark, rich dormant soil patiently anticipating spring, awaiting the seeds of renewal and abundance. Beyond was the coastline, as always dominated by the mood of the sea.

They passed the turning to Burnham Overy-Staithe, where Nelson learnt to sail, and on, almost silently, flitting through the village of Blakeney, from where she could make out across the marsh a windmill without sails standing erect against the horizon.

From the coast road Peter turned down a small track that took them along a deeply cut narrow lane enclosed by high banks, beyond which she caught glimpses of the marsh and cold, gun-metal grey sea. The lane petered out in a small car park made from compacted red carrstone surrounded by a low, dry-stone wall and more arthritic wind-blown hedgerows. When he turned off the engine she slid out from the cosy fug of the car and took a deep breath inhaling the cold, ozone-laden air tinged with the waft of sulphurous, oozy mud.

They crossed a wooden stile and Leda was immediately captivated by the rugged scene that stretched ahead of her. On the horizon, sky and marsh merged, and in between creeks and gullies extended out to the sea half a mile away. A landscape intersected by small inlets and rivulets ran like veins across the surface, which were starting to fill as the sea pumped its way back inland. Peter took her hand to steady her as they walked along a path constructed from wooden slats threaded with cable and she was relieved they were not having to wade across the malevolently glutinous mud. Minutes later, and to her surprise, they came across a low, concealed building designed into the landscape. He took out a key that opened a sliding door in the roof, resembling the hatch of a small boat, and clambered down the four steps easily. As she started to follow her attention was caught by a swan preparing to land. Fleetingly its beady eyes held hers and momentarily she experienced a curious mixture of excitement and sadness. Turning back, she stumbled and fell forward into his hands. He lowered her lightly to the floor where to her surprise and relief she noted that some heating had been activated. It took the edge off the steely cold when he closed the hatch.

Having sealed them in he walked across to the far side of the cabin where shutters covered glazed vision panels. By pulling on ropes he raised wooden blinds to reveal an uninterrupted, hundred and eighty-degree, view across the marshland.

"We should see some Wheatears, Redstarts and Pied Flycatchers because they are all fairly common. If we are lucky perhaps a Red-backed Shrike or even a Barbed Warbler and if extremely fortunate a Great Snipe might pop by."

"But I don't know anything about birds," Leda bemoaned. "You will have to educate me."

He handed her a pair of binoculars and she noticed that he already had some around his neck.

"I am here to be your guide and mentor for as long as you remain interested and are willing to learn."

In the middle of the room, affording a wide-angled view down to the sea, was a long, upholstered comfortably cushioned bench upon which they sat and from where he made muted suggestions as to the direction in which she should look. She concentrated and he guided her binoculars steering her hand with his. From time to time he leaned in close to whisper instructions and she was very aware of his proximity.

"There's an Icterine Warbler," he said in his low bass undertone. "Look – ten o'clock in the reeds just to the left of that stump." He moved her hand until suddenly, and with wonderful clarity, a bird popped into her vision. The little bird was the size of a finch with a vivid yellow colouring on its breast and mixed dark stripes on the plumage of its back and wings. She was captivated, and he told her to listen. When she strained to hear she could just make out its warbling song, it caused her to giggle with delight.

Over the next hour he tutored her in the technique of

distinguishing and viewing the natural life of the marshes and she began to understand why he had such a passion for observing birds in their natural habitat. She was moved by his obvious sensitivity, knowledge and dedication to the natural world and she thought to herself, '*He may be immensely powerful and influential in his world, but just now he is gentle and captivated by these delicate and fragile creatures.*' He seemed more at peace watching birds than blasting them out of the sky.

Leda sat back and observed this complex man more closely as he perched with his arms resting on a shelf below the window, balancing his binoculars, absorbed by what he was seeing. There was no doubt that he was handsome, a man in good physical condition accorded respect by men and women of influence and rank. Clearly intelligent and knowledgeable she knew he held considerable sway in the corridors of power, but this morning she saw only tenderness. Would she want to be seduced by him?

He turned and smiled at her with such intensity that she felt an urge to hug him, but he guided the binoculars back to her eyes and admonished her mildly, "You must be alert at all times." She thrilled at a new idiom she detected in his voice, a suppressed timbre that resonated. '*Yes, very seductive,*' she thought.

Determined not to be considered inattentive Leda raised her binoculars and looked out again across the expanse of reed waiting for him to guide her hand in the direction of the next bird, instead of which she was suddenly acutely aware of his hand moving up the inside of her skirt. She held her breath and stared intensely through her binoculars, closing her legs firmly to convey the message that she would not play this game, but he was not a man to be easily deflected and if she were honest, the anticipation was enjoyable.

With binoculars pressed firmly against her cheeks she studiously ignored this first foray. However, he was persistent, and his next incursion reached the top of her stocking. She heard a small gasp as he touched the soft-warm skin of her bare inner thigh and, still holding the glasses firmly in place, she relaxed a little. He hardly hesitated. Applying a little more pressure, he caressed her pudenda with his index finger, which was when she opened her legs and felt herself tremble.

He stood and moved to the window releasing the wooden shutters, ensuring a cocooned solitude. A small amount of light filtered into the room, enough at least for her to follow his movements until he stood in front of her, which was when he leaned forward and whispered, "Sweet Leda, make me immortal with a kiss." Their mouths met hungrily.

He started to undress, removing his spectacles first, and she experienced involuntary ripples of expectancy, his small errant fringe making him seem beguilingly boyish. Tremulous, she rose and stood watching, aware that her breathing had become rapid, knowing without an iota of doubt, that she wanted him to make love to her. He appeared unaffected by the cold and stood in front of her naked and muscular. She placed a hand against the springy pelt of his chest and ran it downwards revelling in the toned muscle of his abdomen. She took hold of his erection and cradled it gently.

Slowly and tenderly for such an imposing man he kissed her again and began to remove her layers, gazing in awe as she was revealed, "Aphrodite made flesh," he exclaimed. She shivered, both from the cold and in anticipation of him, and when his hand brushed lightly across her nipple the touch stimulated a sudden, urgent, pulsating desire deep within her.

She stood fully naked in front of him and he slid his hand down her back until he found a little hollow of soft, downy hair which was when he pulled her gently into his arms. She moved against him and her legs opened.

They subsided onto the bench and she guided him into her, gloriously and lubriciously. He swelled and they moved rhythmically, matched in tempo as waves of intense pleasure swept over them. She wrapped her legs behind his back, at which moment some instinct caused her to relax and allowed him to penetrate a hidden recess at the core of her being never before accessed. With cataclysmic timing they shuddered in climax and she, clenching tightly as if the world might end, was filled with a white rush that, without doubt, engendered new life within her. She knew, with utter certainty, that she had not just given him her body, something much more profound had taken place.

They clung to one another, incoherent in ecstasy until the heat of their craving slowly abated and they became aware of the cold. He reached for a blanket under the bench.

The second time he entered her they made love as ardently as before, but with more composure and afterwards she clung to him as if he were a god who had plucked her from obscurity with the promise of eternal life.

The cold eventually became distressing and in their dazed state both knew their time had run its course. They must return to the world.

As they dressed and prepared to depart Peter placed his hands tenderly on either side of her head and looked deeply into her eyes. "Understand this, Leda, something of such significance has just taken place that I shall now navigate my life differently. I did not intend to fall in love with you, but I have."

Leda looked down and replied hesitantly. "Peter, I understand because I know I feel exactly the same, but I have to tell you that I will not leave David. I made him a promise and won't renounce my vow. Despite that, I am sure you will never again be far away from my thoughts. I shall think of you when I wake, and you will walk beside me into sleep. But even more than that you will love our child as devotedly as any father, for we have one now."

As they were leaving the hide, they were watched by a pair of swans, the imperious cob scrutinising them, apparently knowingly, its dark, unblinking eyes fixed in their direction. "Tristan and Isolde," quipped Peter as they made their way hand in hand back along the path to the Bentley from where it was a short drive to Holkham Hall and the sociable lunch that awaited.

Back at Sandringham that evening, the last of the weekend, the public interaction between Peter and Leda was deliberately distant, but while they orbited the room on different ellipses, privately each was acutely aware of the other. For both it was as if they were joined by an unseen bond, a thread that would stretch but always connect. At some point their hands brushed and that brief electric contact confirmed an indissoluble union.

She had dressed for the evening with exquisite care, choosing a skin-tight, golden diaphanous, diamante gown with a loosely woven gossamer shawl draped nonchalantly around her upper body. The dress hugged her figure and she exuded sexuality.

"Stylish but not tarty, revealing but not outré," had been her husband's compliment. Jimmy Choo heels and sheer silk stockings emphasised the long, shapely outline of her legs leading to the apple roundness of her bottom. Cleverly applied make-up accentuated the almond shape of her eyes, while her cupid lips and high cheekbones hinted at some distant and mysterious ancestry.

As the evening progressed, Leda went out of her way to appeal to her husband. She was coquettish and amusing, serious and flirtatious, responding vivaciously to his conversation. Having ensured that he did not drink to excess she waited until after dinner before whispering that she wanted an early night. When he returned from the bathroom it was to find her virtually naked covered only by a sheer negligee and positioned with the table light behind her creating an entrancing, provocative silhouette.

David could not help but fall victim to her spell and when some time later he was snoring in the damp exhaustion that followed his exertions she was satisfied that he would recall the events of the evening for a long time to come. Leda had ensured that the fatherhood of the new life engendered within her that afternoon would remain a secret, a secret that she would treasure. What she would never know was that she had conceived a second child. Vivid images of Peter filled her thoughts as she drifted into sleep.

The Boy

In Urdu the plot was codenamed اون ی (fleece) alluding to the return of that which symbolises the right to rule, an allusion taken from Greek myth and passed down through Persian fable. It required meticulous planning and patience and was conceived by a very dedicated and opaque man known only as *The Colonel*.

The boy was selected at the age of four and, while he could not have known it, his life was to be dedicated to a single objective: namely the destabilising and subsequent destruction of a political system. It was his destiny to retrieve the metaphorical fleece that would bring with it wealth, power, authority and revenge.

For the years of his childhood the boy was oblivious to the fact that he had been enlisted, and even as a youth had little awareness of the great cause he was destined to serve.

The selection had been protracted because the screening required was, by necessity, more about the parents and their suitability than that of their infant progeny. The script was to be written upon a 'tabula rasa'.

He was named Iftekhar. It was a calculated genetic gamble, but the hope was that characteristics evident in the parents would be features inherited by the son, qualities such as: physique, sporting ability, high intelligence, charisma and an attractive appearance; all were desired by *The Colonel* who was the architect of the intrigue, the instigator whose hands would mould the man. Very few families were approached and one couple who were initially open to discussion withdrew when they realised their son would be denied a normal life. Another declined because they loved their child too much to sacrifice him to such a cause. In the end the parents chosen were satisfied with the promises made to them and gratified by the belief that their son would serve the same high political cause to which they were dedicated.

With deft political manoeuvring *The Colonel* ensured a political appointment for Iftekhar's father who became Pakistan's Ambassador to the Court of St James's, and so it was that Iftekhar's impressionable early years were lived in England and Pakistan. He was a pliable child who adjusted easily to his binary existence.

Pakistan, 'home,' was dazzling and intriguing, full of excitable people and bright sights and despite being dry, dusty, noisy, hot and monochrome, life there was exuberant. Time always passed in a whirl of vibrant events, which was greatly in contrast to the structured and ordered existence of life in England where the weather was often dreary, and adults mostly coldly stiff and formal. One domicile pulsated with energy and sunlight while the other was filled with order and routine.

And so, the separation that Iftekhar was to become had its genesis in various severances early on in his life as he found himself constantly passing between two hemispheres, east and west. In time it would result in irreconcilable dichotomies and lead to confusion between his sense of self and identity. Caught between different cultures and religions, opposing patriotisms and nationalisms, diverse loyalties and duties, his psyche would be destabilised by inconsistencies and contradictions, but at the age of seven life was still straightforward.

Iftekhar started at a Preparatory School outside London, a boarding school that was popular with a heterogeneous mix of English, Indian and Pakistani aristocracy. It enjoyed a prestigious history and was particularly renowned for having been the alma mater of Lord Mountbatten of Burma, the last Viceroy of India.

On arrival at school Iftekhar was immediately nicknamed Ifty, and the name stuck. He was liked and adapted quickly to the routine of school life with ease and familiarity. The tousle-haired, thin legged seven-year-old, with a charming rueful grin, enjoyed the routine of institutional life, from classroom to shenanigans in the dorm. His favourite part of the day was the games activities and he excelled in all sports, particularly cricket, and it was at Lockers Park that his talent for the game was first recognised. In fact, he engaged enthusiastically with every aspect of the busy and varied days revelling in the variety of school life. While the weeks of term dragged for some, they seemed to fly by for Ifty.

On Sunday mornings after chapel he would sit for an agonising hour in the dining room chewing the end of his pen as he debated what to include in the mandatory epistle to his parents, routinely assuring them of his devotion, listing his successes and expressing the occasional earnest wish for their well-being. Following release from this confinement he and his close friends were free to run wild in the woods and build dens. These were simple, uncomplicated days and, had he understood the concept, happy.

Ifty was a popular boy. His muddy knees were a source of consternation for the undermatrons with whom he undertook a constant battle, but they were always remembered by his mother at Christmas with an expensive gift from Floris. He was considered intelligent and usually surfaced at the top of his class in the regular 'monthly orders'.

From a young age his personality appealed to his contemporaries, for he was ingenuous and humorous. His friends were always delighted when his forays frustrated authority, but they were surprised when censure inexplicably descended on them and he slipped under the radar. As time passed and he progressed through school he stood out for his charismatic disposition and qualities of leadership. By the time he reached the last year of prep school, in his early teens, his teachers valued both his quick grasp of academic subjects and his irrepressible enthusiasm. It was little surprise that he was appointed Head of School before progressing to Eton where he gained election to College as a scholarship boy.

When it came to the end of term, trunks packed and parents milling around, he was met by his remote and ascetic guardian with whom he would stay, his parents having returned to Pakistan when he was nine years old. He went 'home' for the summer holiday but otherwise spent his vacations in England with *The Colonel*, who laid on all sorts of activities that were very different from those undertaken by his contemporaries. He was taught unarmed combat, how to ride and to shoot and he received lessons in Geography, especially in the geo-political history of Asia. He studied long and hard to become a good and worthy Muslim and from a young age adopted the devotions of Islam. In his teens he was encouraged to observe his religion at school and as he matured, he became increasingly devout.

In all areas of his development he was expected to excel, determination having been bred into his character to such a degree that it would define him, his reward being an increasing awareness that he was born with a destiny to fulfil, regardless of any personal ambition or fulfilment.

The Twins

2004

The girls sat head to head in earnest conversation. At thirteen years old they were emerging from childhood into early womanhood; giggling and juvenile one moment, sensible and solemn the next. This particular afternoon, they were sitting on the stone steps leading down to the lawn outside the morning room chattering and laughing in the peculiarly secretive way that twins have of communicating.

They were not identical in any sense, Helen being the first born followed by Clemmie a mere few minutes later and, despite their close relationship, the differences between them were marked and becoming more apparent as they approached adulthood, especially in appearance. It was as if the former had been fashioned from fine porcelain and the latter from clay. However, while the variance in looks, personality and character were discernible, the girls were still emotionally close and continued to share their likes and dislikes as well as the intimacies of their lives. On this occasion Clemmie was telling an anecdote when their mother called to them. "Come inside girls, there's someone here who wants to see you."

Their home, *Swan's Nest*, was a delightful south facing Elizabethan manor house with wide-open sweeping lawns leading down to a stretch of river flowing gracefully along one border of the estate. To the east and beyond the walled kitchen garden was an orchard with an oak gate leading to a perfectly proportioned boat house in which was a small skiff. The girls were forbidden to use this as they were not yet deemed sufficiently strong enough to combat the current that dragged fiercely where the river accelerated towards a weir some few hundred yards further downstream.

The design of the house was symmetrical with wings to the east and west of the vaulted hall forming the shape of an E. The original wide, dark-oak floorboards ran throughout, burnished by centuries of polish and wax as if insulated against time and wear. The unevenly worn York flagstones of the ground-floor passages, kitchen and hall were a further reminder of how the passing of generations had made their mark upon the building, if only imperceptibly.

Most of the rooms had thick rugs and each contained a large fireplace. The more important areas incorporated wide inglenooks supported by massive oak or stone lintels. The two formal reception areas were panelled, and the ceilings were decorated with a preponderance of plaster designs, mostly Tudor roses. During the day the decor might have made the rooms seem dour, but there was a lambent quality to the daylight that illuminated them and imbued them with a quiet serenity. The large windows were lead paned and mullioned, exuberantly exhibiting the skill of Elizabethan masons and glaziers. When closed at dusk the heavy damask curtains created a sense of warmth and intimacy. The red bricked solidity of the building embodied permanence, it had after all withstood the vagaries of peace and war across centuries.

The modern kitchen, warmed by an AGA, was at the heart of the house from where a hidden staircase issued, and one of the joys for the girls was ascending the three flights to emerge through disguised doors onto corridors. The stairs led to small rooms in the attic, originally meant for servants and now used for storage. Once, faithful retainers had been silent observers remaining invisible while their master and guests conducted affairs of state, embarked on affairs of the heart and discussed matters of importance, all far removed from the lives of the scullery maids and the footmen who observed them. A priest hole and large, dark cellar contributed to the mystery and excitement for the girls, especially when they played hide and seek.

The house was their domain. Cook and Bert the gardener, the only remaining retainers, lived in a bungalow in the grounds while Mrs Berry and her daughter, nicknamed 'Nutty' by the twins, visited from the village to 'clean and do' for them, as mother called it, five mornings a week.

Their father, David, a Minister of State (whatever that was) was a remote figure and undemonstrative and their lives were mostly unaffected by him. He had an apartment in London which he used when 'The House' was 'sitting', although he would return for occasional weekends and when Parliament was in recess, however on these visits he was mostly ensconced in his study attending to his red boxes. The twins considered the room rather austere and tended to avoid it, visiting only rarely when he was working at home.

Over breakfast David might emerge from behind his newspaper to make desultory conversation, or at an evening meal declare an interest in their progress at school, but these were occasional interactions and he never offered an impromptu hug or kiss. The girls were neither intimidated by him or saddened when he departed, they were accustomed to him, and were generally indifferent to their father who expressed dutiful affection but avoided intimacy.

Their mother on the other hand was the gravitational force around which their lives revolved. She was their sun and her incandescence was the light that illuminated the house and made it such a happy home. Her *joie de vivre*, her energy and intensity were the polarity to which all were attracted. None were immune and those who visited the house, or joined in her social engagements, or contributed to her charitable activities, soon aligned themselves to her axis. The girls loved their mother with the simplicity and devotion of disciples, although as their adolescent personalities started to emerge an increasing desire for independence was creating some distance and occasional tension.

"Uncle Peter is here to visit for a few days, come and welcome him."

The girls adored Uncle Peter, the big gruff buffalo of a man they had nicknamed 'Gruffabo'. He always brought presents and sweets, sometimes from exotic places and would tell exciting stories that enthralled them. Mother was even more alive and highly charged when he visited, and if she had advance notice then the house would become a whirl of activity in preparation.

"My God, the two of you are even more lovely than when I saw you last," exclaimed Uncle Peter.

"Be careful, Peter," said mother. "You will make me jealous. I shall end up like a character in a fairy story who can't compete with her daughters and has to lock them away until they are old and wizened."

The girls were aware of this lightness and gaiety in their mother's demeanour when Uncle Peter was in the house, it made her seem curiously fey, mysterious and happily capricious, an infectious mixture that imbued the mood of the day with a soothing balm that unified them, rather like a family.

"Leda, let me apologise and I hope that you will forgive me, your daughters have surpassed you. Clemmie, your mind is already as sharply perceptive as that of the keenest legal brains I know, and Helen, as the sun radiates light so do you."

"Oh, Uncle Peter, you are just the best avuncular we could ask for," said Clemmie. "Will you tell our fortune?"

"No. Not now," said mother, "run along as I want Uncle Peter all to myself. I intend to weave my magic to ensure he never escapes our clutches."

Just over fourteen years had passed since the day in Norfolk when Peter and Leda had submitted to the overwhelming passion that was to change the course of their lives in ways more profound than either could have imagined at the time. An attractive and successful man Peter was desirable to women, but he never formed lasting relationships always extracting himself before any emotional obligation developed. Before Leda entered his life so unexpectedly and so profoundly, he had often wondered if he would ever value a woman enough to exchange the uncomplicated, unfettered life of a bachelor, and the freedom it conferred, for commitment to a single person.

But from the day of their first lovemaking Leda, metaphorically, closed the door behind him and kept hold of the key. He wanted her to leave David, but she refused, despite Peter being the biological father of her children.

At one stage the anguish of being apart was almost too much to bear and led them to attempt a permanent separation, but in the end, they had to concede that, as with oxygen, their need was too great.

As time passed, they contrived ways to be in each other's

company, mostly quiet moments at *Swan's Nest*, but also meeting at social events, and when the opportunity arose travelling to discreet rendezvous. Their hunger for one another never diminished.

It took Leda longer than Peter to find acceptance, finally coming to terms with her emotional life by conceptualising it as a passage along which she travelled. On one side were labelled doors that opened on those she loved most: *maternal, filial, matrimonial, sibling, fraternal - close acquaintances and confidants.* On the other side were lesser doors: *affection, duty, devotion, responsibility, admiration,* even *reverence,* and at the end of the passage, always facing her, was the unattributed door that opened into a chamber in which resided her dreams, her imaginings, her reveries, her fantasies and her fulfilment as a woman. In that room was Peter with whom she became whole when she awoke and found him beside her.

Later in the evening when the twins were preparing for bed, their conversation turned to their mother and Uncle Peter. They continued to share a bedroom as they did not want to be parted, indeed they were generally inseparable.

"Do you notice anything different about mother when Uncle Peter is here?" asked Clemmie.

"It is as if Mum burns brighter. What is it about him that gives her such an aura of aliveness, if there is such a word?" observed Helen. "I don't know, but she treats him like a demi-god and he is so tender towards her. Have you noticed how she looks at him in unguarded moments? There is such gentleness in the way he talks to her and takes her hand, they could be in their own world. Do you think they were lovers once upon a time?"

"Are they still lovers?" ventured Clemmie.

The girls speculated upon and discussed the world of adults and their secrets until both were rubbing their eyes and they could feel the enticing tug of sleep. Clemmie went to close the window and pull the curtains tightly shut for it was late autumn and a cold night. She glanced out across the lawn towards the river and illuminated by the silvery gloss of a full moon was a family of swans gliding past. A cob and a pen followed by two cygnets, all pushing upstream on the silvery water, but what held her attention was that while one of the young birds shone like an angel the other was only in silhouette, dark as a shadow. It was as though a wicked secret were hidden in the family, and it made her shiver involuntarily.

Swan's Nest

Ten years later

The house was infused with a fever of excitement. Leda had approached the wedding of her daughter as a general would prepare for a campaign; the logistics had been formidable and every aspect of the arrangements, including contingencies, had been catered for. Everything was ready when the morning of the nuptials dawned, accompanied by an increasing level of activity and overwrought anticipation that spread through the house as infectiously as a virulent bacterium.

The day began early with the fragrance of ground coffee and buttered bacon baps percolating through the rooms before moving slowly towards its apogee. Hair was styled and garlanded, dresses fixed, makeup applied, manicures completed, nails polished in bright colours; all to adorn the young women who were to be the attendant nymphs at the altar of the day's union.

The bride was, of course, the focus of attention, although a difficult, unspoken truth hovered, namely that the mother of the bride surpassed her daughter in beauty and grace. Even more problematic to acknowledge was the fact that the sister of the bride, however much she tried to camouflage the fact, transcended all others in elegance and radiance. When the bride stood beside her bridesmaid, it was as if the moon were striving to eclipse the sun.

Clemmie was not unattractive, but she had inherited neither her mother's personality or sense of style, in fact she was cumbersome and heavy-featured in comparison. Her wedding dress, which had been cleverly designed at inordinate expense, gave her figure shape and femininity, but seemed just a little stretched despite the lace and ruffle that formed a train.

The wedding dress had been months in the planning and contained thousands of sequins sewn individually with a lattice of cream piping and an abundance of lace. At the last minute it required 'easing' to accommodate Clemmie's expanding waistline, although the baby was at an early stage and the signs of pregnancy were not yet greatly noticeable. The alteration, she claimed, was being made more for comfort than expedience.

It had been an option to hold the wedding at St Martin-in-the-Fields with the reception in Westminster Hall, as her father's position in the government entitled, but in the end Clemmie wanted a village affair with a reception in a marquee on the lawn overlooking the river. Given the eminence of the guest list this arrangement had stretched the resources of the security company tasked with ensuring the event passed free of incident.

The bridegroom, Henry de Quincy Adams, was a rising star in the upper echelons of a select banking fraternity that exercised influence and control in the fiscal dynamics of the western world. His marriage to Clemmie would create an allegiance between two very influential families and had the blessing of all those who would benefit most from its merits, wealth and power combining in the union. The couple themselves were comfortable with an arrangement that was to some degree a marriage of convenience for they understood the mutual advantages and benefits it would bring. The hope of those who knew and loved them was that it would also lead to happiness. In one area the two had already discovered that they shared an equal delight, which was why, by dint of some negligence, Clemmie found herself pregnant ahead of the grand day.

Clemmie had learned in her early teens to disguise the jealousy she felt towards her sister, who it seemed to her, was destined to cast a shadow over her life. Helen was born bonnie and had grown into a popular adolescent; an emerging beauty, with a ready intelligence and easy charm. The close friendship that had existed between the twins in childhood had continued because Helen was seemingly unaware of any differences between them, but increasingly their relationship had come under strain as they matured into womanhood. Henry was one man Clemmie considered immune to Helen's Siren effect and he had focused all his matrimonial energy upon wooing the younger twin. Too often in the past young men had feigned interest in Clemmie only to gain an introduction to Helen, salt rubbed deeply into an open wound.

Helen's beauty lay in an exposition of shape and form. Hers was a perfectly symmetrical oval face with high cheekbones and an aquiline, slightly retroussé nose, enhanced by a soft creamy complexion as gentle as that of an infant. Her slate-grey eyes possessed a mesmeric, elven, quality that compelled attention, while her lips were so beguiling, they provoked both men and women to silently speculate how soft and seductive it would be to take her in an embrace. Lustrous, flaxen-coloured, shoulder-length wavy hair framed her face and seemed to focus an inner radiance.

The shape and curves of her upper body surmounted exceptionally elongated legs that granted a languorous grace to her movement; watching her walk was to be reminded of a leopard's stride, slow and full of sophistication. Above all else her smile exuded life and lustre, a hypnotic lustre, a hypnotic magnetism, and amongst her contemporaries she shone like a star in a universe of mediocrity. She would not have recognised herself described in such terms, but the fact was that her appearance seemed a gift from the gods and lesser mortals looked on with both wonder and envy. Clemmie could not help experiencing resentment, although she harboured this feeling silently.

Helen had been approached by numerous modelling agencies but rejected an industry that she considered dull, insincere and full of artifice. Similarly, she showed no interest in becoming an actress and was content working with people she liked on projects she considered worthwhile. She had learned early in life the importance of retaining her independence and was determined to exercise control over the choices she made.

By contrast her twin sister had been less fortunate in her appearance. Clemmie was tall and well-proportioned with an interesting face, but despite dying her hair blonde and blow-drying it regularly, it remained lank. When she smiled, she pursed her lips, and this gave the unfortunate impression of disdain rather than vivacity. Her jowl was somewhat heavy, and cheeks rather ruddy, slightly scarred by teenage acne, a blemish she tried to hide with liberal applications of foundation; also, her nose had a faint crease making it appear a little bulbous.

Her youthful figure was, although plump, attractively provocative and shapely, and she was particularly proud of her pendulous breasts. From behind there was a voluptuousness to her shape and she took pleasure in the knowledge that male libidos were provoked by her physique, which gave her a sense of power as well as ensuring that she satisfied a greedy desire for '*la petite mort*'. But standing beside Helen she seemed awkward and leaden featured.

The wedding ceremony passed uneventfully and for Helen

happily; she felt only love and generosity for her sister. From the moment Clemmie entered the church to a fanfare played by two trumpeters from the Household Cavalry and progressed up the aisle to Jeremiah Clarke's Trumpet Voluntary, she looked radiantly happy. Helen found herself hoping that the rest of Clemmie's days would be a continuation of that moment and when she saw her sister place a hand briefly upon her pregnant front, as though reassuring the unborn child that hers was destined to be a joyful, contented and safe life, the small gesture filled Helen with happiness.

The Queen's Royal Hussars is one of the most senior regiments of the British Army formed from the amalgamation of two other cavalry regiments, the Queen's Own Hussars and the Queen's Royal Irish Hussars. The regiment traces its roots back to 1685 and in over three hundred years has been awarded one hundred and seventy-two battle honours and eight Victoria Crosses; Winston Churchill served in one of its antecedent regiments, the 4th Queen's Own Hussars, and was once described as 'the greatest Hussar of them all'.

The Number One dress uniform is made up of crimson trousers (granted by Prince Albert from his personal livery when the Hussars escorted him to his marriage to Queen Victoria in 1840) and a blue jacket with white belt, silver buttons and shoulder braid. The peaked flat cap is also crimson in colour.

The uniform fitted Captain William Edward Montgomery, the best man, to perfection accentuating his height, his muscular broad shoulders and narrow waist. His blonde hair was a little long and when he removed his cap it flopped to the right, somehow further emphasising a broad smile that lit up his face when he smiled. *'Like a beam of light being switched on,'* thought Helen when she saw him laugh for the first time.

Surprisingly, Helen and William had not been introduced prior to the wedding day rehearsal and her first sight of him in uniform was when she followed Clemmie down the aisle and saw him standing beside his old friend, the groom. Equally his first opportunity to observe her was when he watched her demurely accompany Clemmie.

It was not until after dinner and the obligatory Best Man's speech that William was able to seek out Helen, for she was constantly surrounded by a coterie of young, and some not so young, admirers. His speech had been well received as he trod the delicate line between prudence and indiscretion in respect of the groom. William was amusingly irreverent and caused raucous laughter when he recalled that at school Henry had the nickname Troy, which he resented as it implied a comparison between himself and a dashing but unreliable Sergeant in a Thomas Hardy novel.

"There was no problem with the sobriquet," William recalled, "But in an article Henry wrote for the school magazine his spelling let him down. He wrote that, 'this was a maddening fallacy'. Unfortunately, and to his great embarrassment," confided William, "Our hero confused his *f* with *ph*."

With two glasses of champagne in hand William finally managed to disperse Helen's acolytes and engage her in conversation. To keen observers in the room she seemed more animated once he arrived, and when an infectious Neil Diamond song was playing, he asked her to dance. She accepted and those watching were fascinated as the two matched each other in fluidity of movement and expression. As the music ended Helen became aware of the attention focused upon them and was flustered, immediately conscious that she might be detracting from Clemmie's evening and so she whispered, "Let's take a walk outside?"

Helen had never comprehended why her appearance distinguished her from other women for she did not understand that there was something transformational about her looks; an exquisite intensity, a rare quality, as if, for example, the uniqueness of an orchid or perfect rose had been refined and distilled.

The wedding breakfast continued late into the evening until the departure of the newly-wed husband and wife for a honeymoon in the Maldives. Clemmie, still radiant from the day, turned her back on the guests before throwing the wedding bouquet over her shoulder. It fell into Helen's hands, which caused much merriment and ribaldry.

At one point, late in the evening, Helen was standing next to Gruffabo who smiled kindly. She leaned her back against him as she cradled a glass of champagne and he held her paternally while they watched the dancing. She felt his strength and it made her feel safe.

"He is the one for you," said Peter nodding across the room towards William. "Unlike your sister you have the capacity to be truly happy."

"Thank you," said Helen. "Your opinion matters more to me than anyone else's, other than mother of course."

Helen and William chatted late into the night discovering that they shared common interests especially sport, music, travel and adventure. As the evening approached its conclusion, they returned to the bar for one last glass of champagne, separating as they walked around the imposing ice sculpture of a swan in the centre of the room. Inexplicably Helen experienced a moment of sadness and gave a little shudder as she saw that the decoration was starting to lose its shape with droplets of water running down its neck. It was as if the swan were crying at the union between her sister and Henry.

Helen

Helen's looks were a blessing and also, in her opinion, something of a curse; but if a misfortune then an affliction for which most young women would make a heavy sacrifice. Those who met her for the first time were in agreement that she was uniquely captivating, although they struggled to ascribe a word or phrase to adequately describe the synchronicity of physique and appearance that made her so distinctive. On introduction she made an immediate impression, and on parting she left an indelible image.

From childhood Helen had been aware that her presence could cause a stir, but she disliked being the centre of attention, even more so as she matured and came to understand that there were women and men who resented her; women because they felt eclipsed and men because she was eminently desirable but unattainable. In consequence she tended not to socialise greatly and often found relationships difficult to sustain. She encountered some rogues along the way who behaved deplorably towards her and she learned from experience that there are men who act with malign intent, incapable of valuing women for their intrinsic qualities. In consequence when she met William she had arrived at a stage in her life where she enjoyed the company of numerous men and women but confined her close friendships to a tight circle of confidantes and acquaintances.

As a teenager her horse, Peg, had been the focus of much of Helen's social life and she devoted her energies to eventing. Her mother encouraged and supported both girls in their equine interests although Clemmie never shared her sister's passion for dressage and show jumping, preferring the thrill of the hunt and the satisfaction of a kill.

In those days Helen would often be found with her nose buried in a romantic novel, which meant that her attitude towards love and marriage was idealised, while Clemmie preferred dystopian themes and books with stories of wild adventure. Both girls had boyfriends along the way and Helen thought her heart broken at least twice before she turned twenty.

Now, in her mid-twenties and despite her quixotic disposition, Helen had not met a man who compelled her attention to the degree that she could envisage sharing her life with him. And, so it was that when she and William met for the first time on the evening of Clemmie's wedding Helen found herself disconcerted by Captain William Edward Montgomery. Never before had her interest in a man been piqued to such a degree.

He was six years older than her, and was certainly dashing, but there was another quality about him that caught her attention, an aura of command, a calm restraint and lack of pretence that distanced him from so many of the affected young men with whom she so often mixed. She learned, circumspectly, that as an army officer he had served in some of the most complex and dangerous theatres of war and it was clear that he was battle hardened. She sensed that near him she would be safe and shielded from danger, for authority fitted him as naturally as his uniform. Her interest was aroused by this engaging man who displayed easy and personable confidence, who made amusing conversation and was an entertaining raconteur, but who did not draw attention to himself or need to be the centre of attention. She observed him chatting with fellow officers, most of whom seemed to defer to him, and she could see why he held their esteem. He had obviously earned the trust and confidence of those with whom he served and those he led; he was tempered like a sword.

She also watched William when he was talking with Henry, groom and best man interacting nonchalantly and fraternally. A superficial observation might conclude that the two shared similarities, as indeed they did in their relaxed charm, intelligence and social poise, but, she decided, it would be misleading to think the comparison went any deeper. William seemed resolute, a man used to command, a soldier with sound judgement and moral fibre, rather different from the Henry she had come to know, her new brother-in-law.

Henry was socially emollient, obviously an incisive banker who exhibited every appearance of being in control, but his public persona was, she had concluded, bravado that masked insecurity. Helen's judgement was astute, for in the inner chambers of his own self-awareness Henry did indeed fear there beat a hollow drum. He was self-aware enough to admit to himself that at times he acted with insincerity and he accepted he was morally equivocal; he yearned to emulate his best man's honesty and integrity, but when put to the test he failed.

At the time of Henry's wedding William was on leave having accumulated a couple of months rest and recuperation, which he intended to fill with travel and recreation. Now, having met Helen, he was determined that he would get to know her better before being posted overseas again, and so as the evening moved towards its conclusion he enquired if she was a golfer. Demurely, she said she enjoyed the game and when he asked her if she would like to accompany him to Wentworth later that week she accepted.

William

William was concerned that the West Course might prove too demanding for Helen, but he had underestimated her competitiveness and not for the last time, as he would come to learn. As they left the green on the seventeenth, she was leading by one stroke, which meant that he had to win the last hole to draw the game.

Helen had a naturally languid swing and on the eighteenth tee pivoted with perfect poise, ensuring the length of the club was deployed so that the head of the driver struck the ball in the middle of the 'sweet spot'. The club carried through into a relaxed back swing and she completed her rotation in perfect balance. William watched and was captivated once again.

The redesigned eighteenth hole of the West Course has been heavily criticised, but this fact was irrelevant to Helen who, knowing that she could not outdistance William, was focusing on playing the course cannily. The long, par five of the final hole describes a sweeping dogleg that requires an accurate tee shot. Helen's drive pulled up in the middle of the fairway just short of two bunkers on the left while William, having connected with greater force, drove his ball beyond hers by about thirty yards, clearing the bunkers. For their second shot each took a 3-wood. William's strike was a little wayward which left him one hundred and eighty yards short of the green, but still just in front of Helen.

For her third shot Helen decided to rely upon accuracy laying up short of the treacherous brook that guards the entrance to the green, a shot she accomplished to perfection. A high wedge to the pin and a short putt would leave her with a safe par and, hopefully, a win.

As William walked up to his ball, she looked across at him and in that moment saw a wildness flare in his eyes. She knew instinctively that he was going to throw caution to the wind and attempt the most difficult shot possible to make a birdie, it was to be all or nothing. Despite the danger he would risk all not to be beaten. She was full of admiration for his determination and mettle for he was prepared to step out onto the edge and embrace jeopardy to gamble against the odds. She felt a rising sense of excitement as she watched him calculate his shot, analyse the variables, visualise the trajectory and take into account the conditions. To pull off a win on this hole the ball would have to stop within a few feet of the flag.

As it left the club face and ascended in a perfect parabola the ball reached the zenith of its flight, where it seemed to hang for a moment. To be successful it had to land in front of the brook and bounce once onto the green and lose speed rapidly. A few yards too short and it would be in the stream, mistimed and it would disappear into the lake beyond. As it was, William judged the shot to perfection and the ball struck the ground five yards short of the water from where, in one graceful leap, it landed on the skirt of the green. As its speed bled away it came to a stop within two feet of the flag. Helen surprised herself by throwing her arms around his neck and giving him a hug. He had shown her that he was a bold man, decisive and of good judgement.

Mid-afternoon on their way back to London they were both in a light-hearted and heady mood when William pulled into a pub, for they were hungry and ready for food. Having chosen from the menu they opted for a secluded table near an old inglenook where it was warm and comfortable by the fire. Sitting on a battered settle covered in cushions and, companionably close, they embarked upon their first personal conversation. Time slipped by and their tête-à-tête became more intimate. When they were about to leave William, on impulse, invited Helen to accompany him on the safari he was planning before returning to his regiment. He was delighted when she accepted.

Safari

They flew overnight to Johannesburg where they were met by Hector Perkins, a South African, who had served with William on two tours in Afghanistan. When Hector resigned from the British army he returned to his beloved homeland where, with his partner Sarah, they started a company offering bespoke expeditions to observe the rarest wild animals in Africa. 'Independent Africa', as they named it, was based in the Kruger National Park near the Zimbabwean border and undertook tours advertised as a more authentic experience than those of the 'Hilton' safaris. Hector flew them up to the reserve in his two-engine light aircraft.

William had observed decorum, booking two rooms, albeit adjacent. The camp was in many respects rudimentary and the term 'rooms' turned out to be something of a misnomer for they were little more than discrete quarters separated by reed palisades. The bed and furniture were simple, and the shower was an overhead bucket with holes filled by a hose when a tap was turned on. The toilet was similarly uncomplicated.

Helen was captivated. She adjusted rapidly to the heat, her sensible daytime wardrobe having been chosen to keep her protected from the fierce sun and ubiquitous thorn, however her evening wear was a different matter. For dinner on the first night she wore a cool, gossamer thin trouser ensemble that shimmered as she moved and clung to her every curve. She carried a cashmere pashmina for warmth when the cold of the evening began to bite, as she had been advised. She had applied minimal make-up, with only a hint of mascara, lipstick and blusher to enhance her exquisite features.

When Helen first walked across the compound Sarah happened to be standing beside Hector and he received a sharp poke to the ribs. As she told him later, he looked ridiculous, like a puppy with its tongue hanging out.

Hector had questioned William about the two-room scenario and was agog that William had not yet attempted seduction. "Take my advice mate and ensure the heat of the sun melts her resistance. It's a very fortunate man indeed who gets to drink the honied water at that sweet well," a comment William chose to ignore.

Hector told William that the following morning they would be hunting supper, he provided him with a Rigby .275 rifle, which he insisted was to stay by William's side at all times, this being the bush.

After an exhausting day and good dinner Helen fell into a deep sleep, but in the early hours of the morning she awoke terrified and shaking at the roar of a male lion nearby. It issued a blast of sound that shook the very ground, and lying alone Helen had to fight to impose control over a terror that threatened to overwhelm her, a deep atavistic horror that pushed her to the limit of her self-control. When William called to ask if she was alright, she wanted to run to him, but, screwing up her courage, she assured him she was OK. When the lion moved away her nerves remained stretched, but silence returned and eventually she slipped back into sleep. For the first time she appreciated the vastness of the wilderness and perceived the precariousness of life on the savannah.

She was very grateful to William for respecting her chasteness in such an understated manner. Despite some very determined campaigns over the years she had preserved her chastity, not because she was averse to intimacy, and she was sure she would derive great pleasure from lovemaking, but because she would not give herself away as a chattel. She knew that when she chose to engage in a physical relationship it would be as a part of the total commitment she wanted to make to one man, rather than as an end in itself. Clemmie said she was frigid, but she was sure this was not the case.

The large male lion had been roaring from frustration. That day he had observed the females of his pride attempting to bring down a large cape buffalo, but despite inflicting deep lacerations they had not made the kill and he was both angry and hungry.

At breakfast the next morning Hector outlined the day's expedition which would begin by observing a large family of elephants at their watering hole before moving out onto the plains to track impala, 'the dancing antelope' as Hector referred to them.

"The plan is William, my old mate, for you to shoot a young impala doe for our dinner, the meat is succulent and delicious when grilled."

Turning to Helen, he continued, "However, I fear we shall go hungry because it takes a canny hunter of considerable skill to get close enough to shoot one of these darlings. They are referred to as 'smoke' for a good reason. The moment they detect you, puff, they disappear."

"Are you doubting my skill as a hunter, you straggly old bushman?" challenged William and Helen saw the fire light in his eyes. To add spice to the challenge she said, "Hector, if William fails to make a kill and consequently I am starving this evening, then I shall reserve every dance for you."

Helen was entranced by the elephant family they watched bathing and relaxing in a water hole. Perched in the trees they had a perfect view from the hide, and she could not take her eyes off a little calf who frolicked in the muddy water with babyish abandon, overseen indulgently by a group of matrons. The magnificence of the great, creased, lumbering pachyderms brought tears to her eyes as she observed them bathe, the young trumpeting shrilly while the great males stood to one side and rumbled. She felt enormously grateful to William for bringing her to Africa.

Later, when Hector had picked up the spoor of a herd of impala, William began to understand how nervously skittish the spring hoofed antelope are, so perfectly camouflaged in the long, brown grass. The two men kept low creeping slowly, commando style, down-wind towards the herd until they judged they were within shooting distance. William identified his target, a young female without a foal, and to achieve a clear line of sight he very slowly raised his head above the grass focusing all his concentration upon remaining undetected. They had left the jeep some way back and Helen had opted to stay with the vehicle to prepare Instagram photos to send later.

"Don't go walking around lassie, this is a dangerous place," Hector had instructed, but she had ignored his injunction and had wandered off to shade under a nearby stand of trees.

Unseen in the feather-light, sandy coloured, savannah high grass the wounded bull buffalo had remained still for hours. It needed to conserve energy for it was thirsty and in agonising pain from the deep wounds inflicted by the lions the previous day when they raked its back and loins in their attempt to pull him to the ground. A ton of cape buffalo, in unremitting torment, was looking for a focus for its anger and when a rifle cracked nearby it was incensed. It charged in the direction of the sound accelerating at surprising speed, rapidly becoming an unstoppable force. But the beast was only vaguely aware of the location of the sound that had so angered it and being short-sighted did not make out the camouflaged stalkers. With the reflexes of a trained hunter Hector reacted immediately aligning himself to take a shot, but the animal was angled away from him and his bullet struck its flank. It was not a killing shot and only caused yet greater pain increasing the bull's rage as it charged past the men in the direction of the jeep.

"Go left," Hector shouted at William as he sped off to the right. "Only a brain shot will do."

Helen was startled by the sound of the rifle and decided to wander back to the jeep, but as she did so the ground began to tremble, a sensation that reminded her obscurely of an underground train passing beneath a London theatre. Immediately she was alert and nervous, and sensing danger started to cross the ground towards the jeep, but in so doing she crossed the field of vision of the old bull who was searching for a focus for all its anger and pain. Its primitive brain fixed upon her as the target for its pent-up fury, the object it would tear, rip, and trample.

The buffalo slowed, fixed upon Helen and aligned its run. Then, with the force of an excavator it bore down upon her just as she ducked underneath the jeep for protection. The bull had survived numerous battles, but its present torment was greater than anything it had ever known. It knew no fear and in the dim recesses of its primitive brain, agony inflamed its all-consuming anger. It increased speed striking the 4x4 at the front with such force that the vehicle was shunted six feet backwards. Helen had to scramble to remain underneath and avoid the wheels. Seemingly unaffected by the impact the bull circled twice and then prepared for another charge, this time from the side.

Its run began slowly and as it gathered speed it lowered the thick bone of its cranium to ram the object of its rage for a second time. It crashed into the door of the jeep and used its horns to rip open its enemy. In so doing it managed to tip the vehicle onto its side leaving Helen hopelessly exposed and unprotected. The beast saw her scramble and now she became the single object of its fury. It circled once again preparing for the kill.

Trumpeting with satisfaction it looked straight at Helen with unblinking, baleful, rheumy eyes and lowered its lugubrious head, its horns as penetrating as iron marlin-spikes. An implacable bovine bulldozer it started its charge, oblivious to all else in its intention to satisfy an insatiable desire to trample and gouge until nothing remained except an inert, bloody, broken mess beneath its hoofs.

It was unaware of loud yells from either side and remained focused upon its target, it would not be deviated. All of Helen's vision was taken up with the sight of the mountainous beast bearing down upon her, and in her terror, she yelled out for William. Cantering thunderously the bull was within a hundred yards when William appeared between her and the animal and all she could do was to watch as if in slow motion. With great clarity she saw him drop to his knee, calculate his shot, aim the Rigby, make a fine adjustment and pull the trigger.

The beast was felled instantly, as if it had run into an invisible wall; its knees buckled, and it collapsed. However, its momentum was such that it slid towards her with all the force of a train leaving the tracks. In a single movement William dropped the rifle, wrapped his arms around her and rolled them both to one side. Helen felt the ground shudder and she smelt the animal's last hot breath pass over her as, with one final convulsion it died, mere feet from where they crouched.

That night Helen tapped on the door that separated their rooms. She entered without waiting for a reply and stood in front of William as he lay in bed reading a book. He looked up at her as she untied the delicate shoulder strings of her nightdress and allowed it to fall to the floor.

On their last evening they watched together as the giant blood-red orb of the sun began to descend rapidly as if falling over the horizon. They were sitting closely, side by side, fingers touching as they looked across the vastness of the plain watching a family of giraffe that had been feeding from a baobab tree before lining up and loping past in search of tender leaves elsewhere.

They had dined on grilled liver of Eland, mild in flavour and succulent in taste accompanied by a salad and a chilled bottle of South African Pinot Grigio that Hector had magicked from somewhere. They were relaxed, and their chatter was idle. William told Helen that his next posting was a staff job overseas, not active service, but he appeared unclear of the details and was rather vague, deliberately so she thought. All he would say was that it involved multi-lateral negotiations between Afghans, Pakistanis and Indians and required him to travel around the sub-continent learning about its peoples and politics. Helen mentioned that she had been approached to join a company that organised high level hospitality events and she was inclined to accept, a new and interesting challenge.

Quietly, and almost as a non sequitur, William said, "I shall be away for at least a year, maybe a little longer, but I wonder if on my return you would do me the honour of becoming my wife?"

Helen was quiet for some minutes until there began to be a palpable tension in the air. Having been taken by surprise she was ordering her thoughts as she wanted her reply to be meaningful and honest. She took a deep breath and began.

"Like all little girls, I once believed there would be a prince out there who would sweep me off my feet, but actually I have learned that I don't need protecting and, furthermore, I enjoy a wonderful life of privilege and comfort as a single person. I am no longer that little girl seeking her prince because I have grown into an independent woman who, as a proud feminist, values the notion of herself as self-fulfilling and self-reliant. I don't and won't ever define myself in the shadow of a man or feel constrained because I am female, in fact quite the opposite because I am liberated by my autonomy. However, in the last few days I have come to realise that there is something missing in my life, namely just spending time with a special person who simply wants to share their life with me. And so, to answer your question, I would love that person to be you."

Henry

Clemmie gave birth to a healthy daughter, Iphy, seven and a half months after her wedding, a cherubic infant with pudgy rouge cheeks and a mop of wild curly red hair. From the outset Iphy's nature was engaging and remarkably undemanding, which was a great relief to Clemmie and also to Cassandra, or Cassie as she was known, the nanny who had been employed to live with the family.

After their wedding Clemmie and Henry moved into his apartment in Belgravia where they adjusted to parental life with a minimum of fuss. Clemmie returned to work in less than three months as a buyer with Liberty's of London, a role that required visits overseas and so she was regularly away from home.

Iphy was nineteen months old when Clemmie announced that she was arranging a trip to India to view some exciting new fabrics that might be incorporated into the following season's designs. Henry had already booked a fishing holiday in Scotland and so it was agreed that Iphy would accompany her father with Cassie in attendance.

The Spey river offers, arguably, Scotland's best wild spring and Atlantic Salmon fishing and Henry's family had held a week's rod on one of the Ballindalloch 'beats' for generations.

As Henry, Cassie and Iphy approached their destination along the A95, Ballindalloch Castle came into view with its two Disneyesque round towers. Henry had a love of history and regaled Cassie with stories of the Macpherson-Grant family, the incumbents of Ballindalloch, who traced their importance back to the English Civil War. As they drove past the castle, he pointed out the curiously Z shaped building and mentioned its particularly splendid gardens, but the castle was not their destination and so he did not detour through the grounds. He did though make a brief visit to the recently opened Ballindalloch distillery where he purchased a few bottles of distinctive single malt, a particular favourite.

Earlier, when they had broken the journey for a cream tea of scones, clotted cream and strawberry jam, Henry had told her tales of the 'Black Watch', who were originally based in Ballindalloch where the regiment was originally formed.

He also told her other stories, including a curious one of the disappearance of Captain William Earl Johns from London society after the First World War.

"The dear old flying ace and war hero had in fact rented a house on the Ballindalloch estate with his lover, the exotically named Doris (known as Dol) May Leigh. W. E. was trying to escape his dragon of a wife who was making every effort to track him down, expose his infidelity and drag him through the courts. Penniless, hunted and in love it was here that the 'Biggles' stories were born to stave off penury."

As a boy W. E. Johns' books had featured in the forefront of Henry's imaginative world, and he confided to Cassie that as a nine-year-old he had seen himself as a similar romantic daredevil.

Henry was in a particularly relaxed and loquacious mood as they completed their journey turning onto the B1938 before crossing the river by the stone bridge and arriving at the cottage he had rented near Gorton's Farm.

Later that evening when Iphy was in bed and they were relaxing after a delicate dinner of poached salmon and salad, accompanied by a bottle of burgundy and subsequent tots of whisky, Henry was contemplating one final chaser when Cassie, sitting in an armchair opposite embroidering a small handkerchief, suddenly turned chalk white and shivered; her whole body shook with a convulsion, as if she were undergoing a seizure. Henry leaped off the sofa shocked and concerned and was looking for his phone to summon an ambulance when she began to recover her composure and her colour returned.

"Sorry," she said. "Someone just walked over my grave. I was suddenly convinced that some terrible tragedy is about to engulf us. Ridiculous. It's fine now, please don't concern yourself."

Situated just below its confluence with the Spey the upper River Avon is a stretch that does not require a ghillie and is often fished by four rods. Henry had invited three close friends to join him for the first four days of the week, but he also wanted time to himself and intended to fish alone after they departed. For the duration of their visit his companions stayed at the local pub where Henry joined them in the evenings.

Cassie and Iphy remained at the cottage when the men left to fish and it fell to her to shop and prepare a lunch hamper for Henry and his friends, all of whom were passionate about their sport and liked to party hard back at the pub afterwards. Each morning she drove lunch up to the riverbank after which she and Iphy went for walks and explored.

On the morning after his friends departed, Henry suggested that "the girls" make a picnic lunch and join him on the riverside at midday. He reminded Cassie, unnecessarily she thought, that strict riverside rules apply as fast flowing water is dangerous and Iphy would have to be watched carefully. Furthermore, he said, salmon are easily disturbed and so there should be no noisy distraction from the bank.

Each beat is provided with a small wooden 'ghillie's cottage' for daytime use reserved for the relaxation, warmth and privacy of the party and it was here, he said, they would gather for lunch.

The salmon fishing season on the Spey begins early in February and by March the river, while not in spate, runs fast and deep. Due to heavy rainfall before their arrival the water level was higher than normal for the time of year, ideal for salmon returning upriver to their spawning ground. On the morning of the picnic the sun was shining brightly and there was a promise of warmth in the air.

As he was leaving Henry said to Cassie, "Please don't wear that boring brown uniform today, dress more naturally for the country."

The picnic basket she prepared included Henry's favourite shrimp vol-au-vent, a pasty from the local butcher, and knowing there was a toaster in the hut, some bread and a small porcelain jar of his favourite 'Patum Peperium' brought with them from Fortnum and Mason. A bottle of light white Riesling completed the complement. She made a simple ham sandwich for herself with jam sandwiches for Iphy.

Lunch ready and packed she began to think about what to wear. She had dressed Iphy in toddler's dungarees and high collared shirt, vibrantly coloured Wellington boots and a thick pullover, all of which would keep her warm. Cassie had come to adore her charge who was cute, smiling, lovable and toddling, although collapses to her bottom were not uncommon accompanied by guffaws of giggling.

Cassie had no regard for Clemmie who she considered a hard and callous employer, a bitter and demanding woman and an indifferent mother, but she had formed an affection for Henry who was fun-loving, amusing and irreverent. He was knowledgeable and interesting to be with and always good humoured with an irrepressible sense of the ridiculous that made his company entertaining. He teased her, made her laugh and seemed to take a genuine interest in her life. He was generous in his praise and gratitude and it had occurred to her that, secretly, he might find her attractive as some of his comments were flirtatious.

During her training as a nanny it had been drummed into her that one never harboured intimate thoughts of one's male employer and certainly nanny should never dress in such a way as to attract his attention; indeed, the uniform was deliberately designed to be dreary. To highlight one's femininity was taboo, but that morning she took a delicious delight in planning her wardrobe; a close fitting, calf length, tweed skirt and a Laura Ashley blouse with collar, the top three buttons unfastened. She applied light makeup and over her shirt wore a fitted, tweed waistcoat that gave uplift to her bosom, offering a tantalising but decorous glimpse of cleavage. Under her skirt, stockings with elasticated tops but no underwear, an act of abandonment that always gave her a secret sense of freedom, especially in the country. Her brogues were well polished and sensible.

By eleven-thirty Iphy and Cassie were lying on the picnic rug near the bank playing quietly while Henry continued to fish, dressed in waders and a gilet over his shirt with sleeves rolled up. It was taking all his concentration and skill to judge the flow of the water, temperature and mood of the fish. He was casting frequently, seeking out different currents in the hope of attracting a salmon with one of his own 8/0 'Munro Killer' flies made lovingly from a natural feather and carefully crafted with cotton. He had decided against using his beloved Hardy or Sharp split cane rods and in preference had chosen the sixteen-foot carbon fibre, which was lighter and easier for the switch casting technique he was utilising. He was having to work hard to tease out his adversary.

From time to time Henry glanced at the bank and observed Iphy playing happily with Cassie. They seemed natural and affectionate; indeed, he was sure that Iphy was closer to her nanny than her mother. At about one o'clock he emerged from the river and put aside his rod. Cassie enjoyed watching him as he concentrated on removing his chest waders before walking over to join them.

Cassie spread out the lunch as Henry, in a relaxed and entertaining mood, played with his daughter, chasing after her as she tottered squealing with laughter. Iphy was fed first and then placed in a sleeping position in her Maclaren buggy, where she promptly dropped off to sleep. Cassie poured Henry a glass of wine chilled in the river and they talked easily and naturally while they ate. It was a perfect spring day, warm in the sunshine and wonderfully peaceful with only the gurgle and rush of the river as a background refrain accompanied by the lyric of birdsong from nearby trees. As they lay on the rug the mood was undisturbed without a soul in sight, the next beat hidden from view by a bend in the river. The bottle of wine dwindled pleasantly and soporifically, and the alcohol had the effect of making them lethargic.

Cassie's mind began to wander, and she was teetering on the edge of nodding off, when she felt Henry's hand on her breast gently rubbing and teasing her left nipple through her blouse. Her instant reaction was one of mild panic, but it was a thoroughly enjoyable sensation and seemed innocent enough. She chose not to make a fuss. Her rational brain knew that she should object, but her sensual brain was very pleasurably stimulated. Then he undid her waistcoat and blouse and slipped his hand under her breast, lifting it out of her bra before placing his mouth over her nipple and caressing and nuzzling it in a warm velvety way. A distant voice in her head was telling her to put a stop to this, but so enjoyable was the feeling that she only half-heartedly pushed him away, while casually managing to drop her hand across the front of his trousers where she felt his erection bursting to be released. Her willpower and any wish to repel faded completely as he ran his hand up the inside of her skirt and passed his thumb over her unconfined and receptive vagina. At that moment restraint gave way to a haze of arousal, so much so that when he rose and took her by the hand, she allowed herself to be led into the hut where they abandoned themselves to a vortex of sensual delirium, oblivious to any external distraction. So, when Iphy awoke they were unaware. The belt designed to restrain her in the buggy was not fastened securely and when she wriggled and turned the buckle fell open allowing her to squirm out of the chair. She looked around for the adults but not seeing them wandered down to the edge of the water to look at the gleaming fish daddy had shown her earlier.

The salmon in the net swirled and glimmered, splashed and thrashed, fascinatingly iridescent in the sunshine and she leant down to touch the slippery fish, but at that moment lost her footing and was immediately caught by a fast running eddy that pulled her into the current. She started to panic and shriek, but the more she struggled the more the water flowed into her Wellington boots and soaked her clothing stopping her from regaining balance. She spluttered as water covered her face and she tried again to stand but wobbled on a small rock, and when she slipped the waterlogged clothing held her down. The flux suddenly took hold of her small body and tugged it out towards the middle of the river where she struggled, but in vain. The clutch of an invisible enemy drew her remorselessly into the fast-flowing centre of the stream, where, despite all her diminutive efforts she was pulled below the surface of the churning water.

Andy Macpherson was fishing the next beat when he saw what he thought was a child's doll being tossed along in the choppy water swirling around some rocks. He looked curiously, and then with growing concern, until he decided that he must act. Balancing adroitly, and at some considerable risk to his safety, he waded further into the river, until he grasped what he saw to his horror was an infant child. His efforts to revive her were increasingly frantic, but she remained motionless in his arms.

Iftekhar

It was the end of the working week, a busy Friday afternoon, when Iftekhar Diaz slipped into the back seat of the chauffeur driven limousine waiting to convey him to a large house in Surrey, the residence of his uncle where he had been summoned. The rear windows of the Mercedes were darkened and hid the occupant from the eyes of casual observers, especially anyone who might recognise the passenger, although this was unlikely on this occasion.

Mostly, his uncle had always seemed to Iftekhar a remote, distant figure who existed in the background, overseeing his education, ensuring opportunities and smoothing his path, but there had never been a hint of affection or emotional connection between them. As a child Iftekhar had been unaware of the older man's influence in shaping his future and he thought of him only as an indulgent figure who took an interest in his progress, but he was wary in his company and from a young age knew that he had to be obedient and excel before he would receive any approbation.

In fact, his uncle had followed every aspect of Iftekhar's development with meticulous interest and had worked to shape the boy for his own purposes. He was particularly strict in respect of Iftekhar's religious upbringing, ensuring the boy received assiduous instruction in the teachings of Sunni Islam.

At school Ifty's early spiritual life was 'light touch' and fitted into the pattern of a well organised week but did not impinge greatly upon his everyday world, however, by the time he was an adult studying at Oxford University he was a confirmed Muslim with a strong faith. In the intellectual hothouse of university, studying for a joint honours degree in *Islamic Studies and Western Philosophy*, he mixed with others of his faith drawn from many backgrounds and experiences. He would meet regularly with a group of undergraduates at the Oxford Centre for Islamic Studies, all of whom wanted to better understand their religion and how it interfaced with the modern world in which they lived. One conversation to which they returned often concerned the role and observance of religion in a predominantly secular society. The group agreed that religious practice in the Christian faith occupied a tenuous position in Europe. The inconsistencies between the tenets of east and west were analysed, examined and discussed as they sought to manage the ambiguities they perceived between being a good Muslim and a righteous citizen.

He travelled to visit mosques in other major cities and was introduced to the thoughts of a variety of Imams, some of who were firebrands and maintained that politics and religion were necessarily linked for Muslims. His uncle took great interest in these visits and they frequently discussed issues arising from both Ifty's studies and his experience.

At the end of his first year in college Ifty returned to Pakistan for an extended visit to the land of his birth. During that summer, he spent time with his parents in Islamabad and visited other cities where he was introduced to senior clerics who probed his mind, opinions and attitudes. One particular Imam from Lahore made a profound impression upon Ifty, Ali ibn Musa, named after 'One of the Twelve' who had been famous for his discussions of the Quran between Muslims and non-Muslims.

As well as being tutored as a Muslim, Ifty received intensive instruction in the politics of his country which led to a deep fascination with its history, in particular its violent and bloody birth more than half a century earlier.

He was discerning enough not to be indoctrinated by those he detected wanted to shape and fashion his political or religious experience, and he came to understand that incompatibilities accompanied his binary education. One of these was that while he was expected to be obedient as a Muslim, his education in the western tradition required him to think as a sceptic. Increasingly he strove to reconcile the differences he recognised between the two cultures he inhabited and their various value systems. As a student of philosophy, it was expected that he would not accept deterministic divisions blindly, but as a good Muslim he was required not to question the word of religious doctrine. His natural inclination was to seek a paradigm that could unite rather than divide the two hemispheres of his inner east and west.

His trips to Pakistan each summer included a considerable amount of cricket. His love for the game had developed into a passion having been nurtured at school after his innate ability was recognised. He possessed a superb eye, a grace of movement, nimble timing and electric reflexes. Cricket became an obsession in his final years at Eton and in his first season at Oxford, he was awarded a 'Blue'. His tall, long-limbed delivery made him a fearsome fast bowler and he was a safe middle order batsman, occasionally ratcheting up a high score and maintaining a batting average in the mid-thirties. There was a tantalising possibility, it was suggested, that he might be selected to represent the Marylebone Cricket Club (MCC) if he continued to sustain his present form. Before graduating he made the decision that after university, he wanted to spend time concentrating on his cricket in both England and Pakistan.

Once university was behind him Iftekhar was delighted when an offer to play for a season with the MCC materialised. He accepted with alacrity, and because he was on the players' list, he was offered employment in the marketing department of the International Cricket Council working on an innovative scheme to promote cricket throughout Europe.

The Colonel

When he stepped out of the car Iftekhar was reminded how attractive and orderly were the house and grounds. The building, a large, Georgian mansion of Palladian design was entered through a wide, graceful portico flanked by elegant casement windows. Inside it was furnished tastefully in a variety of British styles, some traditional, others less so. His favourites were the Edwardian drawing room where William Morris 'Ancanthus' wallpaper and plush soft furnishings featured, while in sharp contrast the art-deco dining room was filled with a harsher décor, its linear architecture highlighted in black, white and silver. The highly burnished honey coloured sandalwood floors contributed to an effect of warmth, especially when the sun shone.

As he stretched his recently confined legs, the late afternoon sunlight spread long shadows across the immaculately manicured lawn beyond which grew dense rhododendron hedges covered in purple flowers, the national flower of Nepal.

Ifty anticipated the pre-prandial drinks would take place on the terrace to the rear just outside the library and overlooking his uncle's highly prized and perfectly maintained croquet lawn. From past experience he knew there would be reason and purpose behind today's 'invitation', and it would be revealed soon enough.

Following graduation Iftekhar had been surprised to receive a request to accompany his uncle to Pakistan prior to taking up his new position. They had spent three weeks travelling and Iftekhar was instructed in the rich and ancient history of his country. He was also introduced to men who espoused and argued for a radical new future for their nation, where the state of Pakistan would thrive as a first world nation with a robust economy that would eclipse those of other Muslim nations. Pakistan's old enemy, India, he was told, would decline in significance as his country ascended to first-world prominence.

Gradually it had dawned on Iftekhar that these men were interested in him and not just his politics, he came to realise that he was being evaluated and gauged.

He had spent some time with his parents, especially his father who was now preparing to ascend to the Presidency of his country. He was introduced to men of wealth, power and influence and on one fateful day his place in the destiny of his nation was revealed to him by *The Colonel*.

*

The Butler, George, greeted Iftekhar rather gruffly, a stuffy old retainer from a bygone age.

In his nasal drawl George said, "You will be accommodated in your usual room Mr Diaz, the Locke." All rooms Ifty knew were named after political thinkers and he could not resist teasing George, "Is that the room with the keyboard?" he asked disingenuously, provoking a withering look in reply.

"Drinks will be served outside at 7.00 pm, sir, and as always the dinner guests will adopt evening dress. Yours is pressed and hanging in its usual place in the cupboard. The Colonel will be grateful if you will join him in his study at 6.30 pm, that is in half an hour's time. In the interim please feel free to visit your room and refresh yourself."

When Ifty knocked and entered *The Colonel* rose from behind his desk and, as so often before, Ifty found himself appraising this most enigmatic of men. Elderly but trim and just below average height he was neat in every respect with a carefully manicured attention to detail and wearing an exquisitely cut linen suit and polished brown Oxford loafers. Ifty noted the top pocket silk handkerchief placed with exaggerated care and the knot of his tie effortlessly drawn, while the creases of his trousers were perfectly aligned. His thinning grey hair was brushed tidily (a D.A.) and pomaded, while his thick silver moustache was trimmed with precision. The scent of a pungent eau-de-cologne was distinctive. "Perhaps a trifle egotistical," thought Ifty.

The Colonel's smile broadened. "Iftekhar dear boy. Welcome. Come and sit down and we can chat before the guests arrive. How is the job at Lord's going? I have been following your progress, your three for fourteen last weekend was impressive."

"Thank you, sir. I am enjoying both my cricket and my position at Lord's. Might I be right in thinking that your influence played a part in my appointment?"

"If so then only in a minor way. Talent dear boy is irrepressible, irresistible to all."

"Now," said his host. "One of my guests this evening is very involved in the arena of hospitality and I want you to make her acquaintance; I can assure you this is an assignment you will enjoy. You are to gain her trust and make a good impression, for I cannot underestimate the importance of the association you will strike up."

"What is the name of this lady I am to befriend?"

"Helen Strachan, pronounced, Strawn."

Helen Strachan, the daughter of Sir David Strachan of Stonehaven, recently Tory Minister of Defence and now Chancellor of the Exchequer, arrived slightly late apologising profusely. From the moment of her entrance she had a gyroscopic effect on the dynamics of the assembled dinner guests. Her easy going and unassuming manner drew a coterie of admirers who gathered around, engaged by her personality and charisma as well as her striking physical appearance. During drinks on the terrace Ifty detected a slight frostiness from some of the women present, resentment he thought at the attention she was attracting.

Helen was introduced to Iftekhar by their host and there seemed little doubt to those present that evening that she enjoyed the company of the dashing young man whose tall, athletic physique and debonair, dark good looks had caught the attention of most of the females in the room.

Ifty and Helen were seated next to one another at dinner and he responded to her jocular repartee with a casual offhand wit she found amusing. She was impressed with his astute observations when the topic of conversation turned to more overtly political and serious subjects and she found his epigrammatic turn of phrase amusing. An impressive, intelligent and diverting young man she concluded.

The striking diamond in her engagement ring flashed like a beacon and he trod carefully to ensure that his flirtation did not transgress what he detected would be a rigid boundary.

They both enjoyed the evening and each other's company, their conversation light-hearted and slightly flirtatious, even a little coy at moments. They established that they had numerous friends and acquaintances in common and when he mentioned his role with the MCC she was particularly interested. By the end of the evening she had accepted an invitation to visit Lord's cricket ground, prefixed by an avowed ignorance of the game and its arcane rules.

When the last guest had departed the host and his protégé returned to the study for a final brandy and a cigar from the humidifier.

After a few moments of quiet contemplation Iftekhar enquired, "Will Helen's death be required before we reach the end of this business?"

"That depends," replied *The Colonel*. "Much rests upon your skill and the intransigence of some very big players, but it is not implausible. It may be that it is her demise that proves to be a deciding factor. The stakes are higher than you might imagine."

Clemmie

She would never forgive Henry. The commotion of her emotions went deeper than any capacity for forgiveness could ever offset, coalescing around a deep and abiding anger that solidified into a canker of loathing for her husband. They had been married less than two years and she was childless, any happiness blighted; her daughter, the precious child she had carried, borne and loved with the devotion that only a mother can possess, was "dead by misadventure," as the coroner had ruled.

Henry had explained to the court that he had returned to his car to retrieve some different lures to use during the warm afternoon's fishing. Cassie had *nipped to the loo*, and before doing so checked that Iphy was asleep in the buggy. She could swear, and did, that the buckle was firmly fastened before she left the child alone.

Clemmie followed a line of reasoning that developed into a conviction the more she considered the known facts: "*I wouldn't mind betting Henry was screwing her, that randy goat can't keep his trousers zipped for two days in succession and that girl was mooning after him even before they left for Scotland.*"

A month after the tragedy Clemmie walked out on Henry and rented a place on her own where she could live without constant reminders of her beloved child and where she did not have to have any contact with her estranged husband. She hired a private detective to investigate the circumstances of Iphy's death, and while evidence from the scene was scanty (the buckle was not faulty), the investigator had turned up the fact that Henry was paying rent on a flat in Islington for the disgraced nanny. Clemmie had made sure that Cassie was unemployable in any position of responsibility, an outcast from the world of childcare, but now Henry was staying at her apartment on a regular basis.

In Clemmie's mind Iphy's life had been lost because her useless, negligent father had sacrificed his daughter to his squalid, base desires. As a mother Clemmie was not just bereft but devastated, her mind obsessed with thoughts of her beautiful daughter, imagining her caught in a cataract of water overwhelmed as she was drawn under the surface, struggling to breathe and drowned when her head was driven onto a rock that caved in the right side of her perfect little cranium. The sweet head that she had nurtured at her breast and stroked to sleep night after night. Iphy would be avenged.

Clemmie had lived her life struggling to manage forces that conspired to 'drown' her. The fact that she always came second to Helen in achievement, admiration and love and was undervalued infuriated her. It made her resentful and increasingly rancorous while also stimulating some dark desires that she tried to suppress, but thoughts of revenge were becoming more frequent. She was the second born, she was not physically attractive and while a high achiever at school she struggled with relationships. Her sister meanwhile floated through life receiving attention, plaudits and adulation from all quarters, especially from their mother, albeit unintentionally. It was not surprising that Clemmie had begun to take occasional solace in alcohol and it wouldn't have taken a psychiatrist long to unearth a connection between her increasing sense of isolation and visits to certain clubs in London that attracted dark and malevolent types in whose company she felt comfortable. She had been betrayed. Divorce papers were prepared.

Meanwhile the anger she felt grew like a cancer that untreated started to metastasise. Its malignancy required retribution greater than ruining Henry's reputation or damaging his wealth; a life for a life. To eradicate the source of all her pain necessitated much thought and careful planning, but she had time, she had resources, she had connections and above everything else she had an all-consuming determination.

Lord's

As they had arranged Iftekhar met Helen at the gate to the 'Nursery End' of Lord's. He welcomed her, and they nattered away inconsequentially while they wandered past the practice ground before passing under the Compton Stand and then the Grandstand, from where he led her out to the very beating heart of the game itself, the wicket. Standing reverentially on the hallowed turf he explained they were equidistant between two famous and iconic architectural designs that characterise Lord's and make it so recognisable.

"At one end," explained Ifty, "stands the Pavilion, with its distinctive feature of a large Indian verandah that reminds me of my homeland. That is where the members always congregate at the beginning of test matches to encourage the teams as they make the long walk from the changing rooms. When they pass through the Long Room the players are clapped onto the field, although not always on their return! Until 1999 the only woman allowed in the Long Room was the Queen. It was a bastion of male chauvinism, but no longer, which is still a matter of regret to the old fogeys."

"Sporting their 'egg and bacon' MCC regalia some of these old boys still exist in a time warp," Iftekhar observed, "which is an apposite analogy as directly opposite the Pavilion is the oval media pod, which resembles a large bubble or UFO."

"Now look up there at the wind vane on top of the clock; Father

Time oversees every game. The old boy looks down on the past, the present and the future and presides over triumph and disaster in equal proportions, the ecstasy and the agony. He is removing the bails, a sober reminder for us all!"

He escorted Helen across the grass into the Long Room through the players' door where he showed her the museum with its special artefacts, including the small, precious urn containing 'The Ashes'. As she listened, she could hear his hero worship and it occurred to her that there was something naively charming about this young man with his passion for a sport that most of the people she knew considered unfathomable. He promised to get her a ticket for the next Test Match and as they left the ground through the gates on their way to lunch, he pointed out the statue of the venerated W. C. Grace and said ardently, "Sporting history and heroes are forged here."

"Thank you," said Helen once they were settled in a corner of a little Italian trattoria off the Wellington Road, where, on Ifty's recommendation she ordered a small Wiener Schnitzel with an accompanying salad, and they shared a zesty Pinot Grigio from Lombardy.

"I enjoyed the visit much more than I thought I would," began Helen. "And I begin to see why people feel so involved as a Test Match slowly unfolds because there is a tangible atmosphere in the ground, a sense of the Roman arena, of combat, gladiatorial, and when I stood in the Long Room I could almost imagine the teams being clapped out on to the field of battle. We who are to die salute you!"

"I am so glad you felt like that," said Iftekhar, "because I wanted you to experience the atmosphere, what it is that makes the place so special. The game means a great deal to many people and in my new role I am employed to extend the reach of cricket in a rapidly changing world. In a few years' time the cricketing landscape will be different because of changes being introduced now. A shortened form of the game, 'The Hundred', was introduced recently and the cricketing landscape is changing. Girls have adopted the game and are playing it at school instead of Rounders. In fact the way women's international sport in rugby, football and cricket has attracted support and media attention over the last few years has brought about profound change. Did you know there have been more than ten women's cricket World Cups since 1973 when they were first introduced? There is a rapidly growing interest in cricket."

"But," said Helen, "it takes so long to play, surely it will never really catch on?"

"Ahha, that's why a shortened and more exciting version, Twenty20 or T20, was introduced in 2003, and this is where you and I come in."

"How so?" queried Helen.

"Marketing a new mixed, T20, pan European competition," enthused the young man across the table from her.

As she listened to his earnest vision she relaxed, and her attention began to wander. *If I were not engaged to William I could be intrigued by this young man,* she thought. *His physique is that of a young god and he certainly knows how to charm a woman and make her feel special. I wonder what it would be like to run my hands through those long, dark curly locks?* The wine had softened her mood and she was vaguely aware that she was responding to what he was saying with more intensity than she truly felt. He amused her, and his unworldliness aroused her femininity to the point where she began to react to him in small subliminal ways. At the thought of the firm, muscular body beneath his shirt she felt her nipples harden. Shocked by her inattention she returned to what he was saying,

"So, will you come with me to Paris in January?"

She had to re-orientate rapidly.

"As I was saying," continued Iftekhar, "we are intending to set up a large event in the new year in Paris to promote a new pan European T20 game. With the International Cricket Council, the ICC, we are looking to create a multinational competition in the hope of emulating what the Rugby Football Union have achieved so successfully with the Six Nations competition.

"The launch will be a large and well represented marketing exercise with considerable corporate interest, and I am hoping you will consider leading the planning and organisation for us. Needless to say, there is a lot of money involved and it would be a great account for you to land. We would need to start planning straight away as the time frame is tight."

"In which case a few days in Paris sounds a very attractive proposition," replied Helen.

BDSM

The Rear Entry Club is situated a few minutes from Bromley-by-Bow tube station and is not a venue that might be expected to attract clientele from the aristocracy. It is a club, *'for those who take pleasure in the ritual and eroticism of wearing leather and rubber. You will be refused entry if you do not wear appropriate clothing'*.

Clemmie had been introduced when a group of friends with unorthodox interests persuaded her to join them for an evening as they set out to distract her from her pervasive introspection. Mandy had arrived one morning with an outfit for the evening that included a lace up bodice, a pair of pvc trousers and a leather mask. She instructed Clemmie to forego underwear.

When it was time to change it had been a struggle to squeeze into the ensemble, and as she looked at herself in the long mirror she blushed with embarrassment. She thought her boobs looked inflated and her legs grossly overweight, but at the same time she was eroticised by the feel of the latex and the sight of her body so blatantly clad initiated a sexual tingle. She donned a long overcoat that she buttoned tightly to the neck.

Mandy was waiting for her in a taxi and when they disembarked, they were in a part of London Clemmie had not visited before. They walked down the street and turned into a broad, well-lit alley that led to the back of the building where Clemmie saw a robust door and a group collecting outside. It occurred to her that, as the name suggested, the entrance was at the rear of the building.

Mandy knocked, was recognised and invited to enter a foyer that offered louche exuberance in its welcome with all the trappings of 'kink' - chains, whips, and spanking - as she was to discover later. The décor was a mixture of lipstick red leather panelling highlighted in stark relief by black crocodile skin. Tall mirrors caught the light from disguised lamps that reflected off chromium strips while large candles placed at either end of six steps led up into the atrium of the club. At the top of the steps was a velvet curtain through which everyone had to pass. The attendants carried swagger sticks and were dressed in revealing uniforms with flat, peaked caps that hinted at military correction. Clemmie was introduced to the 'door whore', a person of indeterminate sexual origin who demanded she opened her coat and then nodded, accepting her 'costume'. The man behind her was accused of being a 'tourist' and was required to strip naked and place a slave collar around his neck if he wanted to progress, a demand to which he readily acquiesced. Inside the atmosphere was predominantly dark and vampish with a piquant insinuation of mystery and a hint of clandestine jeopardy.

The evening proved riotously enjoyable.

At first Clemmie was confused and shocked at her first sight of a dominatrix in tight fitting leather with coiffured hair piled high and wearing livid makeup. She was strutting around the room leading a man wearing a dog's collar attached to a leash. He crouched at her side nuzzling her leg.

The music, 'Hard NRG or German EBM', Mandy said, alternated with songs by Nancy Sinatra, Blondie, Pulp and The

Damned. The volume was not as loud as in other clubs, but the incessant rhythm created a primal throb, a pulse that added to the atmosphere. Mandy led Clemmie on a tour of some of the rooms; one with 'feely boxes', long coffin shaped boxes with rubber gloves in which people were sitting while others groped them. There was 'The Dungeon', a room filled with wall harnesses, St Andrew's Crosses and restraints for those who wanted to discipline their partner in front of an audience, again according to Mandy. There were other similarly equipped rooms for couples' personal use and a masked dungeon where 'masters and mistresses' sought new slaves.

Clemmie entered a large room with a small stage on which an S&M play was being performed. She learned that themed nights took place regularly: 'Louis XVth', 'Nightmare Before Christmas' and 'Outer Space' in the previous month alone. She had expected to see a variety of costumes and was unsurprised by the goths and amused by the 'Ann Summers' influence. More perturbing were those displaying weird piercings and tattoos on their naked bodies and for many nudity seemed de rigueur, especially among the fetishists. She hadn't anticipated the number of middle-aged men and women present, some of whom looked distinctly mundane. She avoided the perverts and suspected there were rooms with dark secrets.

Time passed quickly and when she checked her watch she was surprised at the lateness of the hour, followed by the realisation that the bleak despair that had been her constant companion of late had lifted. She had enjoyed the uninhibited, feisty and immodest atmosphere, and when she danced, for the first time in an age, she felt unburdened.

Later on and having consumed a considerable quantity of shots and glasses of white wine, she accompanied an attractive, tall man with very tight clothing and thick chest hair into a small room. She thought he would kiss her, and some petting might take place, so she was unprepared when he lifted a thin whip off the wall and told her to bend over. When the wand struck a sting radiated across the back of her thighs and pulsed through her body initiating a delicious and thrilling sensation that stimulated her as never before. There were two further fiery strokes, and then he placed one hand across her pubis and bent her forward while pulling out his penis which she saw had a large ring through the foreskin. She was aghast and extricated herself rapidly. She was relieved to find the others ordering a taxi in preparation for departure.

Later as she was lying in bed and readying herself for sleep, she allowed her mind to wander back over the events of the evening, and as she did so she slipped her hand between her legs recalling the delicious thrills she had encountered. It would not be long before there was a return trip to the Rear Entry Club.

*

Clemmie had decisions to make. She had received confirmation that Henry had moved Cassie from Islington into the sumptuous apartment in Mayfair that she had only recently vacated. Furthermore, Cassie was pregnant, an outrageous affront against decency that only compounded his previous violations against her. She would not grant him the divorce he had requested, and she would ensure that he came to atone for his sins.

She resigned from Liberty's and embarked upon a law conversion course, articled to a firm in the Inns of Court. Her father was delighted by her chosen path and his influence quietly opened doors that allowed her to cross thresholds that might otherwise have remained obstacles. To her relief she found the intricacies of legal practice, alongside its esoteric language and customs, curiously appealing and it was not long before she knew that she was in her element, although should her peccadillo and visits to the club ever be exposed by the media any thought of a career in law and politics might come to a lurid halt.

What she did not know was that whenever a CCTV camera was installed in a location close to the Rear Entry Club it would quickly cease operation, usually because a pellet from a high velocity air rifle smashed the delicate machinery. With this simple expedient the venue managed to subvert surveillance and maintain anonymity for its clientele, as required by a number of its members some of whom occupied positions of influence. However, certain notorious activities had brought the club to the attention of the intelligence services, and in consequence Section Five installed camouflaged cameras in the brickwork of buildings overlooking both the front and back of the club. The digital record of the club's activities was not considered to be of major importance and was only reviewed occasionally, and so it came as a surprise when a junior section head at MI5 received a request to review the footage covering the previous two months. It was quietly made available and marked for 'Peter Baird's Eyes Only'.

Peter

Their role has been compared with that of the Chorus in a Greek play for THEY observe and track human activities while existing outside the action. Through them is filtered information from which is extracted and extrapolated the intelligence used to keep the United Kingdom secure. THEY monitor all communities and communications and study the actions of those in their ken, and of particular interest to them are those susceptible to the foibles of human nature, especially its excesses, for THEY know that mortals lose their way, sometimes by misadventure and, more dangerously, by design. THEY eavesdrop on whispers carried in the wind and THEY make connections so as to turn the dagger before it strikes. THEY are not warriors, but THEY have access to the sword of justice, and THEY ensure that retribution against subversives is swift. THEY never sleep.

*

The Government's Communications Headquarters is sometimes nicknamed *Avalon* because it's housed in a round-table shaped building. Its public face is a political appointee, but at the hub of the operation's most inner activity is the person colloquially referred to in the organisation as P (for *Prospero*). At an unusually young age, Peter Baird was appointed *Prospero*.

A distant ancestor of Peter's, Sir Giles Baird, served King Charles I faithfully and when the zealous parliamentarians in the long parliament of 1640 forced the King to pay for the army, the Baird family were one of those who came to the King's financial assistance. Later they deployed military backing on the borders of Scotland in support of his cause. When Charles II was restored to the throne in 1660 the Baird's fealty to their King was more than amply rewarded by the monarchy and Sir Giles became the Earl of Northumbria.

Since then some of Peter's ancestors had made a substantial contribution to the nation's affairs while others lacked the intellectual or moral fibre. There had been those who were thrifty and those who were extravagant, but common to them all and bred into the Baird bone was loyalty to King, Country and Church, characteristics deeply imbedded in the DNA of Peter Baird.

An academic, socialite and sportsman in his youth he was unmarried, remaining secretly loyal to one woman, the mother of his two daughters.

Peter's appointment had been made despite his pedigree and not because of it, for he was a man of unusual perspicacity, a brilliant strategist and exemplary patriot who seemed to his colleagues to be possessed of an uncanny ability to read runes, solve puzzles and formulate connections from scant evidence.

When he could not make sense of the fragments that caught his attention he would wait, for he was patient and while he lingered, he would garner snippets. He listened and observed silently, like a ghost, until his understanding began to take form and semblance, but on this particular morning something other than rational construct and logic was at play. Known colloquially as 'gut instinct' Peter's alarm bell was ringing.

Some three weeks previously Robert Gillespie, a low-ranking

local field agent serving out of the British Consulate in Lahore, alerted his section manager to the fact that he had unearthed information about a plot of enormous consequence. In a state of agitated excitement, and employing agreed code words, Bobby made it clear to his senior case officer, Andrew Hall, that he could not speak over an open line, but his tone stressed urgency. There was a note in Bobby's voice that the section head recognised for he had heard it before – fear.

Known as Bobby Gill, because the pronunciation of Gillespie was too convoluted for the Asian tongue to master, he had led an undistinguished career in the Service, but on that Thursday afternoon, Andrew Hall replaced the handset and issued a 'code red' directive. After three hours 'off piste' Hall widened the search until finally he received a report from a local chief of police, concerning the body of a Caucasian man found floating in a backwater of the Ravi River, amongst the detritus of a local slum. A post-mortem established that Bobby's cranium had received a fatal blow prior to entry into the water.

At a local level Bobby's demise was considered a possibly unimportant conclusion to an essentially inconsequential life. He had a reputation for drinking and hell raising and his murder was not initially attributed exceptional significance, but the 'code red' attracted interest further up the chain.

A search of Bobby's clothing revealed nothing of interest except a nondescript notebook that when dried out was still legible. In itself this discovery was deemed to be of little consequence as it contained nothing more than trivial jottings, and Andrew Hall would probably have ignored it except for a local convention that stated if an emergency communication needed to be recorded it should be entered on page seventeen. In this instance page seventeen listed crossword clues, Bobby Gill having been a *Times* concise crossword fanatic. Andrew and his team spent some time trying to make sense of the random words but did not decipher anything meaningful. However, following interest from London, Andrew forwarded the jotter to the head of the 'Asian Book' who in turn sent a copy to Peter Baird. Peter was intrigued and set to work in the hope that Bobby had coded an important message.

On page seventeen, clearly scribbled in haste, were clues to an elementary crossword:

Across
1 Absolute (8)
2 Journalistic writing (7)
3 Mountain depression (3)
4 Death toll (5)
5 Over-runs (7)
6 Word play (3)
7 Injection (3)

Down
1 French contradiction (3)
2 Meaning (5)
3

As instructed Peter dismissed the clues down and gradually assembled a list of words from the first group that when arranged consecutively began to make sense.

Absolute = Definite
Journalistic writing = Article

Mountain depression = Col
Death toll = Knell
Over-runs = Invades
Word play = Pun
Injection = Jab

The Colonel invades Punjab.

Peter was intrigued. *So, a Colonel? Who is this new adversary not previously on my radar? A Colonel, no, to be precise, The Colonel. The use of the definite article invests him with a rank that denotes a specific characteristic and identity. Also, a plot to invade Punjab? If so then who is scheming against whom?*

Peter would wait.

The Taliban

The term *Taliban* derives from the Arabic word for 'student', *Talib,* and refers to fundamentalist Sunni Muslims, mostly from Afghanistan's **Pashtun** tribes. The Taliban, as a military force, originated in Afghanistan and spread along the semi-autonomous tribal lands of the Afghan-Pakistan border at the end of the twentieth century.

From their inception the Taliban sought to establish a puritanical caliphate that neither recognised nor tolerated forms of Islam divergent from its own, scorning democracy, or any secular or pluralistic political process as an offence against Islam. Many traditional Muslims consider the Taliban's version of **Sharia** law to be barbaric because their interpretation of both Islamic law and practice is historically inaccurate, however, the Taliban organised itself into a military and religious force that became dominant.

There was no such organisation as the Taliban in Afghanistan until after the Soviet Union's troop withdrawal in 1989, following a decade-long occupation. By the time the last Russian troops withdrew in February of that year, they left a nation in social and economic chaos with one and a half million dead and a similar number of refugees. The political vacuum was filled by Afghan Mujahideen (Islamic guerrilla) military warlords, who replaced their war with the Soviets with civil strife and the Taliban became established.

Thousands of Afghan orphans were taken by the Taliban to become soldiers, and of these refugee children some were sent to Pakistan's *madrasa* religious schools, which were encouraged and financed by Pakistani and Saudi authorities to foster militantly inclined Islamists. Pakistan nurtured this corps of radicals as proxy fighters, especially for its ongoing conflict in Kashmir but, Pakistan also consciously intended to use the *'madrasa militants'* as leverage in its attempt to control Afghanistan and promote its own Islamist agenda. One such *madrasa* school, a boarding school, was established near the small town of Muzaffarpur in the north of Pakistan in the wooded region not far from the eastern bank of the Indus river where it descends from the mountains. The boys that attended this hidden away school were chosen for their intelligence, their resourcefulness and their commitment to the Muslim cause, and they experienced a more diverse curriculum than that of other *madrasa* institutions for it incorporated training in every conceivable form of terrorist activity.

Some years after its foundation orphaned twin brothers, Kassim and Sadam, arrived aged twelve years old. Their father, a mujahideen commander in Afghanistan had been targeted and killed by a rocket from an American F-35 stealth jet, as had their mother who was travelling beside him in the same vehicle.

The boys were a natural fit for the school, and they thrived. The teaching fuelled belief in the purity of their Islamic faith, the nobility of the Taliban cause and hatred of the west. They proved able and versatile adherents willing to demonstrate their commitment to the Islamic state, which pleased their teachers, and so when the time came for them to leave school, they were transferred to a terrorist training camp in Somalia where their potential as valuable assets was recognised.

The Islamic State of Iraq and the Levant (ISIL) and the Islamic State of Iraq and Syria (ISIS) are jihadist militant groups of fundamentalist Islamists, often referred to collectively as Islamic State (IS) or by the Arabic acronym *Daesh*. *Daesh* is associated with acts of extreme violence and is designated a terrorist organisation by the United Nations. The boys became active members of *Daesh* and before long the elders responsible for their development decided they would be suitable to embed in enemy states.

The brothers arrived on the shores of Europe as refugees from Syria, from where Kassim travelled to Marseille and Sadam found his way to Paris.

They had grown up emotionally dependent upon each other and when separated for the first time felt the need to remain in regular contact via email, text and other social media platforms. During their training they had been instructed not to communicate without permission, but in this one respect they disobeyed their superiors, and so it was that routine monitoring of 'chatter' by *Avalon* resulted in an exchange being picked up and passed on to *Prospero* by a curious controller. It was unusual for such a low-level interaction to arrive on the desk of Peter Baird, but the organisation was functioning in a state of heightened terrorist alert and certain key words triggered a response. In this case it was the reference to *she* that was logged, reviewed and passed on because it was elliptical and might be a coded message.

Sadam had written: *She will bend her knee and the orchid will bleed. Allahu Akbar.*

To which Kassim replied: *The rain will fall and the wheat will wither. Allahu Akbar.*

At first sight neither email seemed particularly notable, but an alert researcher had commented that the orchid might just be a reference to a European city. Peter's advice was sought, and his curiosity engaged, and he initiated a background check on the two young men whose 'footprint' was traced to a school in Muzaffarpur. It was when Peter requested a deeper investigation into the school that he came across the name of its benefactor, a man only ever referred to as سرهنگ , or in translation, *The Colonel*.

ACT THREE

Eurotunnel

The black cab crawled along Euston Road giving the cabbie regular opportunity to look in his mirror for another glimpse of the hauntingly beautiful fare he was driving to St Pancras International Station. From the moment she had hailed him, immaculately dressed in a tight fitting black trouser suit, he was smitten. And so it was that he helped her out of his cab on a cold January morning with a sense of regret before finding a porter to convey her luggage.

The imposing Victorian, gothic façade of St Pancras conceals a modern chromium bright station from where high-speed trains depart on arterial journeys across Europe connecting its great cities and circulating the 'blood' of a continent.

As arranged Helen and Iftekhar met by the statue of the quintessentially British poet John Betjeman, who would have found their rendezvous amusing, embarking as they were upon a mission to strike a victory for Britishness in the very heart of France. Grappling with their luggage they greeted each other with smiles and Helen offered her cheek for a clumsy kiss.

They had some time to spare and prior to embarking decided on a drink at the champagne bar, for they were both infected with a light-hearted mood as if off on holiday. Since their meeting at

Lord's they had spent an increasing number of hours in each other's company planning the important presentation they were to give in Paris, during which time they discovered they genuinely enjoyed each other's company.

William had been away for over a year now and the enforced separation was placing a strain upon Helen who was feeling increasingly alone. He was as devoted as ever in his emails and when they spoke, she always experienced the same thrill at the sound of his voice, but she was finding it a strain to imagine the sensation of his body beside her at night.

A week earlier, Ifty had asked Helen to accompany him to Tate Modern where they had found themselves standing before Rodin's sculpture, *The Kiss*. In that moment each had experienced a heightened awareness of the other, as if sharing in the sensuous eroticism of the naked couple. An unacknowledged but tangible frisson passed between them. It was all Ifty could do to restrain himself from taking her in his arms, and she half expected him to. Aroused by the marble figures so intimately, openly and carnally preparing to make love, they remained silent until Helen broke the mood by saying, "Did you know that at the moment of their kiss her husband discovered them and killed them both? At least that's the story in Dante's Inferno."

As the train sped across the tedious winter countryside of northern France, Helen concentrated on the notes she was jotting on her laptop in preparation for the presentation the next day. Seated opposite one another on two seats at the end of a comfortable first-class carriage there existed between them a sense of seclusion, almost intimacy, and Ifty's mind began to wander, hovering between sleep and wakefulness. Helen's preoccupation gave him the opportunity to scrutinise her without causing offence and he studied her closely trying to decide what it was that made her so uniquely exceptional. On that first day at Lord's he had realised she was captivating, but as he spent more time in her company, he discerned qualities that provoked a much deeper response than mere physical attraction. He had known a number of women and possessed several, but never before had he felt reverence or awe, he had never worshipped.

His gaze focused upon her left breast and he stared in wonder as her fingers slowly unbuttoned her cardigan and then the tight white blouse below revealing pink porcelain skin lightly dusted with freckles. When she cupped her firm, rounded breast and lifted it from her bra he could see it was beautifully proportioned, and he lent forward to take its weight in his hand. She slid forward so that his mouth could suck gently and nuzzle the small erect nipple with his tongue.

With a jolt he emerged from his reverie and shook his head to clear his mind. He looked up and saw that she was contemplating him curiously; for a moment he felt panic as if she had somehow read his thoughts and fleetingly he experienced guilt similar to when, aged seven, matron had caught him in the pantry with his fingers in the honey jar. He avoided her eye and looked away covered with confusion. He coloured and blustered something inane about the meeting that awaited them.

Helen had in fact noticed the distracted way in which Ifty was staring at her. She would have been amused if she could have seen his thoughts, but as it was, she had her own. He was younger than her, a beautiful specimen of athleticism with a physique and looks resonant of a Greek gladiator, but beneath the surface she perceived complexities that intrigued her. There was a winsomeness, a vulnerability, something of the lost boy Peter Pan, the charm and boyish innocence disguising contradictions that she could not pin down. He was entertaining and flippant, amusing and interesting, but she sensed that these beguiling characteristics veiled a corresponding inscrutability, a curious mix of canine devotion and feline detachment. There was a whiff of danger about Ifty that he kept disguised.

The Eurostar drew into the Gare du Nord creeping up to the buffers before silently and imperceptibly drawing to a halt. With a flurry of doors opening noisily a torrent of passengers discharged swelling into a crowd as they strode purposefully along the platform.

Ifty gathered up all their paraphernalia and helped Helen down from the train before heading out to find a taxi beyond the imposing façade designed around a vast triumphal arch.

"Hotel du Quai Voltaire s'il vous plaît," instructed Ifty and the vehicle was rapidly drawn into the river of traffic that flows inexorably through and around Paris, its lifeblood. The taxi stopped, started and bobbed along like a cork in a stream until it drew up outside a modest hotel conveniently situated on the left bank of the Seine near the Musée d'Orsay, opposite the Louvre, the Opera Garnier and almost directly facing the Jardin des Tuileries.

As Ifty gathered their luggage and turned to assist Helen he was immediately aware of danger. She was opening the door on her side into the oncoming traffic, unaware of vehicles accelerating fast from traffic lights some distance behind. He reacted with lightning speed. Leaning across the seat he yanked her back into the cab just as a juggernaut bore down on the vehicle with its air horn blaring. It missed the taxi door by centimetres and the HGV driver shouted wild curses through his window. Helen was dazed but then shock took hold of her and she gripped Ifty hugging him tightly until her fright subsided and he could help her out of the taxi into the hotel.

That evening they dined at a small but charming restaurant, Les Antiquaires, not far from the hotel. At the end of the meal they were pleasantly relaxed and so decided to wander back to the hotel along the embankment warmly wrapped in thick coats and scarves. It felt natural for Helen to take Ifty's arm and lean comfortably against him matching his stride, and so she was surprised when he suddenly stopped and turned to face her, their breath a little fog hovering between them. He took her hands in his and looked deeply into her eyes.

"Helen, I am in love with you. There are dark secrets in my life, but I swear to you that I will leave all that behind and devote the rest of my days to looking after you if you will let me. I want to marry you, and I want to prevent terrible things happening. I know that you say you love William, but I can offer you so much more."

Without disengaging Helen collected her thoughts and after a few moments spoke soothingly, as if to a child.

"Ifty you are special to me, but I am not your confessor and I will not be your lover. I do have deep feelings for you, but they are different from those I hold for William and he is the only man to whom I shall ever give myself. I understand how painful this is for you and you will always be dear to me, but I won't be your mistress or your wife. I'm sorry, I know I am causing you anguish, but please, please respect me enough to understand and accept what I am saying."

They stood foreheads touching and she hugged him because she knew he was struggling not to cry and his voice did waver as he said to her, "My devotion to you Helen is absolute. Whatever happens please believe my promise never to desert you."

His distress was sincere because he knew that if they did not flee Paris that night then his promise would indeed prove a lie.

Stade de France

The roar of the crowd swelled as the ball left the right boot of the fly-half, his calf muscle as rigid as a steel hawser in its power and intensity. In slow motion it rotated elliptically on its axis rising in an arc, end over end. It flew almost a quarter of the length of the pitch, watched by two nations each holding their collective breath. Passing its meridian one half of the crowd willed it to fall between the posts while the others wished as fervently that it deviate or fall short. An audible hush descended across the stadium followed by a muted explosion of sound combining joy and dejection.

Helen dropped her gaze from the screen that was looping silent highlights of great French rugby victories and looked out through the large panoramic window with its superb view of the pitch at the fruit bowl that is the Stade de France with its steeply raked seats and cantilevered glass fringe that circumscribes the roof. In pensive mood she observed that hopes and disappointment, joys and despair are often separated by the tiniest of circumstance, which is why sport is so often called upon as a metaphor for life. Her wish as she stood there was that the day's event would prove victorious.

As it was the presentation passed as well as could have been hoped and with a precision that was a credit to all of Helen's meticulous planning. She made a short introduction to the room, attended equally by men and women from the media, beginning with an extract from a poem:

There's a breathless hush in the close to-night
Ten to make and the match to win
A bumping pitch and a blinding light,
An hour to play and the last man in.
And it's not for the sake of a ribboned coat,
Or the selfish hope of a season's fame,
But his captain's hand on his shoulder smote
'Play up! Play up! And play the game!'

"Ladies and gentlemen, welcome to our event today. In England we understand that the game of cricket is something of an enigma to many of our European friends and neighbours, but those lines I have just read, from a poem by Sir Henry Newbolt, offer perhaps an insight into why the national game has been such an entrenched part of English village, county and national life for centuries for it is a game that enshrines what we believe to be British values. More importantly it is fun to play and can be exciting to watch, which is why it was adopted by many Commonwealth countries where it generates even greater fervency than in the UK.

"It is a game that stirs deep passions and rivalries and its followers are ardent in their support because it excites emotions and pride. It is tribal, it is gladiatorial and tactical, but it has never caught the European imagination, which may well be because the long version of the game does not suit the pace or way of life of Europeans and especially not the modern generation.

"However, when a particular sport does excite public attention then it generates interest in the media, and if it manages to capture international attention then huge financial benefits follow. When television rights are negotiated and syndicated then a sport becomes a hugely valuable commodity.

"We are living through a time of historic social change, and one of the boundaries that is shifting is the range of sports being played by women, especially post-pandemic. These trends are reflected through various media, and we have seen the popularity of women's football and rugby grow enormously in the last few decades. And, following the success of England's women cricketers, a new trend has emerged in many English schools where the girls' summer game of Rounders is being dropped in favour of cricket, which can be played by girls and boys equally. In a few years' time cricket may become the summer sport for all British children, in which case its popularity will lead to an expansion of club and regional competitions.

"It is not, though, the traditional version of cricket that is catching the popular mood, but a relatively new version known as the 100-ball game that has evolved from Twenty20. The 100-ball game is returning cricket to terrestrial television in the UK and is being organised into regional competitions to attract a broad spectrum of players and followers.

"We believe that with the right resources and promotion this new game will capture the interest and imagination of young people, not just in Britain but across nations.

"The 'tablet generation' need to exercise more and it is important that they are inspired through sport to forego their screens, which requires sport to be easily accessible to all. By introducing boys and girls to the 100-ball game from a young age we believe that it will not be long before cricket becomes popular across Europe at all levels, and this will lead to greater international interest in T20 competitions.

"Which brings me to the reason we have invited you here today. The Stade de France represents one of a group of enormously successful commercial venues across Europe where, amongst other fixtures, the Six Nations Rugby internationals are played. This winter competition generates many millions of pounds – and euros – annually. Imagine how profitable it would be for all involved if we could create a summer equivalent? If T20 were to catch the popular imagination across Europe, then there is no reason why we could not in time emulate the success enjoyed by rugby and football. Loving the game as we do it is our belief that with appropriate media interest, sponsorship, sports body funding and grassroots investment then many thousands of young people can be captured by the spirit of T20 and, in turn, they will call upon their nations to play up, play up and play the game! Thank you for listening.

"Now let me introduce Mr Iftekhar Diaz, from the Marylebone Cricket Club in London who will explain in detail how we believe the concept can be developed. He will talk to you about how we can generate excitement for *Europe T20* and how we might look to develop the commercial opportunities."

Afterwards, when lunch was over and all the delegates had drifted away, Iftekhar was animated. The presentation had been well received by the delegates who expressed enthusiasm to pursue the project through a scoping exercise. A proposition to engage with national sporting bodies to investigate the level of interest and to progress marketing strategies was endorsed unanimously.

And now they were alone. Helen was staring through the large panoramic window with its spectacular view of the arena and Iftekhar was standing behind her. He placed his arms around her waist and gently pulled her against him burrowing his nose in her hair. He took a deep breath as if inhaling her.

"That went well, and the success is down to you."

She leant back against him and rested her hands on his arms for a moment before gently prising herself free and turning to face him.

"It did go well, and I think we may have started something big."

He went to embrace her again but, she stopped him holding up her hands.

"Yes, Ifty, it was a great success, but you know that I am not the prize. You also know the rules. To use a cricketing term, it's no ball when it comes to intimacy."

They dissolved into a fit of giggles and she did not resist when he hugged her. "You are very special Ifty and were circumstances different I am sure we would be lovers by now, but I am William's and I will marry him. Ours is a professional relationship and while you are very charming and very attractive, and I like you enormously, I will not go to bed with you."

"Forsooth. Never my intention!" Ifty replied with forced jocularity. "But I do want you to know how much I appreciate all you have achieved today, and it is not incidental that I am hopelessly attracted to the most beautiful woman I have ever met, the most alluring, exciting, sexy female that walks this earth. I only wish I had met you before he did. I shall continue to live in hope that you will take pity upon my unrequited love and realise that it is actually me you love more. Also, whatever happens next remember that I love you."

Helen gently removed his arms and stepped away. "Of course, I don't mind you complimenting me, Ifty, and I'm really touched by your devotion. I promise that if I ever feel the need to be unfaithful to my husband it will be with you."

She saw sadness in his eyes and so changed the mood with abrupt efficiency asking, "What time are we due to leave for London? Do we have an open ticket booked or is there a specific time we need to be at the station? I'm going back to the hotel now."

He answered but seemed unaccountably distracted. "We are booked on the 18.35. I'll meet you at the station at about 17.00. I have ordered a taxi to take you back to the hotel from here and it should be at the main gate in about ten minutes. Just mention my name to the driver."

She gave him a peck on the cheek and made her way to the exit, tottering a little on her high heels as she entered the elevator. They were, she knew, inappropriate for a sports stadium, but they highlighted the musculature of her long, toned legs. The business suit she had chosen for the presentation was tailored by Kathryn Sargent of Savile Row and made from finely woven merino wool, expertly cut so that it enhanced the roundedness of her hips without being voluptuous. A matching jacket over a silk shirt displayed a hint of lace just above her bust and drew attention to her flawless skin. Her buoyant hair was held in a tress by a velvet bow and she knew she had made a strong impression that morning.

As she reached the gate, she could see a taxi waiting, its engine running. The driver confirmed that he was booked for customer Diaz and in reasonably fluent French she asked to be taken to the Hotel du Quai Voltaire. As she subsided into the back seat she began to relax and slipped off her shoes.

Seconds later the taxi turned into a side road and she was totally unprepared when all of a sudden, the driver braked hard. She was thrown forward and dazed but not badly hurt. Confused, she looked through the side window to see what had happened and made out a man lying inert beside a bicycle in the middle of the road. The taxi driver had pulled up beside the injured man who, to Helen's enormous surprise, promptly leaped up, tore open the rear door and jumped into the cab beside her. Bemused, she was unaware that the vehicle had started moving again and was taken totally by surprise when he forced a cloth into her face. She struggled, but almost immediately a fog began to form in front of her eyes and her strength began to ebb. The drug, known as 'Isoflurane', is a fast-acting strong sedative and everything blurred rapidly, so much so that she was only faintly aware of a needle being inserted into her carotid artery as she was injected with another drug, 'Propofol' that induces deep anaesthesia.

The taxi weaved confidently through a number of nearby streets before pulling up sharply and the unconscious Helen was transferred to a waiting ambulance. A saline/sucrose drip, connected to a cannula was inserted into the back of her left wrist to keep her hydrated and allowed for further doses of 'Propofol' to ensure she remained comatose for the rest of the long journey.

The ambulance set off on its route to Germany, via Belgium, and apart from refuelling did not stop again until it reached its destination, Bremen airport. Here it pulled up in a small hangar that housed a private jet, a Gulfstream G600. Once the medical attendant and Helen's inert body were safely stowed in the cabin, the pilot submitted his flight plan and as soon as he received clearance from air traffic control distanced them from Europe as rapidly as possible.

The long flight to northern India passed without incident. The pilot had posted his destination as Chandigarh in northern Punjab, but as he approached Amritsar he advised air traffic control that he was cancelling the instrument flight rules (IFR) and would continue using visual flight rules (VFR) in order that his very important guest could enjoy a view of the hills and mountains over which they would pass. Changing his 'transponder squawk' to A200 (the VFR conspicuity code) he contacted air traffic control again and announced that he would log in again after half an hour, at which point he switched off the plane's transponder and descended below radar cover. In less than ten minutes he made an undetected visual landing at a little used tarmacked runway outside Patiala in eastern Punjab where the weather was perfect. He was only on the ground for a few minutes before taking off and resuming course for Chandigarh. At an altitude of twenty thousand feet, and thirty minutes since he had last spoken to air traffic control, he reported that he had returned to his original course and was now back on their radar. He landed at Chandigarh only minutes after his stated ETA.

GCHQ

Cheltenham - England

Peter Baird's mobile phone had embedded in its electronic brain an application that alerted him in the event of an emergency. Following an excellent lunch with the Minister he was just enjoying a fine piece of camembert, accompanied by a sweet port confit, when his phone began to trill and vibrate with a tone that was guaranteed to raise his heart rate. He knew that his chauffeur would be arriving almost immediately at the entrance to the *Lumiere* restaurant in Cheltenham ready to deliver him back to the office as rapidly as possible. Fortunately, he had almost reached the end of the six-course taster menu, crowned in his opinion, by the Canon Pyon damson soufflé. With as little ado as possible he made an excuse and extracted himself.

He arrived back at 'the office' in short order where a small group were assembled to brief him. News had just arrived of the abduction of a high-profile couple in Paris, the daughter of a senior minister in the UK government and the son of the President of Pakistan. He was informed that Helen Strachan was missing presumed kidnapped. She had been working with Iftekhar Diaz, who could not be traced either.

Peter watched the available CCTV footage that showed Helen climbing into a taxi outside the gate of the Stade de France. A little later the camera on a bus caught the scene of an insensible woman being transferred from the same taxi to an ambulance. By means of number plate recognition the ambulance had been traced along a five-hundred-mile journey to Bremen airport, but twenty-two hours had elapsed since the abduction and the drive would have only taken between eight and nine.

The French gendarmerie had not been alerted to the seizure until an anonymous message was received earlier that day. By the time the authorities had established the veracity and accuracy of the information the trail was almost cold. The ambulance had been found in a car park near a hangar at Bremen airport from where a private Gulfstream G600 jet had departed early that morning. The pilot had filed a flight plan for Chandigarh in northern India, where it had duly landed with the complement listed on the manifest that did not include a female passenger.

The driver of the taxi in Paris was discovered in his vehicle on a deserted plot of land with a bullet through his head. A serious diplomatic incident was brewing and already the press had a whiff of something in the offing. It would be impossible to contain such a story, but there might be a chance of controlling it, or so Peter hoped.

Events whirled and swirled around Peter for many hours. He managed to ensure the CCTV coverage was not made available to the media and took it upon himself to authenticate every single known detail. It was not until late that night, and still at his desk, illuminated only by the pool of light cast from the green glass of a lamp, that he had the chance to unclutter his mind and sift through the facts.

It was being claimed that both the man and the woman had been taken captive, but the recordings only showed the abduction of

Helen. It was established later that Iftekhar Diaz had disappeared at about the same time and could not be traced, but why two separate events when it would have made sense to abduct the victims together? Assuming the snatchers were professionals, why had the two most significant events, Helen being picked up and then transferred, taken place within view of closed-circuit cameras, why not make the exchange in a cul-de-sac or closed building? Why had the ambulance been driven so far when there were airports closer to Paris? No effort had been made to disguise the abduction or where the aeroplane landed, but the trail was cold. Iftekhar had not been seen departing the stadium, but there was no sign or evidence of his kidnap.

This was not a bungled affair; it was a sophisticated and complex operation for which there would be a sophisticated and complex motive. Why two such high profile victims? Presumably because of their eminent families. That being the case then the abductions probably had a political motive, unless events were being orchestrated by some underground organisation whose goal was profit, in which case a ransom demand would be received soon. Something big was building but Peter needed more scraps before he could begin to make sense of what was taking place. He knew from experience that there would be a next stage and so it was now a waiting game. In the meantime, it fell to him to inform the parents of the poor girl at the centre of events.

He leaned back in his chair and allowed his mind to drift. When he set out to seduce Leda all those years ago he had never intended to fall in love. He was a bachelor living life to the full, an active man with high social status, wealth and a successful career; he was respected as a specialist in foreign affairs and his opinions were sought. He was beginning to hold sway in intelligence and political circles and a complex emotional relationship was not on his agenda, and so he was completely unprepared for the turmoil that resulted from their liaison and the consequences that followed.

Peter was a man of principle with fixed points on the compass that guided the decisions by which he lived his life and once he had committed to Leda he never considered another woman, the drawbridge was raised permanently.

Professionally he was equally principled, always retaining high regard for those who work to uphold the rule of law, irrespective of their background, politics or religious inclination. He knew that without the vigilance of a few his country was vulnerable to those who seek to threaten its people and institutions, and he certainly subscribed to the Burkean notion that, *'The only thing necessary for the triumph of evil is for good men to do nothing'*.

"The barbarians lurk outside the gate," he would say, "And to believe otherwise is as good as to invite them in," which was why he had become a *'Fidei Defensor'*, a *Defender of the Faith* or *FD* as they were referred to in clandestine circles.

At school he had not considered life much beyond the estates of his duchy, but his intellectual ability, sound moral character and passionate belief in justice had gradually orientated him towards a life in the service of his country. As he approached graduation the Dean of his Cambridge college suggested a chat with a friend who worked in the Foreign Office and a door opened unexpectedly.

He found the challenges of *'The Service'* fulfilling, although it came at a cost to his innocence, for in the world of intelligence idealism is soon compromised. As he progressed in the murky world of espionage, he could not avoid the depressing conclusion that while modern homosapiens might be generally more humane than their ensanguined predecessors, they repeat the same mistakes because the human frailties of self-interest, perversion and exploitation, are intrinsic.

"Humanity," he espoused, "has to guard against itself and it is only because of the vigilance of the watchmen that the status quo is maintained. Eternal alertness is essential – 'Readiness is all'."

Now, as he sat at his desk ordering the events known so far, he was convinced something dangerous was moving in the dark and it was approaching.

He must speak to Leda. Leda, the woman to whom he was devoted and the mother of his daughter now in great peril. He reached for the phone.

Confusion

Ifty watched from high-up in the stadium as Helen climbed into the taxi and for a moment could hardly breathe as the full implication of his treachery sank in. In that instant he experienced the despair of the quisling who all of a sudden understands he is compromised beyond his ability to control events and knows there is no way back. Up until the last moment he could have stopped her, but he hadn't – why? For so long he had been so sure of the truth behind the cause, but as he stood and watched Helen step into the taxi a feeling of desolation overwhelmed his conviction. He should have stopped her, but he had not. As the full significance of his betrayal sank in and he thought about what was to happen next, he felt utter despair.

He knew he had to subdue his turmoil, but the magnetism of her eyes and softness of her kiss just before she turned to leave were seared into his consciousness.

He told himself that he must focus on the task and remember that he had committed himself to a noble purpose, he could not let sentiment be his undoing, his training required him to remain loyal to the one true cause.

Picking up his holdall he sought out the gents' toilet where he changed his appearance before, apparently, stepping off the edge of the world.

From a public payphone outside the stadium he called a number and when the line connected, he asked the simple question,

"*Où, et à quelle heure?*"

Ifty descended the steps into the Metro and was sucked underground. He bought a ticket for the 'Pont de Bezons' in the north west sector of the city and sometime later emerged following a tortuous route to the Rue des Freres Bonneff where he stopped outside an old tenement building. Ahead of him as he opened a small nondescript front door was a passage that led to another entrance where he was buzzed in. A staircase spiralled up to an apartment on the first floor.

*

Two days later Leda lay cradled with Peter Baird's arm wrapped protectively around her but there was no further news of Helen. They were naked, their warmth shared under a duvet as the urgency of their lovemaking began to diminish, and in Leda's case give way to despondency. Fear for their daughter had found expression in the need they had for each other.

Her head rested on his broad chest and slow tears began to trickle into the springy mass of hair that covered his upper body. She thought back to that winter's day in Norfolk when he had first taken her, and she had abandoned herself to him so willingly. From the beginning she had been honest, telling him that she would remain David's wife because to divorce would have compromised the future careers of both men and undermined the stable bedrock of her new family. And so, while David lived his remote and increasingly ascetic life in London, dedicated almost exclusively to the Government and his passions for opera and fine art, much of Leda's energy remained directed towards her daughters, upon whom she focused all her maternal devotion.

The first she had known of Helen's disappearance was when Peter broke the news to her forty-eight hours earlier. Neither he nor David could offer any firm reassurance that Helen would be found safe and well, indeed there was no indication as yet to her whereabouts and Leda was distraught with worry.

"Will you find her for me, please Peter? I can't bear the thought of our beautiful, lovely girl being hurt or disfigured by some evil menace."

"You know that I will," said Peter conveying all his strength and determination. "Have you told Clemmie?"

"She knows, but I can't seem to reach her anymore. Since Iphy it is as if she has closed her emotional doors and wants to exclude everyone, including Helen and me. She is drifting away from me and in my darkest moments I fear that she is capable of some desperate act. She seems so very alone."

"Clemmie is certainly confused and at the moment is in danger of rejecting us for something else, but I shall watch over her," said Peter. "In me you must trust for I am your rock."

India

East Punjab

A perfect media cyclone was growing around the breaking news that the daughter of the Chancellor of the Exchequer of Great Britain and the son of the President of Pakistan had gone missing in extraordinary and mysterious circumstances. The broadsheet newspapers were trying to adopt a reserved and dispassionate response, but the tabloids were frothing with excitement at what they hoped might turn into the story of the year.

The *Daily Mail* took the high ground in its opinion columns and one columnist even went so far as to imply that Helen was a woman of loose moral conduct. A reporter paid a member of staff at the hotel in Paris in which the two had been staying for a photograph that drew attention to the fact that there was an interconnecting door between their separate bedrooms, the salacious implication being that this represented evidence of an amorous affair. Was she indulging in a dalliance and cuckolding her faithful fiancé while he risked his life in foreign lands; was the beautiful but fickle and indulged daughter of wealthy parents cavorting in Paris with a pampered Pakistani playboy? One obnoxious commentator even suggested a spurious parallel with Princess Diana who had spent her final days in Paris with the son of a rich middle eastern. Online comments fuelled further speculation. The story was a tale destined to grow wings and the more sensationally it was spun the more the media salivated. After days when lack of new information meant the narrative might lose oxygen the papers turned their attention to the fiancé.

And then, six weeks after her abduction a YouTube clip flashed around the world and spread faster than wildfire. It headlined all news programmes and soon became the image that would define a seminal moment in journalism for years to come. Helen, looking dishevelled and ethereal was tied to a post. Dressed in an orange jumpsuit there was a copy of that day's *Times of India* hung on a string around her neck.

The Americans who ran the internment camp at Guantanamo Bay had initially dressed their 'non-compliant' prisoners in orange overalls, and this mode of dress was adopted by various terrorist organisations as a symbol of hated American imperialism. The message was implicit.

Behind Helen stood a man with a turban wound around his head and face, leaving only a slit for his eyes that shone dark and malevolent. On his left breast was an insignia, *PSM*, the letters printed with straight lines resonant of the lightning style adopted by the Nazi Gestapo. The man held a large commando knife, the cutting edge of which glinted with vindictive intent and looked as sharp as a razor blade. The top edge of the heavy weapon was fashioned with serried, steel teeth designed to tear through flesh.

As the video ran the man leaned forward, grasped Helen's hair and forced her head backwards. Without hesitation he drew the blade slowly across her exposed neck leaving a crimson line that started to bleed copiously where the honed edge passed. When the wound stretched across her throat, he released his hold allowing her to fall forward and collapse. Seen on virtually every television, mobile phone, laptop and tablet across the globe was the face of a transcendently beautiful woman being desecrated by a homicidal Jihadist.

In another video that followed two days later the son of the President of Pakistan, also dressed in an orange jumpsuit with the letters *PSM* printed on the chest, was made to kneel and place his neck on an execution block. Beside him stood the same man, this time holding a heavy scimitar which he raised with the obvious intention of beheading his victim. The camera focused on the face of Iftekhar with his eyes closed before panning back to show the executioner in full length. The killer, apparently a Sikh, changed his stance and raised the blade, swinging it downwards with as much force as he could muster. The screen went blank accompanied by the sound of a heavy weapon cleaving wood.

And so, the political agenda of the *PSM* or *Punjab Separatist Movement* was suddenly thrust into the centre of world affairs when the *PSM* claimed to be the inheritors of Jarnail Singh Bhindranwale, a Sikh leader killed in 1984 after the Indian military stormed the Golden Temple of 'Akal Takht' in Amritsar during 'Operation Blue Star'. Bhindranwale had plotted to create 'Khalistan', an independent country and homeland for Sikhs, free from the rule of Hindus, in Punjab. He plotted with the government of Pakistan who were supportive of his ambition and military objective.

The Prime Minister of India, Indira Gandhi ordered the army to launch Operation Blue Star on the first of June, and it took until the eighth before Bhindranwale was killed and the siege lifted, by which time almost five hundred Sikhs were dead and eighty-three soldiers. The clean-up that followed, 'Operation Woodrose' was extensive throughout Punjab and the political fallout was long lasting and extensive, including the assassination of Indira Gandhi when she was shot by her Sikh bodyguards.

When the agenda of the *PSM* was launched with the videos of Helen and Ifty being executed the Indian government was quick to distance itself from any historical association and claimed ignorance of the movement. The government of Pakistan, on the other hand, was vociferous in its outrage arguing that the activities attributed to the *PSM* were nothing more than a cynical land grab by India itself who wanted to disenfranchise West Punjab.

International tension began to ratchet. The purported execution of the son of Pakistan's President brought howls of anger, while the prospect of the brutal execution of an English Rose by callous Indians resulted in demands for military action from Her Majesty's Government.

As a consequence of the abductions the political tension between east and west was raised at the United Nations and debated at NATO, resulting in a resolution that agreed a pact of cooperation. A motion was approved that if another egregious act were to take place anywhere in Europe then NATO would act collectively and defensively, and America would, of course, stand by its allies. In that case Russia was almost certainly going to sense an opportunity to further its expansionist ambitions in Asia. Perceptive and veteran members of the UN understood that the building blocks of international stability were under threat.

A Proposition

Peter Baird received the flight plan for the only private jet to depart Bremen for Chandigarh on the day of Helen's abduction. When he read the report from air traffic control the dots started to arrange themselves and he realised that something was askew. He requested a copy of the communication log between air traffic control and the pilot when it entered Indian air space, at which point it became immediately obvious to him that there was an unaccounted for half hour, time enough to have made an unofficial landing. His next step was to order an intelligence analysis listing all non-commercial runways and landing strips within a thousand kilometres of Chandigarh. When he received the report, he scanned the list eagerly, finally concluding that it was most likely the jet had landed outside the city of Patiala, near enough to Chandigarh to deviate and be back on track in the time available. Assuming his conjecture was accurate it raised the question of why Patiala. He would investigate. In the meantime, he ensured that an immediate embargo was enacted on any information relating to the investigation and issued a gagging order in the event that any details were leaked to the press.

*

William reported, as instructed, to the Ministry of Defence in London on the Tuesday morning eight weeks after Helen's disappearance. Dressed in 'civvies' he was escorted to a room deep within the building where he was met by Sir David Strachan, which was the first time the two men had seen each other since Helen's father welcomed his prospective son-in-law into the family at their engagement party. Another man was sitting quietly in the corner and there was no introduction. William was waved into a chair.

"You have my most sincere sympathy, dear boy," began Sir David. "I have not slept since I first heard the news and I imagine that you are frantic with worry. Helen's mother is distraught. The only positive we have is that we know she is alive. HMG is doing all it can to trace her whereabouts and of course no stone, not one, shall be left unturned. We shall do everything in our power to return her to you as soon as possible, which, I am sure will be before long. Believe me every sinew is being stretched and all the considerable resources of HMG are being expended in the effort to ensure her safe return. As yet there is no firm information upon which we can formulate a plan of action, but I want you to meet an old friend of mine, Peter, who is an expert in this field. Awful mess, but don't lose hope, keep the faith dear boy." With that he walked out without acknowledging either of the men who remained.

William was aware that he was being appraised by the well-built, silent man who now emerged from the corner to take a seat on the other side of the small conference table that separated them. William could not avoid the sense that he was being evaluated and noted the stranger's expression, it was as if he was making a judgement. He was being studied intently and quizzically.

To William's surprise Peter addressed him abruptly, almost rudely and demanded, "Did she run off with this Pakistani fellow?"

Hesitating for a few seconds before replying William kept his tone equable. "I can't say for certain, sir, but I don't think so. She may have been attracted to him, but I believe she is essentially a loyal, honest woman not known to be unpredictable or unduly impetuous. In all the months I have been away I have received at least one text or email a day detailing plans for our wedding and listing schemes for the décor and furniture of the house we are buying in London. Her missives have been consistently positive with nothing to suggest a change of heart. Furthermore, she has been throwing herself into planning the extended trip we intend to take around South America once we are married and I have left the army. She has made oblique references to family life and parenthood, all of which suggest commitment and plans for a stable future rather than doubt and uncertainty. Occasionally she has referred to this man Iftekhar but only as a work colleague, and I have never detected any particular spark between them. My opinion is that it would be out of character for her to behave as has been suggested by some in the media."

"Hmm," grunted the big man, "I agree, but that raises the more problematic question as to what exactly has happened. If I am right in my reading of the situation, we are looking at something much darker and more complex than has yet become obvious, indeed events suggest to me that Helen has been drawn, albeit unwittingly, into an intrigue with dire consequences. Of one thing I am certain, though, she is nothing more than an innocent pawn in a deadly game, but it is one in which she is expendable. And so, I have a proposition for you. Would you be prepared to put together a small cadre of men, highly trained and equipped with whatever you need to effect Helen's rescue? You would have to operate outside the remit of the regular army and would be deniable in the event that you are caught up in an action that would embarrass the British Government. I will place at your disposal every resource you may need, both financial and military and the theatre of operation is northern India. You have served with distinction in Afghanistan and so have some understanding of the people and how they live."

"Yes, sir. Unequivocally so, sir," was William's reply, which was the answer Peter had hoped for and expected if he had judged his man correctly.

"Good. Pick two men and report to Hereford. In the meantime, don't falter in your constancy. I know Helen well and of one thing I am sure, she is your woman."

That evening William emailed Hector, a note designed to be innocuous to a casual reader, but which Hector would recognise instantly as a plea for help and a call to arms. Hector and Sarah talked late into the night. He had promised her that his military days were behind him and that she would no longer have to live with the fear that he could be injured or worse. And this at a time when their combined energy and efforts were concentrated on their safari business, which was just turning a corner and showing signs of success.

But Sarah would not listen to his protestations. Like almost everyone else in the world she had seen the video clips of Helen's throat being brutally cut, and although it seemed that she had not been killed, everyone was aware that such a fate probably awaited her soon. Sarah was fond of Helen, but above all else she knew her man and was aware that if she held him back it might result in a breach between them that would later prove difficult to reconcile.

Sarah looked Hector in the eye and took his hand.

"You and I both understand that William could call on someone else, but I know that if Helen is killed and you have not been with him then you'll never forgive yourself or be able to hide from the shame and disloyalty you feel. I am selfish and don't want you to go as I understand there is considerable risk, but I cannot sit here and watch you, day by day, agonising as to what is happening. I am perfectly capable of running the business side and you have trained young Angus well enough for him to cover your duties for a while. It will be good for him."

The following morning Sarah drove Hector to the Oliver Tambo airport in Johannesburg. He lifted his rucksack on to his back and gave her a long, lingering kiss before walking into the terminal, and then he was gone.

Ray Gould was on leave and in a Glasgow pub when he received a similar email. Lance Corporal Ray Gould, affectionately known as 'Grouchy Achilles' because of his tendency to sulk and his extraordinary turn of speed, was due to spend his R&R in a remote crofter's cottage in the highlands of Scotland but immediately changed his plans. Ray, a hardened soldier, a scarred and toughened NCO, had first met William when they were both serving with Hector in Afghanistan.

Afghanistan

William's first patrol in a dusty, brick baked Kandahar took place during a time of Afghan insurgency known as Operation Kamin. The coalition operation mounted in response was named Operation Falcon Summit and was supported by special forces. Tensions were high as the Taliban undertook successive attacks against British and Canadian forces.

At the end of their first day Lance Corporal Ray Gould, a Glaswegian, observed to his younger but senior officer, "You'll nae survive long if you think soldiering is a poncey polka like you used to dance at officer school. You were lucky today not to be shot by that there sniper on the hill, he's a bugger. I kept you out of his line of sight. Also, if I had allowed you to take a walk down that wee alleyway we passed you would have ended up spread across the neighbourhood. Fred is taking short odds on you only lasting a month. Personally, I wouldn't put my money on more than a week."

As time passed William found himself teamed regularly with Lance Corporal Ray Gould and Staff Sergeant Hector Perkins, and by the end of his first tour he had matured from a cocksure young subaltern into an experienced soldier. The three men were considered a small, operational, independent unit and rapidly gained a reputation as an effective cadre. From time to time they were deployed to infiltrate the enemy, their orders being to 'remove operational opposition targets', a euphemism for active jihadists and

Taliban leaders.

On one notable occasion the three men slipped out of camp before dawn disguised in *khet partug*, the traditional dress of local men, accompanied by Abdul, a mountain guide, and under the cover of darkness left the city. Travelling in a disguised truck they headed north east for two days until they reached the remote village of Lagham in the foothills of the Hindu Kush where they hid the truck in a gulley concealed from view and the local population. They made a reasonably good job of camouflaging and disabling their transport while Abdul was detailed to visit the small town and buy a donkey, which, on his return, they nicknamed Ben because, as Ray commented, "He's a bluddy stupid and obstinate ass, just like Sergeant Major Ben Stephens." Ben was loaded with provisions and munitions as their journey was to continue on foot.

In the caves of the mountain range towards which the men trekked lay the camp of Mullah Mawlawi Rehani, leader of the Taliban's Quetta Shura. This sect of the Taliban imposed extremely strict Sharia law and was committed to exterminating the infidel invading force. The faction was ruthless and merciless, and many tales of their extreme violence were told, especially of their callous, misogynistic repression of women. A few months earlier an Afghan girl named Bibi Aisha had been promised to a new family through a tribal method of solving disputes known as 'Baad'. When she tried to run away, her new family chased and tracked her down. She was caught and returned, and the family requested judgement from Mullah Rehani.

He ordered she be punished as an example: "So that any other girl who might choose to disobey the will of her husband will remember what happened to Bibi Aisha." He ordered her ears and nose be cut off and she be abandoned in the mountains not too far from her village. Hugely disfigured she survived and made her way home, thereby delivering a message, loud and clear, to the local community.

Ruthless in the extreme the soldiers serving under Rehani had no regard for their own safety and were hardy mountain warriors whose ancestors had lived in the mountains for generations. They showed no mercy when it came to the fate of enemies they captured often handing prisoners over to their women, who were even more feared because of their cruelty and skill with their sharp little knives.

Rehani had led numerous attacks against British forces and was accountable for a growing toll of British deaths and casualties. High Command wanted his operation terminated.

William, Hector and Ray travelled on foot up the valley that leads from Lagham to Sunderrwar. At Sunderrwar they veered east, following a dry river course until finally they skirted Nurah Lam and began a long and steep trek into the arid mountains. Following small tracks, they avoided human habitation but had to halt regularly to secrete themselves when roving groups of Taliban were heard approaching from either ahead or behind. Fortunately, the noise the Afghans made announced their presence well in advance.

The three Europeans had grown beards, wore traditional *pakol* headdress and were deeply suntanned, but any encounter had to be avoided at all costs as a close inspection would immediately expose their true identity.

During the summer the sun hammers down on the bare mountains of eastern Afghanistan where the rock is barren and rough-hewn, as if formed from pig-iron fashioned by an almighty cold chisel. The heat reverberates off the surface of the rocks in waves and, in the folds of the mountains increases as it would in an oven. As the task force progressed it was as if they were battling a physical force, requiring them to halt during the extreme heat of midday when they rested in the shade of a valley out of sight of any passing shepherd or soldier.

Abdul navigated with unerring confidence and as evening dawned on the second night he assured them their destination was less than two days march ahead. Every thirty miles the soldiers built a small cairn under which they secreted water and rations for their return journey.

The three soldiers and donkey traipsed behind their guide following goat-worn trails away from the beaten track through ever more treacherous mountain passes where shale made some of the steep tracks even more onerous. On the third day they walked until the sun dropped abruptly out of the sky, when, under the cover of darkness they made camp high in the mountains. Before sleep overtook him, William looked up at the heavens, at the cold, pin-pricked immense dome, and the enormity of the firmament served to remind him of his insignificance, at least as far as an indifferent universe and hostile enemy was concerned.

He awoke early on the final morning of their journey as the sun was rising, gilding the far-off eastern peaks in the distance. In between stretched a vast panorama of desolation, an inimical sterility that weighed upon his spirit. He noted that the shining transparency of the early morning light had a blue tinge which appeared to enhance the leaden quality of the landscape and he was reminded of Milton's description of hell in *Paradise Lost,* lines studied at school: 'The dismal situation waste and wild, A dungeon horrible, on all sides round'. *Appropriate*, he thought.

Their final day followed the same pattern, although now they travelled more slowly, acutely aware of the increased danger of accidental discovery; their hearing attuned, listening for the slightest sound that might be out of place knowing that a stone carelessly dislodged could be enough to alert the enemy. They employed anti-tracking techniques to cover their spoor in case any *Pashtun* happened on their trail.

At last the blessed cooler air of evening returned and William conferred with Abdul who checked their GPS co-ordinates to confirm they were approaching the interlaced complex of caves where the enemy had their stronghold. It was here the despots formulated their plans to wreak death and destruction on the infidel, specifically upon the army of occupation.

Just before midnight the men moved into position silently and settled on a ledge from where they could look down upon the entrance to a series of tunnels where the 'intelligence' had assured them the Afghans had their mountain retreat. An attack from the air would have been futile, which is why such a daring and extremely dangerous plan had been devised.

Before the moon rose to illuminate the frost covered mountain, they bound Ben's hoofs with sackcloth to muffle any sound. William established where the desultory watch was placed and directed Hector and Ray to circle round behind the guards. Their agreed call was that of the short-eared owl, not uncommon in the area, this being the signal to inform of a successful dispatch.

When it came to it the indolent night watchmen were not alert to anything out of the ordinary and their first awareness of danger was momentary as a wire garrotte tightened across their throat before slicing through skin and carotid artery, releasing a spurt of crimson blood accompanied by a hiss of severed wind pipe. There were six guards in total, four of whom were on patrol in pairs, while two relaxed around a small fire near the entrance to the caves enjoying a cigarette and exchanging highly embellished tales of their deeds. All were dispatched silently and with ruthless efficiency.

When the team regrouped in the darkest period of the night and were sure the entrance to the cave was unattended, Ray led Ben forward along the path into the access tunnel, illuminated by occasional flickering torches. William did not anticipate an alert soldier sounding the alarm, but he and Hector were positioned to give covering fire if Ray had to escape pursued by tribesmen. 'Achilles' had been chosen to lead this stage of the operation as it would be necessary to run for his life once the action started and Ray was a sprinter with a remarkable turn of speed.

William had placed a small percussive charge on Ben's rump and he watched until man and compliant beast rounded the last corner and passed out of view, praying that Ben would remain silent.

Slowly and with extreme caution Ray made his way into the entrance of the first cave from where he could make out lumps on the ground, the outline of recumbent men. As quietly as possible man and beast progressed until Ray judged it no longer safe to progress, which was when he initiated the timers attached to the packs on Ben's back. The small explosive on the animal's rump had a short fuse to give Ray a minute's grace.

When Ben felt the detonation on his flank and the sudden pain that accompanied it, it had an electrifying effect on the donkey who charged forward into the cave braying loudly, at which moment Ray was running in the opposite direction. The noisy arrival of a donkey amongst the sleeping men caused pandemonium. Rehani, and those most attuned to danger were instantly awake, but long before any order could be imposed the Semtex packed into Ben's saddle bags exploded gathering force rapidly and reverberating through the passages that radiated from the central cave creating a violent, deadly expansion that extended into every nook, corner, grotto and cranny.

The initial blast detonated the ammunition and fuel stored in adjoining caves releasing an ever-greater paroxysm of kinetic energy that amplified in force and magnitude, intensifying many times over. By the time it reached the mouth of the tunnel its original potency had multiplied, and it disgorged like a superhuman expulsion. It caught the fleeing 'Achilles' and rolled him headlong down the side of the mountain, however its anger and rage was diminishing as it rumbled down the pass leaving behind total annihilation in the caves.

Having picked Ray up, dusted him down and ensured that he was not badly hurt, the men turned their back on the destruction they had unleashed and began the long trudge back.

"Mission accomplished," said Hector. "With special thanks to Ben the Trojan Donkey!"

"Over the pass the voices one by one faded, and the hill slept."

London

England

Peter's analysis of the initial evidence available to him from Paris resulted in three conclusions: those who had abducted Helen wanted their actions to be observed; Iftekhar had not necessarily been taken hostage; the planning involved was coordinated and sophisticated.

Most curious was why Helen had been selected? Her abduction was clearly a deliberately planned exercise and therefore her disappearance served a purpose, which was not kidnapping for financial gain. Very little political influence could be achieved, so why go to so much trouble? The answer must lie with Helen's particular profile: a beautiful innocent woman, socialite and daughter of a senior member of both the British government and establishment. Her bloody assassination would swell world outrage at this quasi-separatist movement self-styled as the *PSM*. In which case there was no intention to release her.

At the back of Peter's mind was a niggle that raised further questions. Were other apparently unrelated events germane, and had he just not made the connections? He had received reports about growing instability between Pakistan and India that was having a destabilising effect on the economy of the former.

Reports had reached him of sabre-rattling by extreme elements in the Pakistani military and it was documented that right-wing elements, the hawks in the Indian government, were restless leading to increased tension between the old enemies, especially in Punjab. Could Bobby Gill's crossword relate in any way to present events? If so then matters of iceberg proportions might be on the move, although as yet all he could make out was a shadow beneath the surface.

More information was required. What, for example, was the involvement of Iftekhar Diaz? If at all possible, and assuming he was alive, contact needed to be established, urgently. The *PSM* seemed to Peter a spurious militant group, a perplexing organisation in this unfolding drama, furthermore the choice of the city of Patiala, where the aeroplane from Bremen had landed, needed further investigation. Patiala, a city ruled by a Nawab with a reputation for misdeeds.

Peter had a sense that some momentous occurrence was in the offing, one designed to raise the international temperature and precipitate confrontation somewhere, but, when and how? He needed more information, especially to inform a plan to rescue Helen.

*

Lingering over a second cup of coffee and enjoying a relaxed breakfast at his club before a series of meetings at GCHQ's secret London base, a nondescript building in Palmer Street that nestled bizarrely between a Starbucks café and a pub opposite St James's Park Tube station, Peter was reading *The Times* when his attention was attracted by an article in the world section.

Financial investigators in America suspect that a spectacular internet bank heist may have damaged the economy in Pakistan where millions of dollars would appear to have been spirited out of the banks that operate in that region. The Indian government has been implicated.

Investigators examining an audacious international cybercrime have found similarities with two smaller but comparable penetrations of security, the first being a robbery in Bangladesh and the second a hacking attack on Netflix film studios. The FBI have noted parallels and the investigation has recently shone a light upon a very sophisticated group ostensibly operating out of India who are thought to have perpetrated multiple IT related offences.

Hackers working for this unidentified group have also been implicated in attacks on Polish banks. 'If that linkage (between the attacks on Pakistani banks, Polish banks and Netflix) is proved, it is possible that a nation state may be sanctioning strikes', commented Michael Aubrey a deputy director of the National Security Agency, last week. 'That's a big deal. It's a whole different game. We have seen the Russians and Chinese involved in international cybercrime but never the Indian government'.

It seems hackers sent orders to the Pakistani Federal Reserve mandating the transfer of $20 million. These appear to have originated from an Indian public sector bank. Irregularities in the transfers initially did not cause suspicion and a few small transfers were swiftly shuffled through off-shore accounts but then vigilant clerks in The Bank of West Punjab in Pakistan stopped a $5 million payment having noticed a misspelling in the transfer documents. At that point greater scrutiny was undertaken.

'Skilled hackers go to great lengths to disguise themselves and their places of origin, and so it is almost impossible to identify individuals responsible for a particular attack, but in this case a

link may have been established that suggests a connection between an Indian government department and the hackers. If proved then a major international incident will result', said Aubrey.

When asked to comment, the Indian government was emphatic that it had never engaged in any such activity, while a representative of the Pakistani government made a blistering attack on its neighbour's aggressive attempts to undermine the economy of Pakistan.

"Once again," thought Peter, "India is specifically implicated in a hostile act against Pakistan. While perfectly possible, neither GCHQ or MI6 are, to my knowledge, presently aware of any malign intent by India beyond the usual sabre-rattling. Acts of international cyber aggression are not uncommon, but an act of sophisticated fraud on this scale brings no obvious benefit for the Indian government, indeed exactly the opposite."

Peter Baird put the paper aside and buttered his toast before applying marmalade and reaching for one last coffee.

Later that day Peter established that the internet raid he had read about had been thwarted, but he showed the article to his Deputy and asked for his thoughts.

"Bank hacking, I understand, but leaving a trail as obvious as this is immensely provocative and potentially explosive. It could be that what is going on here is provocation, although I can't see who benefits?"

"I am beginning to be of that opinion," said Peter. "Someone is orchestrating a complex web of deceit of which this may be just one strand. Perhaps this and other events relate back to whatever Bobby Gill was trying to warn us about? If so, then *The Colonel* is the spider at the centre of a complex web, and we need to find him before he pounces."

Two days later a credible source passed information to the department that changed everything. A large amount of a deadly toxin, it was reported, had been smuggled into Europe in preparation for a major act of terrorism.

Central Asia

In mid-April, a routine intelligence report reached GCHQ (where it was filed) noting the progress of an eight-wheeled, unremarkable, flat backed heavy goods vehicle loaded with building materials. The information seemed of minor significance and little attention was given to a vehicle following a tortuously slow route that began in Pakistan before passing through Tajikistan, then Uzbekistan and on through Kazakhstan and crossing southern Russia to Smolensk and into Belarus. After weeks lumbering across Asia it reached the customs crossing at Bruzgi on the Belarus/Polish border where its paperwork was scrutinised, and it was searched.

The large concrete crossing point on the Asian side of the Kuznica border is well equipped and the guards thoroughly trained. Checks were made against the HGV's bill of loading manifest, which specified building materials mined in Pakistan and destined for Germany. The driver's passport, personal history and identification papers were studied and only when the border control was entirely satisfied was the vehicle allowed to cross a short strip of no-man's land and enter Europe where it had to submit to similar verifications undertaken by vigilant EU authorities.

The customs officials did not unload the cargo although rigorous checks were undertaken. A number of the large containers were opened and inspected but nothing appeared untoward or aroused suspicion. However, buried in two of the many large plastic transport flasks were inner packages sealed in waterproof plastic cartons. Each contained two hundred and fifty kilograms of fentanyl in powder form.

Fifty miles beyond Kuznica the articulated vehicle entered a large indoor storage facility where it parked overnight at the extreme end. During that night the contraband was carefully removed and transferred to an unmarked Ford transit van where it was disguised amongst other chemicals destined for factories in France.

The following day, in the third week of June the deadly containers embarked upon the last stage of their journey, passing innocuously through Germany and finally arriving at a large farm to the east of Paris in the early days of July.

*

Peter was fascinated by the texts intercepted between the brothers, Sadam and Kassim, who were quite possibly known to the elusive Colonel:

'She will bend her knee and the orchid will bleed.'

'The rain will fall and the wheat will wither.'

Emails between the siblings were infrequent and elliptical in content, but when received confirmed that the brothers were still in France. Further research unearthed the fact that Sadam had a private pilot's licence, but Peter thought it unlikely there was a plot to strike using a commercial aircraft because since 2011 such an attack had become almost impossible. Something else was afoot.

Time and again Peter had re-read the original exchange between the brothers which, he had become convinced alluded to some kind of plot. *'She'* - a pronoun possibly referring to a nation or a place rather than a person? *'Will bend her knee'*, might imply being brought to submission? An *'orchid'* - London or Paris? *'They will bleed'*, an act of terrorism? *'The rain will fall'* and *'The wheat will wither';* Biblical as in a plague that brings mass destruction?

Relaxing at his flat a few days later watching television, Peter idly switched between channels and happened across one of his favourite films, *Goldfinger*. Lying in bed later that evening and drifting off to sleep his mind segued between scenes of low flying aircraft and people being gassed from the air and, all of a sudden, he sat bolt upright. *'The rain will fall and the wheat will wither'* suddenly took on another connotation. A fanciful association perhaps, but nonetheless he reached for his phone.

A week later, the eighth of July, Peter convened a top priority *COBRA* (Cabinet Office Briefing Room A) meeting in Whitehall attended by the Cabinet Secretary, various senior members of the Ministry of Defence and Heads of both MI5 and MI6. The Chancellor of the Exchequer was in attendance.

Peter began. "From the analysis we have undertaken we now have reason to believe that we know the location where Helen Strachan is being held. Concurrently, and not necessarily unrelated, we believe we may have stumbled across a jihadist plot to kill a large number of people at the July fourteenth celebrations in Paris, which our Prime Minister is due to attend."

General Braithwaite asked, "Where is Miss Strachan being held?"

Peter nodded to his second in command, a seconded Brigadier, who answered for him.

"In India, in the Punjab to be exact, a city called Patiala where we think she will be executed. Her killing will be public and brutal and is intended to initiate a series of events that escalate tensions between India and Pakistan, possibly to war status. We speculate that she will be kept alive until the forces that are manipulating events are ready to trigger an invasion, which may be a few months off."

There was a sharp intake of breath from David Strachan, who asked, "Can she be saved?"

"That is our intention and we have a plan," said Peter.

"Why is she being held captive in a predominantly Sikh part of India?" enquired the Head of MI6.

Peter answered. "That is a very good question and the answer we think lies with a Muslim initiated plan to destabilise the region. However, let me return to Miss Strachan later because we need to consider the more pressing matter of a major terrorist act in Paris."

The Brigadier continued. "Acting on information received from a deep undercover agent in Pakistan we have tracked a vehicle that we believe has transported a large quantity of a lethal substance from Pakistan to France where it is intended to be used to inflict an act of mass destruction. A terrorist cell may be planning to spray a deadly nerve agent from the air while the July fourteenth celebrations are underway. If successful, the death toll will be considerable, and the evidence trail will lead back to a group in India who will claim responsibility for the atrocity on behalf of disenfranchised Muslims in India. London was the original target, but Paris has proved more vulnerable."

"But that's ridiculous," said the head of MI5. "Neither India or Pakistan would undertake such an atrocity."

"I'll return to that point later," said Peter.

"Do you know where this substance is being stored?" asked the Head of MI6.

"No."

"Then any aircraft approaching Paris on that day will have to be diverted or blown out of the air."

"Neither is an option, for if the plane carrying the deadly toxin were to crash as a result of an aerial attack or as a kamikaze act of self-destruction, then the casualty count would be unacceptably high."

"What have the French got to say?"

"We are holding a meeting later today and they are examining all the options, but as yet they have no idea where the terrorists are located. They are directing all their resources to finding the plane, and of course we are supporting with as much intelligence as possible."

"So, what happens next?"

"We do all we can to assist and at the same time prepare for the worst. We conjecture that Helen Strachan's abduction and this present threat to Paris are in fact related, designed to bring about all-out war between India and Pakistan. At another level is the intention to provoke ever greater social and military instability between Islam and the rest of the world."

At the conclusion of the meeting David indicated to Peter that he wanted a private word. "Can you tell me with confidence that Helen will be safe, at least enough for me to look her mother in the eye and make a promise?"

"No," replied Peter, "but what I can promise is that I shall try as hard to save her as I would if she were my own daughter."

WMD

The *Direction Générale de la Sécurité Extérieure* (DGSE), or General Directorate for External Security is France's external intelligence agency, the French equivalent to the United Kingdom's MI6 and the United States' CIA. The DGSE operate under the direction of the French Ministry of Defence and work alongside its domestic counterpart, the DGSI (General Directorate for Internal Security) whose function it is to provide intelligence and safeguard homeland security, like the MI5 or FBI. As with all intelligence agencies, details of the organisation and their operations are veiled in secrecy.

*

At the eastern end of the *Avenue des Champs-Élysées* is one of the major public squares of Paris, the *Place de la Concorde*. During the French Revolution this was the site for *Madame La Guillotine*, (where the statue of Brest can be found today) and was the place of execution of King Louis XVI. Known then as the *Place de la Révolution* it was later renamed the *Place de la Concorde* as an act of reconciliation.

Since 1880, and almost without exception, the Bastille Day Military Parade has taken place on the fourteenth of July. The *Défilé militaire du 14 Juillet* passes down the Champs-Élysées from *L'Arc de Triomphe* to the *Place de la Concorde* where the President of the French Republic, his government and foreign ambassadors stand to take the salute. This national event is widely broadcast on French television and there is very tight security indeed.

For Parisians the *Place de la Concorde* has powerful symbolic significance, and for this reason *The Colonel* chose it as the location for an act of terror to rival September 11th in the USA.

*

In 1960 Paul Janssen, a Belgian chemist, developed a drug he named fentanyl, an opioid that is seventy-five times stronger than morphine. Since then fentanyl has contributed to numerous beneficial applications in medicine, especially in the aid of pain relief and for anaesthesia. During the 1970's fentanyl analogues were further refined to create a medication many times more potent than the heroin-based opiates from which they originated. A unit of carfentanil, first synthesised in 1974, is ten thousand times more powerful than a unit of morphine.

In 2012 a team of researchers at the British chemical and biological defence laboratories at Porton Down found traces of carfentanil and remifentanil on clothing taken from two British survivors of the Moscow theatre hostage crisis, and in the urine of a third. The scientists concluded that the Russian military had used an aerosol mist, combining a mixture of fentanyls, to subdue the Chechen hostage takers. One hundred and twenty-five people exposed to the gas, mostly hostages, died from respiratory failure and since then the toxicity of the drug has caused international concern because of its potential as a weapon of mass destruction.

For some weeks a Gippsland GA200 aerial crop sprayer, a small aeroplane designed for agricultural use, had been stored in the back of a forty-ton truck and kept on the move around France. It had been purchased two years previously and on the morning of

Monday eleventh of July it arrived at its destination, a large, remote farm building east of Paris, adjacent to a strip of grassland eight hundred metres long. Here, in secret, the aeroplane was reassembled and prepared for its only flight.

This particular Gippsland had first been used in Australia where it was put to work in the outback until it was sold and taken to east Africa. There it was bought and brought to France by a bogus organisation who had purchased it through a shell company and smuggled it into the country through Marseille. A certificate of airworthiness had never been sought from the French civil aviation authority and so it was unregistered. In fact, no record of its existence or whereabouts existed.

With its single seat the Gippsland needs less than seven hundred metres for take-off with a full load. Each wing has an integral fuel tank and with a combined capacity of 200 litres it can be refuelled from one two hundred litre drum by means of a simple hand pump.

On Tuesday twelfth July a container of powder, a mix of carfentanil and remifentanil, was delivered by a Ford Transit van to the barn where it was carefully lowered into the tank of the aerial crop sprayer. Water was added and the protective wrapping dissolved releasing two hundred and fifty kilogrammes of deadly toxin that dissolved.

In the barn Sadam watched intently as the plane was prepared and when all was ready, he clambered into the cockpit to check the instruments and familiarise himself. All that was required now was fuel, which would arrive on Wednesday evening. The plan was audacious. With a flying time to the centre of Paris of thirty-five minutes he would ascend to nine hundred metres before descending to five hundred at exactly twelve noon on Thursday fourteenth July. He would fly along the Champs-Élysées, to the Place de la Concorde and then across the Jardin des Tuileries, releasing the 'rain' on the many thousands who had collected for the annual Bastille Day or La Fête Nationale. Those lining the route would look to the skies as a low flying aircraft passed overhead ingesting the vapour released. He knew the chances of making a getaway were extremely slim, but the chaos, panic and disorder that followed might offer a slight opportunity. Either way documentation would be found in the cockpit afterwards linking the pilot with a freedom movement in India known by the initials *PSM*. The *PSM* would claim responsibility for the atrocity in the name of a united Punjab and on behalf of all disenfranchised peoples demanding independence.

Balayeuse de Voirie

It is said that a terrorist only has to get lucky once, but luck is not the exclusive preserve of terrorists. In a rare outbreak of cooperation, the DGSE and DGSI in Paris collaborated. Having been presented by GCHQ with a warning that an act of mass destruction on French soil may be imminent the two organisations went into overdrive, supported by Interpol and with the full cooperation of every security agency across Europe.

The first priority for the team formed to counter the threat was to determine the level of risk, and the second was to discover whether a nerve agent had actually been smuggled into the country, as conjectured by the British. The evidence supplied by GCHQ was compelling and demonstrated how a substance (such as ricin or sarin, both chemical weapons of extreme potency) could have been transported across Asia and into Europe. The expert opinion was that ricin was the more likely as it is easier to manufacture and move and less straightforward to trace. However, after much debate and, allowing for an attack by air in the form of vapour, both sarin and ricin were finally ruled out. Sulphur mustard gas was another strong possibility, but numerous large drums would be required, and it would be difficult to smuggle such a quantity. Therefore, whatever the deadly substance was it must have been chosen because it could be disguised and transported relatively easily amongst a consignment of legitimate goods. It was agreed that the risk of an imminent attack was 'code red' and the focus of the search should be on vans rather than lorries. It was a risk to make this assumption, but time was short.

The evidence supplied by the British, supported by records and permits from border and security forces across Europe, was analysed and a list of possible carriers for the final stage of the journey was narrowed to twenty-five vehicles. All were tracked and having submitted to intensive searches proved legitimate, and the scent was lost.

In the absence of a 'hot' trail it was decided that the only remaining approach was to search for a supplier of fuel. All efforts were concentrated intensively on finding companies that had or could provide a few hundred litres of aviation kerosene in a drum.

Frantic efforts were undertaken to unearth potential suppliers, and within a few hours a shortlist was compiled. Investigators descended on each company to scrutinise their order books and to everyone's relief the process proved more straightforward than was initially feared, for one receipt stood out. It was established that a single two-hundred litre drum had been delivered that morning to a small garage compound in the impoverished area of Goutte d'Or behind the Gare du Nord rail station. A frantic and furtive investigation was launched, and it revealed that the drum had not yet been moved from the lock-up. The zone around the garage was placed under intensive surveillance.

Late in the afternoon of Wednesday thirteenth of July the gate to the compound opened and a white van emerged. It turned left. A team of six ordinary looking vehicles followed in tag rotation and a seamless surveillance began. Satellites were moved to track the tiny GPS device attached to the drum and helicopters and emergency services were on standby to respond should an emergency arise.

The driver took the Boulevard Périphérique and then headed east on the N6 out of Paris. In total the van was driven a hundred and sixty kilometres on main roads before turning into a series of increasingly narrow lanes that posed difficult challenges for the followers who had to adapt their tactics. After two and a half hours, it came to a halt beside a farm gate that was opened by a watchman loitering nearby, and after the van passed through the gate was closed and padlocked. The Ford Transit was seen driving slowly around the edge of a field towards a bulky farm building large enough to house a small aircraft. Through powerful binoculars watchers saw two large doors slide open and the van was absorbed, just as dusk descended.

The lead vehicle of the tactical surveillance squad had remained at a distance, a large Renault that accommodated a driver and three heavily armed service men. Instructions were communicated.

During the scenario planning numerous options had been considered. The most imaginative of which was to deploy helicopters to bomb the small aircraft with sand so that contaminated material would be contained, but this was considered too open to the vagaries of chance and finally it was agreed that a simple plan would be best. An invisible ring of steel was now placed around the airstrip.

The team back at base studied maps to glean as much information about the terrain as possible and on that evening it fell to Jacques Parmentier, previously a member of the GCP (the elite unit within the Foreign Legion), to make his way under cover of darkness to a designated spot where he was to observe and wait.

Carrying a high velocity weapon, he inched into position concerned that a tripwire mechanism might have been employed as an alarm, even though this seemed unlikely given the number of small mammals moving through the woodland adjacent to the landing strip.

*

Back in Paris, at two o'clock in the morning of the fourteenth of July, a large *balayeuse de voirie* - a road sweeper - lumbered along the Rue de Rivoli and turned left into the Place de la Concorde. It progressed slowly until it was adjacent with the obelisk, where it turned into the service road that leads to the Jardin des Tuileries. As it arrived at the gates to the gardens they opened silently. The ungainly vehicle passed through and drove down the slope beside the octagon, its statues watching mutely, and then turned left, drawing up in front of the large white marble memorial dedicated to Pierre Waldeck-Rousseau. Kassim switched off the engine and began his long wait.

The weather was perfect, a cloudless sky with a breeze blowing from the north. He knew he would only have one opportunity to sweep through the gardens and into the Champs-Élysées before total chaos erupted, but he was ready and if he was to meet his maker then he was prepared.

The second canister of the nerve agent had been placed in the large water tank of the sweeper where it dissolved. It would be released at ground level as the road sweeper progressed through the assembled crowd, timed to coincide with the aerial attack.

The large vehicle had been stolen from a transport depot in Marseille some weeks earlier and was now huddled like a giant beetle ready to crawl forward at exactly eleven forty-five am.

Kassim could not relax for his body coursed with adrenaline, and each time he thought of what was to transpire the tension ratcheted. It was reassuring to know that he would be remembered for his courage and great dedication to God, and would be welcomed through the gates of Paradise, but now he was nervous and trembling at the thought of what was about to unfold.

By four in the morning he felt an overwhelming need to communicate with his brother. He could not resist the urge to send a last text. Before destroying the sim card he took out his phone and typed: *The cloud and the scythe. Allahu Akbar.*

At GCHQ Kassim's text was picked up and passed immediately to Peter Baird, despite the fact that he had to be woken by an aide-de-camp. In minutes Peter was dressed and pondering what was meant by Kassim's apparent sign-off message traced to the very centre of Paris.

Then, in a moment of pure intuition, it came to him. He had interpreted *rain* falling and *wheat* dying as one action, but what if they were two? Deadly rain would fall from the *cloud* but what if the wheat was also to be *scythed* at ground level? With a sickening lurch he realised that while they had focused exclusively on one attack, two were planned. Peter called Paris.

Place de la Révolution

Jacques Parmentier shifted his position minutely to reduce the cramp in his left leg. He had been almost motionless since daylight and knew that if something were going to happen then it would be soon. He considered the possibility that the interpretation of the evidence had been erroneous or perhaps they had been duped, in which case many innocent people would lose their lives on this perfect July day when they looked up into the clear sky and inhaled a lungful of deadly toxin. Men, women and children of all ages would die painfully and in great numbers unable to breathe, and others would be trampled in the panic that followed. The emergency services would be overwhelmed and unable to cope with the number of casualties.

The dangerous decision to allow crowds to form along the route had been taken in the belief that if the terrorists were alerted, they would alter their plan and make a suicide attack elsewhere. So, it came down to him to stop the aeroplane leaving the ground, and if all went well the public would never know how close to mass destruction an enemy of the state had come.

At ten-thirty in the morning the door to the barn slid open and three hundred metres away Jacques moved his eye to the telescopic sight. The scene jumped into the foreground as he watched two men wheel out a small aircraft with a large tank suspended over the fuselage. The plane was prepared for take-off and one of the men, presumably the pilot, walked around making a visual inspection.

Endless discussion had taken place between the top brass as to the options for neutralising the plane. A tracer bullet through the fuel tank, troops swarming across the site to capture the perpetrators, even tanks to block the grass runway; it was vital the plane did not leave the ground and that the container carrying the toxin remain undamaged.

At eleven-thirty the pilot checked his watch, clambered into the cockpit and started the engine, which whined for a moment before engaging and running smoothly. He aligned the aircraft for take-off. Jacques heard the engine surge as the pilot increased the revs preparing to release the brake and begin his run.

Listening intently to the pitch and tone of the engine Sadam was not immediately aware of the thrump, thrump from the rotors of two approaching helicopters, and by the time he looked up and realised what was happening, two Super Pumas were almost overhead. Confused he panicked as large concrete barriers were lowered in front and behind the Gippsland, which was when a single shot rang out that Sadam never heard.

*

Strategically placed along the streets around the Place de la Concorde were large military vehicles in which men waited patiently, men whose shape was distorted by the PRPS they were wearing. Powered Respiratory Protective Suits are multi-layered and contain their own oxygen supply, designed to enable highly trained operatives to work in a hostile chemical environment.

The search was on, but with only a few hours' notice, and nothing definitive, the police presence on the ground still had no idea what they were looking for or where to find it. The signal from Kassim's phone had been recorded but not triangulated, and the target area was over a kilometre long.

The recent good weather had continued warm with clear skies, ideal for family excursions to enjoy the July celebrations in the centre of Paris and large numbers flooded into the city swelling the spectators along the route. The mood of the crowd was relaxed and genial, families, many with picnics, out to enjoy the day.

It was eleven-forty and Kassim's long wait was over. The park was filling, and as he had no indication how his brother's plan was progressing, he concentrated on his task. During the long night he had wondered if he would remain calm when the moment for action came, and now that it was approaching his breathing was shallow and he was sweating. Coiled like a spring wound to breaking point he was experiencing a combination of physiological responses, all caused by the anticipation, excitement and adrenaline swirling through his veins. At the appointed moment he placed a gas mask over his head and started the engine of the large road sweeper.

He was aware of an unusually active police presence but was not unduly perturbed. "For the love of God and my country may Allah protect me now," he prayed, and he began to recite verses from the Quran.

Kassim engaged first gear and the large vehicle edged forward as the crowd parted meekly to allow the unwieldy machine through. He would engage the spray when he made his turn around the eastern carousel and began his run along La Grande Allée.

The Chastain family had decided to visit the gardens, enjoy the early summer warmth and join in with the holiday spirit that accompanied the annual celebration. Chantel was steering the buggy and Constance, their three-year-old daughter, was on Francois's shoulders. Constance started wriggling and so her father reached up and lifted her down, keeping hold of her hand as she ran along beside him until her attention was caught by a pigeon strutting on the path. She loved to watch birds flutter into flight when she chased them and so she let go of her father's hand and started to run. At that moment her mother became aware of a vehicle approaching from behind and a sixth sense alerted her to danger. Abandoning the buggy Chantel ran to pick up her daughter.

Kassim was staring ahead of him in a state of religious rapture, his focus entirely on the task and not his surroundings. In consequence, just at the moment he floored the pedal, he was unaware of a small child and its mother running into his path. He was only mildly aware of a double bump, ecstatic that his jihad had begun. He accelerated towards the fountain.

A small crowd watched in horror as mother and child were crushed beneath the wheels of the large vehicle. A group of outraged men ran towards the sweeper catching up with it as it slowed to make its turn around the fountain. One, an off-duty soldier, managed to pull open the cab door, at which point Kassim shot him, at point blank range and he fell back gravely, if not fatally, wounded. The crowd were incensed and just as Kassim went to operate the spray mechanism another brave heart reached for the handle of the passenger door and yanked it open. With both hands occupied Kassim could not defend himself and his foot slipped off the clutch, causing the vehicle to stall. He was pulled from the cab and manhandled to the ground.

Near to the site of mass execution in the late eighteenth century an enraged mob dispensed Parisian 'justice'.

The French authorities released details of the thwarted attack, knowing that to try and hide the events would lead to public outrage when they were leaked, as would inevitably be the case. News of the death of a young mother and child, and the shooting of an off-duty soldier was splashed across the media. Better to claim credit for foiling an outrageous Islamist assault than be accused of institutional cover-up, although there was no mention of an attack from the air.

Timed to coincide with the Paris shock was the release of a message on social media from *#freepunjab,* a group referring to themselves as the *Punjabi Separatist Movement.* They claimed responsibility for bringing the attention of the world to the suffering of those living in Punjab and demanded that all governments support the reintegration of east and west Punjab as an independent state. The Indian government's response was measured but Pakistan was furious and railed against Indian imperialism demanding the United Nations support a motion condemning India's bellicose intention towards Pakistan. Fuel had been thrown on a fire and heightened rhetoric was beginning to draw the sub-continent closer to armed confrontation. A tipping point was becoming a dangerous possibility.

ACT FOUR

Swan's Nest

Peter returned to *Swan's Nest* having snatched some hours to be with Leda and to give himself time to think without distraction. He needed to apply his mind exclusively and arrange the interconnecting threads so that when they aligned he could make sense of the snippets, scraps and fragments he had garnered. Moreover, he and Leda needed space to be with each other, she being his balm and he her strength. For a short while they would retreat behind the barricade of their mutual and enduring absorption.

It was late and they were now sitting in the snug, a small cosy room at the back of the house with only a reading light for illumination. It had rained solidly for two days and despite being July there was a distinct chill in the evening air, and so Leda had laid a small fire in the grate where flames were soon leaping, and tendrils of warmth reached out to them. The wood was not fully seasoned and small pockets of gas exploded unexpectedly like pistol shots.

Following a supper of home-made steak pie, accompanied by a bottle of Châteauneuf-du-Pape, Peter was sitting at the end of the Chesterfield sofa and she lay curled contentedly against him, his left arm draped around her shoulder. They had chosen to listen to a collection of arias from *The Magic Flute* and were relaxed, allowing the music to float around the room, but as the harmonies became more exquisite Peter detected a change in her, and when it came to the aria between Pamina and Papageno the turmoil of Leda's troubled mind seemed to increase. The voices rose in perfect counterpoint and she hugged him tightly, her wretchedness, he thought, provoked by the sublime composition.

When the opera concluded she looked up at him and asked despairingly, "Why is all this happening, Peter, I just don't understand? Is Helen the target or is she an innocent victim? Is it because of David's position, is it to blackmail him, or has she been kidnapped for ransom? Explain it to me please, I just want to know."

He thought for a moment. "Unfortunately, I can't give you a rational explanation but in our cosy, democratic, western world we forget that beyond our borders are dangerous sparks that if we don't control will flare up hoping to engulf us. Our enemies, like your fire, constantly spit and crackle hoping to ignite a fire that will endanger us."

Leda was pensive. "I get that," she said. "But if life in Britain is relatively comfortable why don't such people aspire to live like us rather than attack us?"

"Well," replied Peter, "Western societies are founded on order, the rule of law and the rights of the individuals, but many of those who threaten us live in worlds that do not value principles of equality and they don't want their citizens to have rights. It is not in the interest of those who hold power to bring about change. To adopt our values would weaken their control."

"But why do they hate us? We are no threat. I know that religion is a major issue, but Helen has not been taken because of her beliefs."

"You are right," replied Peter, "the answer is that it's not us they fear, it's what our society represents. In such countries corruption is the way of life. It is perpetuated because of a collective code that suits the economic behaviour and protects the status of all its hierarchies. From the dishonest minor official who takes money to issue a licence, to the fraudulent politician who holds the power to make life saving decisions, the imperative is personal gain. The gap between rich and poor remains unbridgeable, reinforced, as you say, by the subjugation of a population through religion."

Leda looked puzzled. "You seem to be saying that a combination of corruption and religious practice deny citizens in these countries their rights, and a mixture of custom and tradition outweighs individual liberties, so it is never in the interest of those with power to adopt our values. Actually, I can understand that also, but it still doesn't explain why Helen's life is in danger as she is no threat to them."

"It is because of the deep state," said Peter, "which goes beyond endemic corruption. At the hub of the 'deep state' in some countries are criminals and politicians as well as military and religious men who are committed to bringing about the downfall of their enemies no matter the cost. They are avaricious and ideological, devious and patient, and utterly ruthless, and they hold the reins of power. Such men bring anarchy and despair in their wake and I fear that our girl has become a pawn in one of their deadly games for some dark purpose we don't yet understand."

"But will she die?"

Peter pulled Leda towards him and wrapped both arms tightly around her. "Not if I have anything to do with it," was his reply.

Later, once Leda was asleep and breathing evenly, Peter slipped out of bed and returned to the snug. He raked the embers and watched as flames took hold of a log bringing renewed light and warmth.

He was sure the plot that had netted Helen was part of something much more complex than hostage-taking, it emanated from the 'deep state' and he had come to believe its purpose was conceived and coordinated by a single intelligence who was controlling events. Could it be the elusive Colonel? Who was *The Colonel* and was it possible that these apparently disconnected events bore his imprint? A long time had elapsed since Peter had received the intelligence that cost Robert Gillespie his life. 'Bobby Gill' had warned that the Punjab was the prize, and now the Punjab was a common denominator.

The aeroplane that had transported Helen had its destination in northern India and, as he had disclosed at COBRA, it was almost certainly in the Punjab that she was being held. But, despite implicating the Indian government, the events as they were unfolding had the hallmarks of a plot that originated in Pakistan, or at least the 'deep state' of Pakistan.

He reached for his laptop and wrote an email to the senior duty desk officer at GCHQ requiring the results of a search he had initiated earlier in the week into the background of every Colonel in the Pakistani army promoted between 1970 and 1979, with a list of their subsequent appointments and biographies.

Before dawn, and back in bed, Peter's mobile phone alerted him to an email that contained the encrypted results of the report he had requested. He lay there reading it through time and again and making meticulous notes. When at last he put down his pen he knew, with absolute certainty, the identity of his adversary.

Venus Fly Trap

Clemmie planned the meeting with scrupulous attention to detail. She rented a room on the thirty-fourth floor of a large skyscraper in Canary Wharf near to Henry's offices. A large picture window offered an uninterrupted, postcard view of central London.

She arranged for a wide table to separate the two parties and the blinds of the internal windows were drawn to ensure complete privacy. Along the back wall of the room was a sumptuous sofa. Coffee and pastries were available on a sideboard.

It had taken considerable negotiation before Henry would acquiesce to the notion of mediation and attend a meeting at which the two of them would settle the terms of agreement for their divorce. Once it was made clear to Henry by his solicitor that it would be considerably to his advantage, especially when it came to making a settlement, he agreed to meet, albeit reluctantly. Mr Archibald Compton was engaged to arbitrate between the two parties.

As requested, Henry arrived promptly at ten-thirty in the morning to find Clemmie and Mr Compton already seated on opposite sides of the wide conference table. She rose to greet him and insisted that he sit beside her in the vacant chair on her left. Henry was relieved that she seemed relaxed and friendly, for he had anticipated extreme confrontation accompanied by blame, bitterness and rancour. Moreover he was taken by surprise at what she was wearing for he had expected her to be severely dressed to reflect the ruthlessness of her purpose, instead of which he could not help noticing that she had chosen a very short skirt, above which she wore a flimsy blouse without a bra. He was immediately aware of a provocative fullness to her breasts, the outline of which was obvious. A dowdy Mr Compton in a cheap crumpled suit appeared discomfited by her attire, in fact he was uncomfortable with the whole situation in which he found himself. As proceedings got underway Henry could not help glancing sideways at Clemmie's breasts and he was increasingly distracted by inappropriate thoughts of her body.

"Mr and Mrs de Quincy Adams, we are gathered here today in the hope that we may find some resolution to the difficulties that have beset your previously loving relationship, and to do so without recrimination," intoned Mr Compton.

"Sounds like a bloody wedding service," grumbled Henry. Clemmie kicked him under the table and hissed at him to keep quiet.

Distracted also by the shortness of Clemmie's skirt, Henry was having difficulty following Mr Compton's meandering explanation of the purpose of the meeting, recalling vividly how active and inventive their lovemaking had been. He found himself unexpectedly and uncomfortably aroused.

Mr Compton droned on, a tedious preamble aimed at bringing the couple to a point where they might discuss their differences, but neither Henry nor Clemmie appeared interested in what he was saying. Clemmie wriggled constantly, and each time she moved her skirt inched upwards revealing a further tantalising display of thigh that began to dominate Henry's attention. After a few minutes he could do no other than focus exclusively on her legs, and in so doing lost the thread of what Mr Compton was saying. He found himself hoping her skirt would ride up further to the point where the next wriggle would reveal her underwear; the prospect of which increased his discomfort because, sitting down, his burgeoning erection was thoroughly uncomfortable. She squirmed once again, and he gasped involuntarily as her pubic hair was suddenly and gloriously revealed. Previously, she had waxed, but now long, dark, silky pubes parted to reveal the soft rounded cleft that had held such pleasure in the past.

Mr Compton knew that he had lost the attention of the two and was certain that some undercurrent was at play that he did not comprehend. It made him increasingly discomposed and annoyed. Clemmie wriggled once again, but this time to Henry's disappointment she tugged her skirt down and without warning stood to announce that the session was over. As she pulled her skirt straight, she thanked Mr Compton and assured him that he would be generously remunerated, after which she walked around the table, shook his hand and ushered him out. He departed with relief.

She closed and locked the door and as she turned back to Henry undid the buttons of her blouse. She removed the scrunchy from her hair and shook it out before taking a few steps to stand in front of him with her large breasts inches from his face. Seated he swallowed and without hesitation cupped the one on the left before placing his mouth firmly over her nipple and sucking like an infant. His left hand slid up her leg, at which point she reached behind and unzipped her skirt. With a little shuffle and a tug from Henry, the skirt fell to the thickly piled carpet where it was joined by her blouse. Henry's vision, filled with the sight of her bosom and full nakedness accompanied by a now extremely painful, pulsating erection; his lust had become so urgent that all rational thought deserted him.

She stood in front of him voluptuously and leaned forward to help him out of his jacket and shirt before kneeling and undoing his shoes and then, lasciviously opening his fly, slipping her hand into his pants and stroking his hardness, which resulted in a small moan. When he was fully naked, she led him to the sofa and lowered herself with legs splayed. He noticed little droplets of moisture in her pubic hair, which stimulated him further still. It was obvious she wanted him to enter her, and he did so with carnal force and urgency.

Moments later he ejaculated with wild abandon and she knew, with absolute certainty, that she had conceived his child. A child that she would ensure grew to hate his or her biological father. A paternity test would prove to Cassie and Henry's family his infidelity and he would be required to accept responsibility for the parenthood of his legitimate heir. The de Quincy Adams name and wealth would be passed to her second born, she would make sure of that, the first step of her revenge.

"Now get out," she hissed at him venomously.

Aegisthus

Clemmie was unsure of the distinction between the verbs 'avenge' and 'revenge' and so referred to a dictionary, from which she learned that the former requires 'inflicting a punishment in the pursuit of justice', while the latter is a matter of 'inflicting harm or punishment for personal retaliation'. The difference was too subtle for her to distinguish between, because as far as she was concerned Iphy's death had to be both avenged and revenged.

The intensity of Clemmie's anger was fuelled by a need for retribution that burned like acid, caustic and corrosive. Her rage did not diminish as months passed, it only increased, provoking within her an animus that urged her to excise the cause of her pain and suffering, which was Henry. It was his negligence that had caused their daughter's death. Clemmie's thirst for vengeance extended also to Cassie, the strumpet who had failed in her duty to protect Iphy and was now carrying Henry's illegitimate child. Iphy would be avenged by her mother who sought a reckoning for a wound so deep that it could never heal and so cruel that she could feel it in the centre of her very being, in her womb.

Clemmie returned to the Rear Entry Club unaccompanied and although she felt bashful, having purchased suitable attire online, it seemed appropriate and when seen in front of the mirror made her feel exceptionally libidinous. Before leaving the house, she donned a long raincoat and on arrival adopted a simple leather mask to disguise her identity. Hailing a taxi, she gave an address two roads distant from her actual destination.

The feverish excitement she experienced as she entered the club and handed her coat to a cloakroom assistant made her shiver with anticipation, although she was still apprehensive. She was poised for flight when a man sidled up to her and offered to buy her a drink; she accepted the drink but declined his offer of a visit upstairs. When she saw a glimpse of herself reflected in the various mirrors around the room, she was both horrified and proud: a buttoned waistcoat without bra so that her breasts bulged, fishnet stockings and a thong that drew attention to her long legs and firm rounded buttocks. She wondered frequently what she was doing flaunting herself in such a flagrant fashion, but also observed that she was dressed conservatively by comparison with some of the women who ranged in age from young and flashy to old and saggy. Some of the men leered and appeared desperate and, she observed that, the more unattractive they were the more outrageously they dressed. *'Sad. God, I hope no one thinks that looking at me.'*

It was on the evening of her triumph over Henry that she saw him for the first time. He stood out from the crowd on the other side of the room. He noticed her also and smiled; she acknowledged his greeting with a small gesture. It took him half an hour to make his way over to the bar and join her, during which time she had been approached by three men all of whom made lewd propositions that she rejected with crushing disdain. He was tall and muscular and when he spoke his rich accented baritone excited her. His garb was not excessively revealing, but it highlighted his powerful masculinity, and naked, she thought, he would look very different from the ineffectual, fleshy, metropolitan, Henry. There was something of the street fighter about him and a hint of danger that stimulated a tremor of excitement in her.

When he invited her to join him alone in one of the rooms upstairs, she accepted. She was still wondering if it was in her nature to be dominant or submissive when they entered a dimly-lit but opulently decorated room with pornographic wall coverings. In the middle of which was a small sofa with a bed to one side that featured a moulded iron fretwork headboard. Hanging on the wall were a number of the club's accoutrements, all within easy reach.

When the door was firmly shut and bolted behind her Clemmie sat resting against the back of the sofa with her legs open. She unfastened her clutch bag and withdrew a small bottle of red nail varnish which she handed to him instructing him to apply the varnish to her toes. As he knelt at her feet, she outraged herself by opening the buttons of her waistcoat and rubbing her nipples between finger and thumb before placing her hand down the front of her thong and starting to masturbate. Never in her life had she ever been so brazen. She watched him closely to judge the moment his lust began to flare. Raising him up she undid his trousers and stroked his erection squeezing it hard until she knew he was bursting with desire. At the moment she was sure he was about to take her she slapped him across the face. He did not flinch but reached behind for a horsewhip that he flicked across her thigh, and with that sting she could no longer contain herself as he effortlessly stripped off her underwear. He turned her around and over and forced himself where no man had been previously. The surprise brought with it such sexual pleasure that she shuddered to a climax.

His name was Aegisthus and he had been born in Greece. The

relationship that developed between them was full of complicated contradictions, but as it grew over the following weeks it strengthened and they became increasingly dependent upon each other. She was financially dominant and when he asked her for money, she exacted a high price, while submitting to his physical ascendancy willingly.

It was not long before she was beguiled and her craving for his strength became potent. She withdrew from the social circle that had supported her previously and the two were inexorably drawn into an increasingly hedonistic cycle that included both cocaine and controlled violence. By day Clemmie continued with her employment as a solicitor, but increasingly she withdrew from contact with her family, until she was merely sustaining a nominal relationship via social media.

Clemmie told Aegisthus of her pregnancy after three months and to her profound relief he was unmoved. When she explained that he was not the father he was unperturbed, however he was astonished when she asked him to marry her promising to settle a very large sum of money on him to give him his independence.

Clemmie had come to understand that while she could generally control Aegisthus there was a dark side to his character. In fact, she had concluded, he was morally deficient; intensely loyal and cravenly obedient to her commands, but indifferent to the feelings of others. He had no empathy and was unaffected if his actions inflicted hurt. She had witnessed this most vividly when he became enraged one day driving her Range Rover down a country road. A cyclist, affronted by Aegisthus' aggressive use of the horn, had raised a finger to him. Instead of ignoring the gesture Aegisthus was instantly consumed with rage. He slowed the vehicle and when the cyclist turned off into a narrow lane Aegisthus followed, accelerated and bore down on the man sending him flying. At the very least the rider must have been injured, but Aegisthus showed no sign of remorse, instead she noticed him smiling to himself as if vindicated.

Clemmie told him the sum of money she had in mind for the settlement and he was astounded, but there was a condition attached. Her proposition required, in return for access to her wealth, the death of her previous husband and his paramour, Cassie. Aegisthus had no hesitation agreeing to the contract outlined by his future wife and the woman who was to be the mother of his putative child.

Tirana

The British Airways flight banked and circled the Dajti mountains that ring the city of Tirana, the capital of Albania, before beginning its steep descent into the airport where Aegisthus was met by a smartly suited young man wearing the ubiquitous dark glasses of his type. He was ushered from the concrete terminal into a Toyota Landcruiser with tinted windows, a vehicle that may well have been smuggled into Albania, he thought, such is the country's reputation for international crime. The vehicle was comfortable, but the roads congested, and every driver made liberal use of their car horn. In the absence of traffic lights or roundabouts, the sense of ordered chaos was confirmed when his driver cursed all other road users.

Along the main route into the city Aegisthus noted two centuries of market economy juxtaposed; along one side of the highway were tawdry shops trading hub caps for ancient cars, while on the other were glittering showrooms displaying prestige vehicles that long ago dispensed with hub caps. Forty minutes later he was ushered into a comfortable apartment in the centre of the city made available to him for the duration of his stay.

The history of Albania is one of oppression and bloody opposition: Greeks, Romans, Byzantines, Ottomans and during the twentieth century the Italians followed by Nazi occupation. After the second world war the political vacuum was filled by Enver Hoxha and his Stalinist party who oppressed the people and tore down much of the city, replacing the ancient buildings with soviet apartments constructed from inferior materials. During the communist era the centre of the city was walled off and reserved for Hoxha and his apparatchiks, an oasis of comfort hidden from the populace behind a heavily guarded wall. The narrow car-less roads of the soviet era were eventually replaced with boulevards in the city centre when the country chose to return to democracy in the last decade of the twentieth century. However, many of the social adjustments were cosmetic and the pervasive soviet culture remained, evidenced in the architecture and the ubiquitous tangle of cables strung above every pavement, a metaphor for the convoluted and disorganised politics of a historically complex society.

The narrative of the Albanian people is about resistance to invasion and invaders and their emblematic hero, Skanderbeg (who sustained a twenty-five-year rebellion against the might of the Ottoman empire) has his own statue in the centre of the modern city. It is a history of resistance represented by 'isms': opportunism and cynicism, communism and capitalism, nationalism and pragmatism; populism and totalitarianism, a nation in modern Europe with the bloody history of the Balkans in its veins.

Aegisthus had lived in Albania as a young man and felt at home amongst its people. He enjoyed its culture, its terrain, its food and the lurking Balkan danger that padded below the surface of its declared aspirations. Poverty-stricken men, women and children still garnered a living from rubbish bins, scouring them for plastic bottles while the privileged and influential looked down impassively from the glittering Sky Tower and affluent modern apartment blocks. The metro-elite glided around in air-conditioned cars secure in the knowledge that their homes were guarded by armed men who not so long ago had been bandits.

The heavy, imperial public buildings from the Italian era might give the impression of solid authority in a city that espouses law and order, but the Albanian mafia operate with considerable impunity and it was into that world that Aegisthus came to seek assistance from men of his acquaintance. His business was soon brought to a mutually satisfactory conclusion.

Untouchables

The small, and mostly insignificant intelligence outpost in Patiala, had never been called upon by Her Majesty's Government to undertake any meaningful service, at least not since Partition which was well beyond living memory.

Major Rasheed (retired), the Indian editor of *The Patiala Chronicle* and station head of a far-flung British outpost, was therefore electrified when he received a top-secret memo, a most urgent command from Whitehall. All that had ever been required of him previously was to report on 'population shift' or 'demographic drift' and, just occasionally, an analysis of border relations and troop movements in the region. But now he, Major Rasheed (retired), was being called upon, himself, to serve Her Majesty Queen Elizabeth, the monarch of Great Britain, in a matter of the greatest secrecy and importance. A significant honour. The magnitude and value of the task was made clear to him in a telephone call from London, as was the need for total confidentiality. He must carry out the assignment in complete secrecy and do his duty no matter how onerous, dangerous or complex it may prove to be.

In India, for millennia, the caste system has been the organising principle of society. Determined by birth, caste draws distinctions between communities that determine a person's profession, level of education and potential marriage status. Privileges are reserved for the upper castes and denied to the lower. The lowliest in this pecking order are the 'Dalits', once called 'untouchables' who are consigned by the Hindu hierarchy to the lowest and dirtiest occupations. Theirs is a sizeable community of some two-hundred million people, the term 'Dalit' deriving from a Hindi word meaning 'oppressed, suppressed, downtrodden'.

Vashram Sarvaiya was a Dalit who lived a quiet and humble existence taking care not to draw attention to himself. He was content with his life and did not want more than he possessed, and so it was a surprise and matter of some consternation to find Sahib Rasheed waiting patiently for him in his humble abode when he returned from work.

Vashram had never received a formal education but was blessed with an extraordinary eye for detail and a prodigious memory, photographic in its accuracy. He was also virtually invisible as he went about his duties in the service of the Nawab of Patiala for whom he was employed as a cleaner. Mainly he swept and then settled the dust by spraying water, or he mopped the courtyards and watered the gardens at the lavish Palace of the Nawab of Patiala, whom he had only ever seen from a distance. Over the many years of his service he had swept and cleaned every area of the ancient fort.

The report prepared for Major Rasheed by Vashram was duly forwarded to London. It was meticulous and extensive with detailed drawings of the layout of the Nawab's palace that included accurate proportions of the buildings as well as defences, numbers of soldiers, location of state rooms, offices, billets, gates, guard and sentry positions, fortifications and administrative areas, all neatly noted. The positioning of the main and other gates, defences, passwords, duty rosters, patrols, guard stations, as well as the location of utilities; electricity, telephone, internet switch cabinets, water and even sewerage were annotated. Over two-hundred men he reported were employed at the palace and only rarely were visitors welcomed, for it was a fortress. A helicopter was kept and maintained in the large parade ground, mostly used to transport the Nawab to an airfield some miles outside the city. This airfield had been built by the government for heavy transport aircraft after the last war with Pakistan and was kept in readiness in case of future tensions and the need for deployment of a rapid response force. The runway was just over five-thousand feet in length and was leased to the Nawab, who housed a Learjet 45 in the hangar for his private use.

Most importantly Major Rasheed (retired), could confirm a visual sighting in the prison wing of the palace of, *'A white memsahib with an extraordinarily beautiful physiognomy and resilience of character who always wears a scarf around her neck as if to hide a scar'*.

The East India Club

St James's Square, London

William was in London and had asked Henry to host him and one other for dinner at the East India Club in St James's Square where they could dine and talk more confidentially than at his club, the Army and Navy. As William approached the colonnaded entrance, he passed the tribute to WPC Yvonne Fletcher, killed in 1984 by a gunman who shot her from a window of the Libyan Embassy. He was reminded that nowhere is truly safe, as Helen now knew.

Henry had arrived ahead of him and they greeted each other in the lobby with all the warmth of close friends for whom there are no barriers to trust and loyalty. Henry had booked a discreet table near the dining room window and not long after being seated they were joined by Peter Baird. William introduced Peter to Henry as an old family friend of Helen's mother, and as a tactician and advisor on a joint project they wished to discuss.

When the sommelier moved away, and speaking in soft tones, William addressed Henry across the table. "Of course, you are aware of Helen's situation, and you should know that I have put together a small team that intend to rescue her from where she is being held in captivity."

"Is it funding you require?" asked Henry. "Because have no doubt, appropriate resources can be made available."

"No," said William, "money is not the issue, or at least not money in the sense you mean it, but I would like you to listen to a proposition from Peter when we have finished dinner."

Henry turned to Peter with interest trying to appraise the large, enigmatic man sitting on his right. He remembered that Peter had been a guest at his wedding, but they had not been introduced. What could his involvement be, he wondered?

The meal progressed cordially, and William admitted to Henry that he had never really sought to understand what type of banking he undertook. Peter, he commented, had assured him that Henry's reputation was formidable in the city and if he could be persuaded to assist then he might prove central to a plan to save Helen.

William had heard from Leda that Henry's relationship with Clemmie was now toxic and he avoided the subject, partly because Henry's marital difficulties were none of his business but more importantly the subject was a digression from the purpose of the evening which was to ensure Henry's help in putting together the operation to rescue Helen.

Having concluded their meal they retired to a private room, passing on the long-curved stairway the large array of public-school shields that adorn the wall. Coffee and brandy were ordered and duly delivered during which time William uttered a silent prayer that the noblesse oblige that had bound them through their school years, and as close friends since, would resonate with Henry.

"Now," said Henry, "perhaps the two of you will outline for me whatever it is that you are cooking up."

"Let me explain," began Peter. "You understand finance, and the man we believe is holding Helen captive likes to trade. He likes to be known by his title, which is the Nawab of Patiala."

"Do you mean Indolent Indi? If so, then he was in my house at

Harrow. A lazy sod but I never thought him wicked."

"One and the same," continued Peter. "These days he doesn't often venture far from his home city of Patiala, which is in south eastern Punjab. He may have been lazy at school but is now very actively dedicated to enhancing his not inconsiderable wealth. He enjoys nothing more than playing the markets and speculating on the financial exchanges. We know that in the past some of his deals have flown very close to the regulatory wire and we suspect that he has been implicated in a couple of substantial insider trading transactions that have netted him a small fortune, but he has never been caught with his hand in the cookie jar. We believe that he has been offered a number of sweet and juicy incentives to become involved in the plot that threatens Helen, and because he is greedy, we hope that he is open to a tempting proposition. This is where you come in."

"Of course, you know the story of the horse," interjected William. "And how it was used to lull the Trojans into a false sense of security. Well, what we are intending is to infiltrate the Nawab's stronghold where Helen is incarcerated with a modern equivalent and the hook is good old-fashioned greed."

"Indolent Indi," said Peter. "Will be in London in a week's time and we want you to make him an offer that he truly can't refuse. Let me explain."

Infection

The head of the cybersecurity unit at GCHQ delivered his report to Peter Baird in person as requested, a verbal briefing.

"Well Brian," began Peter, "I need to know all that you have unearthed and all that you conclude. Even if you don't have the evidence, give me the threads. Your conclusions may be vital to an operation I am running."

"I am hesitant Peter," replied the boffin. "Because as yet I don't have the complete picture, but I'll outline what we have established and what I suspect. Forgive my use of technical terms but they are necessary. I will try to keep the explanation straightforward.

"Firstly, the plan is simple. Over the last eighteen months a small piece of armoured malware has been introduced to the computer infrastructure of banks across Pakistan; armouring is a technique to avoid detection by antivirus protection. Further to this it is polymorphic, which means it changes its signature each time it replicates. It has been incredibly effective due to a zero-day exploit in the core operating system of the terminals, so no one other than its designer and us knows it is there. Every time a terminal has been accessed this Trojan 'bug' has been circulated and become resident, although it is as yet dormant."

"Excuse me for interrupting," said Peter. "But what happens when the bug is triggered?"

Brian looked at him quizzically. "It will freeze all the accounts of the Bank of Punjab making them inaccessible. The banks all connect to the WAN, or Wide Area Network, for the purpose of clearing funds, and the virus has exploited vulnerable systems installing itself in the rootkit, but as it is in effect operating outside of the rootkit it is completely invisible to it. It tunnelled out and spawned when connections were made."

"So, what will trigger it?"

"A simple logic bomb which can be deployed upon command when a certain port is opened on a remote server on the Web. Of course, none of this would have been possible if the firewall's firmware update hadn't been hacked in the first place to allow the traffic to flow. But, as interesting as the disruption it will cause when initiated, is the fact that it will leave behind a false trail. The footprint will implicate the Indian government as the originator, although we believe it has come from somewhere in Pakistan itself, but that is a very political conclusion and so one for you to play with, it's not for us in our techie eyrie."

"OK to simplify," summarised Peter. "Are you saying that an agent from somewhere has hacked into the IT systems of the National Bank of Pakistan?"

"Yes."

"Are you saying this Trojan bug is primed but not yet activated?"

"Yes."

"Are you saying that when triggered it will stop all access to personal accounts for all customers of Pakistani banks?"

"Yes."

"Furthermore, are you saying that when traced it will have the fingerprints of the Indians all over it?"

"Yes."

"But, in fact it originated in Pakistan?"

"That's it in a nutshell."

Peter was silent for a while. "I feared something like this and many congratulations, Brian, for an excellent job unravelling this one. The two questions I have for you now are, can you come up with something that will stop this little monster? And can you come up with it in time?"

Graphene

William leaned back and moulded himself into the leather driving seat of the Maserati Ghibli. He had ordered the car while serving overseas and it was awaiting collection on his return. As he accelerated onto the M40 the deep throaty roar of the three litre V6, 410 horsepower engine was immensely satisfying and he settled comfortably into the four-hour journey to Manchester knowing that he would enjoy the journey. He turned on the Harman Kardon surround sound system and relaxed listening to his playlist.

He parked in Booth Street as close as possible to the glassy, unbalanced cube that is the National Graphene Institute of Manchester University and was on time for his meeting with Professor Nicola Watkins, a meeting that had been arranged by Peter Baird at William's request.

"How can I help?" asked the Professor once they were seated in her office. "The Marquis has made a generous offer to fund an extension to our facility and asked that the department offer you every assistance. If we can help, then we shall. How much do you know about graphene?"

"Well I know that it is ten times as strong as titanium, that it is conductive and that it is stretchy."

Nicola Watkins smiled and replied. "It was first discovered here at Manchester by two scientists in 2004. They understood its properties might have commercial applications, but never imagined how important it would become. It is a layer of carbon atoms locked together in a strongly bonded honeycomb pattern one atom thick. It is five percent as dense as steel and yet possesses ten times its strength, one layer can support the weight of an elephant.

Initially it was only a two-dimensional product, but scientists quickly realised that by layering graphite its applications could be much more versatile and this they called graphene. The world was ready and scientists at other universities started experimenting. At the Manchester Institute of Technology in Boston they developed a hexagonal lattice of graphene that gave three-dimensional form. Believe me when I say that we are talking about the future. A mobile phone the thickness of cling film has already been devised. But how can we assist you?"

Their conversation lasted for over two hours and Nicola made the promise that the Institute would do all it could to assist in the very tight time frame available.

When he left the building, William was satisfied that important progress had been made and as he approached his new car, he admired the Maserati once again, its sleek lines and power, like a leopard ready to be unleashed he thought. He set the sat-nav for Credenhill in Herefordshire, the HQ of the Special Air Service.

*

The trio had not met for some months and greeted each other in the Mess with a cordial fraternity that disguised the strength of loyalty and affection they shared.

After dinner and seated in large comfortable wing back leather chairs secluded from the rest of the officers, each was enjoying their individual choice of single malt whisky. Observing protocol and the need for secrecy they avoided the subject of the undertaking that awaited them and their banter was light-hearted and irreverent.

William turned to Hector and said, "Did you know that in the Iliad Homer describes Achilles and Hector as bitter enemies who end up in a fight to the death?"

Ray was quick to respond. "Well, sonny, I happen te know that Achilles whipped Hector. Hector, he was a mummy's boy who certainly never visited Glasgae on a Saturday night and nae learned to fight properly when the pubs closed."

"Actually," responded Hector, "Achilles was a sulky bastard while my namesake was the greatest warrior in ancient Greece. In the end Hector was tricked by Achilles who, judging by his behaviour, might have been born in that heathen, bog filled, whisky drinking, skirt wearing extremity of the civilised world known as Scotland!"

William intervened. "My point gentlemen is that I am in the fortunate position of having the two greatest warriors in history serving on my team. Unbeatable."

"Hmm," replied Hector, "but was Achilles a Scotch git?"

The training programme William had devised was comprehensive and arduous. Peter had supplied them with a floor plan of Bandargarh Fort marked with the position of guards all of whom would be heavily armed and present in overwhelming numbers. They had identified where Helen was being kept captive, "But," Peter informed William, "a guard is placed permanently outside Helen's cell and in the event of an armed attack is under orders to kill her. One glitch will result in her immediate despatch. Getting inside the fortifications will be a feat in itself but getting out with a woman who is weak and confused is quite another matter."

The three-man team were training with the Special Air Service, their authority having been issued from a dizzying height. Mock-ups of the key areas of the citadel, and the building where the prisoner was being held, were created and dry run situations rehearsed. Numerous scenarios were envisaged in case the plan had to be adapted on the ground and only six weeks were allocated to the training. Peter was convinced Helen was safe only until the first of November. Everything had to be in place for the 'missionaries' to depart on the twenty-sixth of October.

New Delhi

India

The 22.30 British Airways flight from London Heathrow to the Indira Gandhi airport, New Delhi, landed on the inside of the three parallel runways and taxied to Terminal 2 where it parked up at exactly 08.40.

As he disembarked Peter Baird thanked the crew for a pleasant flight, and reached the Arrivals Hall in short order, his diplomatic passport having seen him smoothly bypass immigration. He was met by a Brigadier of the Indian Army who escorted him from the concourse to a waiting car that was ignoring all parking restrictions. The airport's military presence tolerated this breach of security only because the number plate and the driver's credentials included a code that ensured priority.

The car swept through the crowded streets shrouding him in air-conditioned comfort and insulating him from the heat, smells and dust that sought to suffocate those less fortunate outside. He was taken to a nondescript looking building used by the Indian Defence Agency since it became operational on the fifth of March 2002.

Ushered through a maze of corridors he was finally shown into a secured room somewhere in the middle of the building where two men and a woman were awaiting his arrival. They were seated in comfortable office chairs set around a large conference table and the vacant seat was clearly reserved for him.

Chairing the meeting was Doctor Aziz who introduced herself and her two male colleagues, both of whom were four-star Generals.

"First," began Doctor Aziz, "let me welcome you to Delhi Lord Marquis of Northumbria and thank you for coming all this way to visit us."

"It's Peter, please. Let's leave all that title nonsense to one side."

"Thank you, Peter. Then let me cut through the preliminaries, but, for the record, your exalted position is relevant to us as you are the UK's leading intelligence and security exponent. Furthermore, we recognise and respect the rank you hold in the British establishment and know you work alongside the Americans who hold you in high regard.

"Now, you have asked to have a discussion with us concerning a threat that you say could jeopardise the security of our country. As I have stated already, we are conscious of your illustrious position and keen for you to share with us any matters that might affect the stability of our beloved country. So please then, begin by outlining the situation that so alarms you."

"Well," began Peter, "let me seek to connect a number of specific events. In isolation they may not seem to pose a major threat to your country, but when viewed in conjunction they are a matter of grave concern to the British Government.

"Your agency, alongside the Indian Defence Image Processing and Analysis Centre are highly regarded security organisations, and so the matters to which I refer will have been observed by you, but our explanation may offer a new interpretation of apparently disconnected issues.

"Firstly, there has been a systematic undermining of confidence in the Bank of Punjab, driven by suggestions that India is seeking to destabilise the economy of Pakistan. The implication is that hackers, not necessarily sponsored by the Indian government, but perhaps unofficially sanctioned by them, have been stealing from the bank, and despite Indian denials the notion has gained traction. Articles to this effect have appeared in financial journals around the world contributing to an escalating political tension between you and your neighbour to the west. Indeed, recriminations from Pakistan are becoming ever more vociferous and strident.

"What is not yet known is that a further crisis of confidence in the Bank of Punjab is being prepared, which, when triggered, will result in a dangerous undermining of the financial sector in Pakistan and a run on the bank, probably leading to widespread civil unrest. The government in Islamabad will direct the blame against your government, fuelled by fake evidence of Indian complicity.

"Secondly, the disappearance of the daughter of the Chancellor of the Exchequer of the UK and the son of the President of Pakistan, and their televised mock executions, has caused international outrage from governments around the world. The girl's incarceration is known to be somewhere in the Indian Punjab, and it is supposed that the son of the President is being held with her. From intelligence received it is our belief that the two will be executed and evidence released implicating a fanatical group known as the *PSM*. The international outrage that will follow the killings is ostensibly to draw attention to their cause, but its real motive is to reinforce mistrust in your government. Again, false evidence will be unearthed after these murders purporting to prove the *PSM* have received covert support from your government.

"This organisation, the *Punjabi Separatist Movement,* or *PSM* claim they want to reunify Punjab and make the region an independent, multi-denominational state within India, as it was before Partition. If your government were believed to be supporting such a political agenda then, under international law, India would be condoning an illegal act, namely the secession of West Punjab. This would be an act of aggression and would legitimise a military response from Pakistan.

"The abortive July fourteenth outrage in Paris was laid firmly at the door of the *PSM* and brought international prominence for their cause. As I have said the *PSM*'s declared aim is to create a unilateral state of Punjab, and while the Indian government's response may be incredulous and dismissive of such a preposterous idea, Pakistan is posturing, claiming that the *PSM* is nothing more than a proxy for a state sponsored land grab by the Indian government, which they will resist at all costs. In bringing their cause to Europe the *PSM* have made India appear complicit in their ambitions.

"In fact, we believe the *PSM* are a spurious faction of Muslims. The purpose behind their activities is to manipulate international support for Pakistan so that Pakistan is perceived as the innocent victim of India, who they will claim, undertakes kidnap, assassination, terrorism, economic sabotage, cyberwarfare and territorial misappropriation.

"A case is, therefore, being carefully constructed that prepares the ground for Pakistan to claim the legitimate right of self-defence, as a sovereign state, in response to threats against it, and it is that plot that represents the third strand.

"The political temperature has been ramped up and as you are aware questions are being raised at the UN. When Europe and the USA start to express concern, you can be sure that Russia won't be far behind hoping to foment dissent.

"We have ascertained that Helen Strachan is being held in

Indian Punjab and, as I have said, when her captors are taken, as they will be following her execution, further false evidence will emerge to suggest complicity between the *PSM* and the Indian government.

"At that moment the situation will become perilous; a tinder box that only requires a spark to precipitate a war that threatens to draw in east and west. I must emphasise, however, that the present government in Pakistan is not orchestrating these events, it is the work of a secret cabal preparing to seize power triggered by an outrage that gives unambiguous credence to Pakistan's claim of Indian collusion. We don't know what the atrocity will be, but there will be one used to precipitate a military coup in Pakistan and justify a build-up of troops along its border. When ready, a pre-emptive strike will annex Indian Punjab, which has been the prize all along. The perpetrators are bargaining that India will not retaliate immediately because its allies will not support hostilities between two nuclear powers, especially when the evidence points to India as the aggressor.

"We are of the opinion that all these interconnected elements are strands of a single coherent plot orchestrated by one man who has devoted his life to the purpose of reuniting Punjab as a Muslim territory under the aegis of Pakistan. His parents were killed in 1947 and the family's lands seized during the ethnic cleansing that Partition became. Surviving members of his family were killed in the war of 1965.

"We have identified this man who is only ever referred to as *The Colonel*. He has been well funded for many years by a group within the deep state of Pakistan and he divides his time between there and Europe.

"As you are all too well aware the ongoing geo-political

instability of Afghanistan, its support by Pakistan and the dominance of Muslim fundamentalism across the Middle East all represent a growing theocratic threat on your western borders. If the Indians in Pakistan's Punjab were supplanted by radical Muslims, then the security of your country would be greatly weakened; their dream but your nightmare of an Islamic caliphate would be brought a step closer.

"So, in conclusion, civil strife in Pakistan is being stoked and a wedge is being driven between India and the west as a prelude to the annexing of East Punjab by a new, bellicose Pakistani military junta.

"I am here to offer the hand of friendship and, on behalf of the Prime Minister of the United Kingdom, to suggest that we work together to avoid a catastrophe."

The three people around the table looked stunned. They had listened avidly without interruption, but the questions came thick and fast.

After five hours of intense discussion Doctor Aziz leaned back in her chair and drew the conversation to a conclusion.

"Peter, we are enormously grateful to you. Of course, we have looked at the same information, but it seems through a different lens. We have been increasingly nervous at the way events have been unfolding, but knew nothing of this elusive Colonel, a monster who threatens us all. The scenario you have painted could unfold as you describe, and it is a horrifying possibility. We shall now draw up plans to neutralise this danger and contain it as far as possible. We wish you a comfortable return journey and we shall set up an encrypted link between our departments."

"Before I depart may I request one favour," said Peter.

"Of course. We are in your debt."

"We know where Helen Strachan is being held. I have a small

team of highly trained men who I would like to call upon to extract her safely. This means launching an exercise on your sovereign territory."

Doctor Aziz looked at each of the Generals and they nodded their acceptance.

"Please keep us informed and request whatever help or equipment you may need," said the Doctor as Peter rose to leave.

The comfortable limousine, with the Indian pendant flying proudly on its bonnet, whisked Peter back to the airport.

Options

"What is a 'Put Option'?" asked William.

"Good thing you asked," replied Henry, "because it is central to the proposal Peter and I are going to make to the Nawab tomorrow."

"Please enlighten me but use straightforward terms so that I understand."

"Well then simply put, and no pun intended, it is a device that gives the owner the option to sell assets, including currencies, at an agreed price on or before a particular date."

The Nawab of Patiala was ushered into Henry's office, high up in a tower block in Canary Wharf. The company had deliberately chosen a less imposing and more reassuringly contemporary set of offices than investment banks traditionally opt for with a location that offered easy access to central London, including the added benefit of being conveniently close to London's City Airport.

The Nawab, a short, rotund, puffy man with centre parted over-long hair, dark moustache and round glasses, arrived with a small entourage who Peter thought were employed more for personal protection than financial acuity. It was unlikely that the Nawab would want any witnesses to the discussion that was to follow, and it was no surprise when he sent them to wait elsewhere.

"Welcome, Indi my old friend," Henry began, "It's been a long time, but I have followed your progress with interest, and it is in the belief that we may be able to put together a project of mutual benefit that I thought it would be helpful if we had a chat. I heard you were passing through London."

The Nawab replied in a jocular tone, but with an edge, "Henry you and I were friends at school, but I suffered regular humiliation from your crowd, and I have to say that I don't feel any warmth or affection for most of our contemporaries. I have only come along today because your enigmatic invitation was suggestive of a tantalising opportunity and I am curious enough to want to hear what you have to say."

"Well old chum you are right to be intrigued because my business partner, Peter, and I want to talk to you about a project that will expunge any latent hostility, in fact I am certain it will cement our future mutual prosperity. Please sit and we shall explain."

The three men took seats facing one another, but before Henry could start Indi addressed him directly, almost rudely.

"Why me, Henry? There must be many others with whom you could put together a deal."

"Well Indi you are right to ask but let me allay any suspicions you might have about our motives. The reason this one has your name written all over it is that we need both your Indian wealth and your position as a dealer on the sub-continent. It could make us all a small fortune, but to pull it off we need you. If everything goes well then you will add substantially to your Ali Baba coffers."

"Go on," said the Nawab.

"Well, let's say, for sake of argument, that an Indian company with interests around the world has been having a hush hush conversation with a certain American conglomerate that is well known for its sale of fossil fuels and has just struck it lucky off the coast of Morocco. Moreover, let's speculate that the former is going to make an all cash proposition for the latter somewhere in the region of a hundred billion dollars, then our hypothetical lovers are dancing a delicate little tango.

"However, if our Indian lover is to entice the little American beauty into the bedroom then he's going to have to do the deal in dollars, which means exchanging his sparkling little rupees. A cash transaction of such enormity has rarely been seen before in the Indian market and the impact of selling such a number of rupees will inevitably result in major pressure on the value of the Indian currency which will fall. Once speculators get wind of the transaction the pressure on the central bank will be so massive that they won't be able to hold the currency stable. Our estimate is that it will fall by about twenty percent and, as you can imagine, any Put Options will explode in value. Now if a third party, say an investor such as myself and Peter had happened to have some millions of dollars, alongside a similar amount from you, to place on out of the money Put Options based on the rupee/dollar exchange rate, then the gearing on those futures options could become many times the investment when the currency falls.

"For us to make such an investment we need someone who can manage a rupee/dollar transaction without suspicion. We need an Indian prince to act on our behalf. Obviously our Indian prince would need relevant and helpful information and he would have to purchase the Put Options through several third parties. The options would need to be bought very discreetly with absolutely no trace or the authorities will be deeply suspicious and investigate with some potentially very uncomfortable consequences."

The Nawab interrupted. "How could your Indian prince trust that events will fall out as you predict because he would be at great risk if his options expired before the transaction took place, and then his investment would be worthless?"

"I can't give you exact details yet," Henry replied cordially, "But were you and I to walk down the aisle hand in hand then, as I have said, my risk matches yours. Peter and I are each prepared to put up five million dollars on the twenty-eighth of this month which we will lodge with you personally. This is our show of good faith. We will know if and when the bid is to be made and there will only be a short window of opportunity to transact. We have people on the inside in both parties and we are the only players who know for sure that the bid will be accepted and when it will be tabled. How much you invest is up to you.

"Assuming you agree my dear Nawab," continued Henry, "then we shall arrange the funds and you will purchase the options when we tell you to during the last few days of October. We can track the market and make our decision at what moment to maximise the profit on our Put Options. And all of this is as old friends working together, we will be one hundred percent certain of each other and the transaction.

"What do you think? If a prince, his old school chum and new friend Peter were to look to a golden future rather than a tarnished past then their bond might become very strong."

"Indeed, they might," said Indi, "but I know of no such deal, there has been nothing in the press, not even a whisper around the markets."

"Of course not, and were there any such talk then our conversation would not be taking place for I have no intention of spending the next twelve years in an Indian jail."

"You can take my word for it," Peter interjected. "There will not be a whisper and that's why we need to act quickly so that we control events." He spoke with impressive conviction and confidence.

"So," said Henry opening his diary, "let's pencil in October the twenty-eighth when we can meet with our expert associates and together purchase the options."

The Nawab was still wary. "This matter must remain absolutely watertight, so I insist you come to me in India. My palace is a fortress from where we can progress with complete secrecy and concealment."

"So be it," concluded Henry. "We will be with you on the twenty-eighth."

Cygnet

On the evening of the twenty-fifth of October a plain white transport plane, nicknamed 'Cygnet', was parked in the Oxfordshire mist out of sight at RAF Brize Norton. In the evening dusk it looked as though it was huddling against the perimeter hedge to escape the wind while being equipped, purportedly for a routine trip. In fact, the C-17A Globemaster III harboured, like eggs, an adapted and unmarked three-ton truck with the livery of a well-known Indian distribution company, and an apache helicopter. Also, within the fuselage was a small aeromedical evacuation facility that included an emergency operating theatre.

With its reverse thrust the Globemaster can be turned on the ground in a small radius, and with its four Pratt & Whitney engines it only requires five-and-a-half thousand feet of runway for take-off, making it ideal for unusual transportation operations delivering cargo to relatively small airports. The aeroplane dwarfed the four men who had collected at the rear, three of whom were obviously military and appeared relaxed, and one who was neither a soldier nor unperturbed, namely Henry.

William, Hector, Ray and Henry were joined by the rest of the team and William made the introductions. The line-up included a doctor, a military nurse, two RAF helicopter pilots and the Globemaster's air crew, all of whom had 'volunteered' for this most unusual and potentially hazardous mission. The flight complement listened attentively as William outlined the mission and explained that they would not reassemble until they were nearing the end of the operation. He and his contingent would be travelling by commercial airline to maintain anonymity. When they next rendezvoused, a rapid departure would be required.

It was not until the pilots were running their pre-flight checks on the twenty-sixth of October that they received their high security briefing, including details of their destination.

"Well this will be interesting," commented Wing Commander Justin Moore to his co-pilot. "Apparently the Indians have granted us a 'no questions asked' permission to land and park up at an old airfield outside Patiala in the Punjab where there will be a tanker standing by to refuel. The runway is in fair condition because it is used occasionally by their military but is only five thousand, three hundred feet in length, just short of what we need for take-off. There will be no margin for error, and we will have to lose as much air speed as possible before touchdown. It is anticipated we shall be on the ground for two days and may have to depart with casevacs. Our call sign is 'Dustoff', and we know what that means. Departure from Patiala, according to the top brass may be, and I quote, 'in unusual and rushed circumstances', which, in my book, is a euphemism for by the seat of our pants. Sounds exciting."

Disquiet

Leda had never before contacted Peter during working hours and so when he received her carefully worded request, he made space in his schedule and that evening drove to *Swan's Nest*.

It took Leda a while to work round to why she was so agitated and even then she began hesitantly, embarking upon a preamble while she organised her thoughts.

"I have tried speaking to David, but he no longer appears to have any substantive interest in me. He hardly ever comes home and when he does, he is so preoccupied that it is almost impossible to engage him in conversation. It seems that any mutuality we may have had has faded to a memory and so, of course, I have turned to you as I always do when I need strength. I am concerned, because while we have all been so preoccupied with Helen's situation, we haven't spared a thought for Clemmie.

"We both know that she lacks Helen's graces and can be difficult and wilful, but there is something else about her at the moment that is worrying me greatly, I'm sure she needs our help. She has never really recovered from the loss of Iphy and over the last few months has become increasingly distant and cold, it's as if she has disconnected, unplugged herself from us emotionally. She has such black moods. But it's more than that now, she is retreating into a world that excludes us all. I can't seem to relate to her anymore and she has little interest in Helen's plight.

"I was driving in the vicinity of her apartment yesterday and thought I would pop in to say hello. Admittedly I didn't call first, but when I arrived, she was frosty and unwelcoming and clearly didn't want me to enter. I insisted on a cup of tea and there was a man in the flat who I think may have moved in. He hardly said a word to me; I thought him coarse, but she is clearly attached to him. She kept touching him and stroking his arm. I think they had been drinking. She told me she has given up her job.

"She wouldn't talk about Helen dismissing her as vain and attention seeking and the architect of her own downfall, all of which is so untrue and unfeeling. I think she might be pregnant. The atmosphere was all wrong, it was horrible.

"I have never seen Clemmie like this before, so angry, bitter and resentful. Her attitude was malevolent towards us, her family, and I very definitely could no longer connect with our girl. I don't know what to do."

Peter thought carefully before replying and giving her a protective hug. "I am not sure there is much we can do," he said. "But we will try."

"Oh, and by the way," confided Leda, "David and I have agreed to a trial separation."

Torment

Iftekhar was plagued by a single image that was etched onto the retina of his memory. Just before she climbed into the taxi cab Helen had turned and looked up at him; she had smiled and waved, and in that moment there was about her such an aura of innocence and radiance that each time he recalled it his feelings for her swelled, like wind filling a main sail.

From the evening when they had first been introduced at *The Colonel's* dinner party thoughts of her discomposed him, and then he became fascinated by her. In the weeks that followed he detected no flaw in her character for she showed no sign of conceit, spite or malice. He was captivated by her vivacious ebullience, which he considered both artless and ingenuous; he perceived purity and it enamoured him.

What he was not conscious of was the effect she was having on his emotional equilibrium. Without knowing or comprehending it, she triggered a deep emotional dependence in someone who had never known sympathetic attachment.

The sequestration from his parents and indoctrination he received as a child had been deliberate, designed to foster detachment, for it was *The Colonel's* design to cultivate indifference in the boy. The intention was to create an ideologically driven, cold-blooded automaton, a dangerous chameleon committed to one goal and devoid of conscience. However, the Machiavellian manipulator had never looked for, nor understood, that in Ifty's nature there dwelled an unfulfilled need for emotional connection.

The Colonel never perceived the complexity of Ifty's psyche and did not recognise that the affection deficit the child experienced would cause a lasting vacuum of maternal deprivation. Into this void stepped Helen. When *The Colonel* inserted her into Ifty's life a latent craving for reciprocal tenderness found a home, and the potency of that need multiplied. Moreover, his emotional upheaval was accompanied by an increasingly physical enchantment that acted like fuel thrown on a fire. Ifty was confused and had no understanding of what was happening. By the time he started to acknowledge his feelings it was becoming too late to save Helen.

On that fateful afternoon in Paris he looked down at the departing taxi and suddenly understood that he was about to destroy what he had come to love, which was utterly dysfunctional. It confounded him and left him feeling debilitated for he had allowed events to overtake any chance he might have to manage outcomes. If only she had reciprocated in some way when he declared his feelings, but now she had passed beyond his control.

He spent the night after his disappearance in hiding and turmoil. The following morning, he was picked up by an anonymous Citroen and driven to the home of a makeup artist who transformed him into a man thirty years older who would pass through the airports of Europe and beyond without being recognised or challenged. His new passport gave his age as fifty-three.

It was a few days before he arrived in Lahore where he was immediately absorbed into the ancient walled city, a teeming metropolis of souls that paid him not one jot of attention.

Lahore

The apartment allocated to Iftekhar in the old city of Lahore was comfortable, although not extravagant, and for the first time in a long while he was at a complete loose end, cooped up with only a television and a few uninteresting books to occupy him while a noisy, ceaseless flow of humanity passed by in the streets below.

Rather than finding himself energised by an enforced break, he was restless and troubled by vivid images. Despite all his attempts to think positively, thoughts of Helen and concern for her future continued to haunt him. Moreover, the more he dwelt on *The Colonel's* mission the more his doubts began to challenge his certainties, threatening to unravel the threads of his zeal. The dependable cloth of his convictions started to fray, and not even devout reading or prayer could offset his misgivings. Above all else he wanted to see Helen so that he could explain that he craved her forgiveness and needed her absolution.

The maelstrom of conflicting thoughts and emotions that swirled around him granted no peace, and by the end of the week he could bear the confinement no longer. He decided to take a stroll, despite having been instructed to remain indoors. He had no purpose in mind other than to mingle with ordinary people going about their normal business and to experience the mood of the city and its people, his people as he kept reminding himself, those for whom *The Colonel's* cause was forged.

From the moment he closed the front door he sensed the embrace of the city and was rapidly absorbed into the river of people flowing towards the heart, the interior. Entranced, he wandered along busy, bustling thoroughfares and alleyways that were filled with a discordant confusion that exuded energy and life. Entering a labyrinthine bazaar, he jostled past traders and merchants who competed for his attention and made slow progress through the melee. He was captivated by the vibrancy of the people and the place and could not help but be overwhelmed by everything around him.

The air was filled with a multitude of pervasive smells, mostly alien to his senses, made redolent by the heat of the afternoon. The musk from numerous types of spice was inescapable: curry powder, peppers, cardamom, chillies, cumin, cloves, cinnamon and ginger, beneath which was the mild reek of meat and vegetables that had remained on display all day and everywhere there was the odour of unwashed bodies.

As he moved through the market, he was conscious of colours competing for his attention: an array of vegetables, flowers of all shades, clothes, fabrics and bolts of flamboyant textiles, all clamoured to be noticed, while the commotion of people bartering, berating, debating, and arguing was incessant. Everyone it seemed was bellowing, bawling, bargaining or just conversing, and all of them loudly. A multi-hued weft of dense human interaction surrounded him raucously, watched over by elders who sat or squatted and drank tea with the motionless, rheumy indifference of old men and the patient serenity of elderly women.

At every street corner men with long ladles spooned and stirred ingredients in large pans that bubbled, steamed and sizzled, pungent and evocative, while women sat kneading dough before spinning it on the ends of their fingers and laying it on hot coals from which emanated the tantalising smoulder of chapatis. Numerous other spiced foods were being cooked in flat pans.

The streets funnelled the human traffic between high buildings and swarmed with activity. The roads were frantic with those on bicycles stridently ringing their bells and weaving between overladen mopeds transporting precariously perched goods and families. Those on scooters or driving Tuk-Tuks beetled and beeped criss-crossing between the jetsam that flowed inexorably in all directions and everywhere people barked into mobile phones. Dust rose, swirled in little vortexes before settling momentarily and then rising again.

The walls of the older townhouses were decorated with intricate and elaborately carved wooden designs, mostly decaying, inspired by the Moghul tradition of Haveli, that spoke of histories and cultures long passed.

Through open doors and windows Ifty observed adults, children and animals mingling inside buildings, all living in close proximity. It felt to him as though the whole metropolis had been crammed within the city walls and he was a piece of driftwood taken by the current. He dodged vehicles, people and animals that intersected miraculously without collision, all part of the impatient, noisy confusion that surrounded him.

Taking a turn away from the tumult of the main thoroughfare, he found himself in an open space dominated by a domed mosque, magnificent in its design and imposing presence and in complete contrast to the street. He stopped and marvelled at its size captivated by the Persian design of its turrets and frescoes. Parallel worlds - the streets: earthy and in constant flux, random, discordant and incoherent; juxtaposed with calm, geometric order and tranquillity. The temporal and the spiritual, a metaphor for his emotional chaos he wondered.

He recalled reading that the two-and-a-half square kilometres of the original city of Lahore is contained within high defensive walls that connect twelve magnificent, fortified gates most of which are still intact.

Passing out through the massively imposing Roshnai Gate (one of the original twelve) he stopped at the awe-inspiring Badshahi Mosque, astounded by its size, architectural magnificence, dominance and antiquity, a match for any of the great cathedrals of Europe. He entered, reverently, dwarfed by the vast vaulted interior and surrounding columns, all intricately decorated with marble inlay and glowing golden in the early evening sunlight that slanted through the west window as the afternoon waned. The space was cool, quiet and contemplative, which suited his mood, and he kneeled offering prayers for both his guidance and Helen's safety.

Later, when night had fallen, he finally wended his way back to the apartment retracing his journey through the walled city, musing on its long history and tempestuous past. He knew that beyond the ancient walls modern Lahore was developing fast, aspiring to build a strong progressive economy, but what he had experienced that afternoon seemed like an animated pageant of centuries past.

Lahore's history had been revealed to him through its magnificent formal architecture; regular, intricate and calm signifying stability and spiritual permanence, a living testament to human creativity and harmony, but also as a vibrant, chaotic, metropolis seething with energy, noise, dust, heat and confusion, seemingly little changed over centuries; sensual and vital, in constant turmoil and circumscribed by poverty. He had experienced the city's diversity, richness and also its destitution, so very different from life in the west. He felt uplifted, for he loved his people, but he was also saddened by the deprivation.

As he neared the apartment his highly sensitised attention was drawn to a stand selling magazines, and there, from the cover of one periodical, as if staring straight at him, was a picture of Helen. Her hair was dishevelled, and she emanated ethereal fragility. Behind her stood a man poised to draw a vicious looking knife across her throat. Helen seemed to stare straight into his eyes as if pleading.

Inside Ifty something lurched and with the force of a slap across the face her image drove out all other thoughts. *The Colonel* may not have been holding the knife, but it was he who was planning her death in the name of all that had brought Ifty to Islam.

Returning to his rooms he was reeling from his excursion, uplifted by his homeland, its culture and its people, but pained by its lack of progress, poverty and brutality; ruthlessness in which Helen was caught like a fly in a web. Above all else his mind was dominated by the fear, horror and vulnerability he had seen pictured in the face of the woman he loved.

*

When Ifty awoke the next morning after a night of disturbed sleep, it was in a state of confused exhaustion. He lay restlessly awake as thoughts spun like clothes in a drier.

He had been schooled to hate the imperialists who denied his country its rightful place in the world and taught to mask his hatred, but did the flames of extremism burn as brightly within him as his masters expected? Ifty had been told numerous tales to justify why those responsible for the burning inequalities in his country should be brought to justice, but he could not help questioning whose justice, and, furthermore whether the term 'justice', as they used it, was interchangeable with 'revenge'?

From a young age Ifty had been taught that in Islam the explanation for all that is ordained is found within scripture and then revealed by sages and clerics. He was to suppress the perfidious voice of western scepticism because it challenged the notion of unconditional obedience expected of all Muslims. However, as he matured, he could not ignore the fact that different interpretations of doctrine exist and this opened him up to the heretical question, whom should he trust?

As a young man his anger and his scorn had been provoked and nurtured for a purpose, to vindicate extreme action. He had been instructed that violence is not only justifiable for a Muslim but is his duty, and so it was that he was introduced to Jihadism, the anvil upon which the spear that would be Ifty was forged.

But, schooled in two philosophical paradigms, those of both east and west, his masters, unknowingly, fashioned a dichotomy. As a follower of Islam, he was required to submit to the Will of Allah, but at the same time, as a product of western education, he was attracted to the compelling concept of freewill.

Virtually from birth he was immersed in the Salafi teaching that required him, as a *Ghuraba,* to be a right and truthful Muslim in a world of wrongdoers, one who accepts Jihad.

But, was he, he asked himself, unequivocally a Muslim (*al-wala wal-bara)*, one who held enmity towards non-Muslims? Did he accept *Takfir* - the licence to kill? He had been taught that his religious obligation of *Hakimiyyah,* required him to establish God's government on earth, but did that justify taking the life of non-Muslims for his cause?

Islam was the rock to which he had adhered like a limpet, but did his God truly want him to kill in the name of all that is omnipotent and destroy everything that he had come to value living in the west?

He was plagued by insecurities and needed guidance. Twice a day he returned to the Badshahi Mosque in the hope that God would speak to him directly, but he knew in his heart that Allah required him to come to his own conclusion.

Ifty was a good Muslim who prayed according to the declaration of faith, the *Shahada,* religiously observing *The Five Pillars of Islam.* In the mosque he was conscientious in his observance and undertook to submit willingly to the *Istislam* (the surrender) in the hope of achieving *salam* (the peace). And despite his intellectual uncertainties he accepted that it is only through surrender to God that the soul finds peace, but, however hard he tried, his soul was far from being at peace because at the root of his uncertainty was the question of moral authority and how it was mediated.

Time and again he returned to his mentor, Ali ibn Musa, to explore the question that lay at the core of his confusion, *"I know what men are asking of me but do they speak with the authority of God?"*

"In answer to your dilemma," concluded Ali ibn Musa. "What you need to ask yourself is whether your Jihad is undertaken to defend Islam, in which case it is legitimate and has the authority of Allah. But, if you employ scripture and scholarship to legitimise a personal interpretation of the Muslim cause, I am telling you your Jihad can't be justified. Islam gains its legitimacy from the authority of its true spiritual leaders, but if undertaken wrongly under the guise of Jihad, then what you may believe is a moral action is actually no more than a justification for killing using the name of Islam."

*

One morning in the first week of October an official looking car forced its way along the road outside Ifty's apartment and stopped, blocking the traffic. A rough looking soldier in combat uniform emerged and knocked harshly on the door. Opening the front door Ifty was faced with a muscular man with narrow black pitiless eyes, a walrus moustache and bulbous, pitted nose.

"Mr Diaz, you must come with me, now."

Ifty was immediately unsettled by his visitor but had no choice other than to accompany the unsavoury escort. Without pleasantry or explanation, or any attempt to make conversation, he was driven to the outskirts of the city where the car entered an industrial area. It turned into a road lined with large commercial units and finally into a gated compound surrounded by trees and a tall fence topped with razor wire. Ahead was a large building with sliding doors that closed behind the car. Men with automatic rifles patrolled. In the centre of the empty warehouse was an enormous glass-sided tank full of water and illuminated by arc lights.

Ifty tried to disguise his anxiety challenging the man to show his authority, but to no effect. The monosyllabic thug, his hand menacingly on the butt of his pistol, merely told him to change into an orange jumpsuit that had been laid out on a table beside the tank. Ifty recognised the coverall immediately with the initials *PSM* clearly evident. Two cameramen were poised, ready to film.

"We are going to make a video to show the world we are serious," said the man. "You should not fear for you are far too important to be allowed to die."

Beside the tank, suspended by a winch, was a metal cage into which Ifty was instructed to climb. It was not large, and he had to bend his legs to squeeze in sideways, after which the hinged access was closed above him and, to his consternation, locked.

The soldier gave a signal and a man operating the winch raised the cage that was then lowered slowly into the water.

Ifty looked down upon his tormentor and saw the man staring up at him with a look of such malevolence that he was filled with a sudden, unnerving fear.

He knew he could manage a minute, perhaps a little more without air and so expected the torment to be brief, but it wasn't. As the seconds ticked by his rational mind began to give way to instinct and he struggled, a natural but futile action that only increased his need for oxygen. Desperation multiplied as his lungs began to scream for relief. The pain in his chest was like fire and his pulse detonated between his ears. He thought his head would explode.

As carbon dioxide accumulated in his brain he started to hallucinate; rational thought replaced by fraudulent imaginings that spuriously encouraged him to open his mouth and take a gulp of sweet invigorating air ... all he had to do was to suck in a draft of blissful fresh, clean air.

When the water entered his lungs blackness descended and following an involuntary expulsion of air his body started to sink. A video camera zoomed in on a string of bubbles that flowed upwards from the corner of his mouth.

When released on YouTube the clip showed the son of the President of Pakistan drowning, an image designed to inflame further outrage around the world. Most horrific was the casual indifference of the turbaned man, with the initials *PSM* emblazoned on his uniform, who stood watching and smiling impassively.

Whispers

While the main focus of Peter's attention had concerned Helen's disappearance, Iftekhar's synchronised evaporation disturbed him greatly for it raised two unanswered questions: If both were hostages why were they not taken together? And why, if Helen's capture was so obviously visible, was Ifty's so veiled?

As Peter probed deeper into Ifty's history he began to wonder if the young man's involvement was more intricately woven into this plot than had been hitherto obvious? What if Ifty's role was more than a lure to ensnare a valuable hostage, as had been originally conjectured?

Peter formed a team to delve into Ifty's background, and as the file grew a strand emerged that unearthed an elusive guardian with whom Ifty had spent numerous holidays during his years at school. A new enquiry was launched into '*The Uncle*' and Peter began to speculate that perhaps Iftekhar might be more of a central character than minor attendant in this unfolding drama.

However, this line of investigation was abandoned when another vile video showed almost conclusively that Ifty was dead. *The Uncle* it transpired had sold his estate and left the country, his imprint 'wiped'.

But, just as Peter was resigning himself to an unresolved loose end, the team received a 'whisper', their term for information received, obliquely through the deepest, darkest web of international espionage. The interception was deemed 'cold' by the decipherers, but when it reached him Peter had a very different interpretation because it was signed '*The Nephew*'.

Bandargarh Fort

Patiala

Punjab

Following her abduction Helen returned to full consciousness only slowly and without continuity of recollection. Her awareness of events and sense of time were initially fragmentary, although she soon began to piece together fleeting images and started to make observations about her surroundings. Having been insensible for days her cognitive function was impaired, and it took time for her to recover.

At first, only semi-sensible, she perceived that she was lying on some form of palliasse. Somewhere in the distance she could hear men's voices shouting in an unknown language and she thought she could make out boots stomping. The brightness of the light puzzled her as did the heat, the dryness and the dust, and she was tortuously thirsty. She needed to empty her bladder.

Returning to fuzzy wakefulness she started to focus on her surroundings and concluded that she was indeed lying on a mattress in what looked like a cell dressed in a pair of overalls. Near her on the floor was a bottle of water and within arm's reach a bucket, which she assumed was meant for use as a latrine. Since peeing was the priority, she started to raise herself, only to discover that her left arm was manacled by a cuff attached to a chain and a ring in the wall. Her wrist was red, swollen and painful.

She was physically weak and struggled to remove the overall with one arm tethered. Finally, making it to the bucket she gained blessed relief, after which she drank every drop of the warm life-giving water, emptying the bottle in a few long greedy draughts.

As Helen organised her thoughts, she began to make sense of her surroundings; it was obvious that she was no longer in Paris. She was a prisoner; there was the shackle and the window was barred. When she made the effort to look out of the window all she could see was a beaten-earth parade ground within the walls of a stronghold where troops were being drilled. The heat and light suggested Africa but on closer inspection the soldiers she could see in the distance looked more Indo-Aryan than Negro. She was being held captive in a cell, but for what reason?

Memories tugged at the edges of her recall – she was struggling with a man inside a taxi. Images, thoughts and flashbacks swirled, but in no logical order as she tried to make sense of her situation. She must have been drugged. What about William? He would surely come for her soon. But when she analysed the evidence, reality dawned, and she was forced to conclude that whatever had transpired had happened for reasons way beyond her understanding and it had been carefully planned. She would only make herself miserable thinking of William and their plans; he would want her to be strong and so she forced herself to focus on the immediate.

At some point she heard a key in the door and a disreputable grinning gaoler, missing most of his teeth and dressed in a dirty robe, brought in a plate of unappetising looking rice slopping around in some kind of liquid. She bombarded him with a stream of questions, but he was uncommunicative, either because he did not understand or because he was mute. He left her another bottle of water, replaced the bucket and departed in silence.

Over the days that followed Helen had no alternative than to resign herself to inactivity, although she made the decision to keep as physically fit as possible. She devised a limited and painful exercise programme that became a ritual during the seemingly interminable days that followed in dull succession. She asked for something to read, a radio, paper and pen to write with, but all requests were met with impassive indifference and no favours were forthcoming. Her left arm remained chained to the metal ring on the wall and the cuff continued to rub painfully.

As days passed, her most fierce battle became psychological, struggling not to be overwhelmed by dejection and despondency. She did not understand the motive for her abduction, and a creeping loneliness was accompanied by a growing sense of abandonment. As the days ticked by without any change to routine or any distraction to alleviate her boredom, she forced herself to face the possibility of a bleak future, but she also resolved to be resilient and remain strong, she would not succumb to self-pity.

Once every few days a sharp-faced female escort of saturnine disposition walked her to a nearby shower block where she was allowed to wash her hair and use soap, an experience she began to long for and which never failed to revive her spirits. In the early evenings when the heat of the day began to wane, she was taken for exercise attached to the same female guard. They walked the perimeter of the parade ground five times before she was returned to the cell in the tall tower.

As Helen reflected on her situation, she arranged her thoughts into comprehensible order in the hope that she could make some sense of what was happening. She had been abducted, that was clear, and transported across the world, but for what purpose? Might it be something to do with her family? If so, she could not think of any obvious reason other than for ransom, or to gain political influence over her father.

Accepting that she was a prisoner in a fortified encampment, she wondered if perhaps she was being held by a Muslim group, Isis or Al Qaeda? However, she had not heard an *adhan*, the traditional Muslim call to prayer from a muezzin and a number of the men she saw through the window wore turbans. She was at a loss to think of any motive for being taken captive by Sikhs. The more she considered her situation the less sense she could make of her circumstances.

She had lost track of the days but she reckoned it was probably a couple of weeks into her interment when a squad of soldiers marched noisily into her cell, heads swathed in niqabs, and all she could see of their faces was hostile eyes glaring at her vindictively. The leader unlocked the chain and threw down an orange jumpsuit. In English he ordered her to change and she suffered agonies of embarrassment as lascivious men watched her strip down to her underwear. She was not immune to the symbolism of the orange garment and for the first-time felt a tremor of fear that undermined her resolve.

The armed escort surrounded her, and she was marched down the turret stairs leading out onto the dusty square that served as a parade ground, in the middle of which she could now see a telegraph sized post dug firmly into the ground. She was immediately conscious of the heat of the sun and a chill of terror made her shiver when she recalled seeing a video of a woman being stoned to death.

She was taken to the post and from behind her arms were pulled roughly and bound tightly, securing her to the post. A newspaper on a loop of string was placed around her neck and her hair was grasped and yanked backwards, stretching her bare neck. Before she had time to react a stinging blade was drawn across her throat and she felt blood trickle down her front. Her arms were released and she was returned to her cell where a woman she had not seen before was waiting with an emollient paste that she spread gently to the long wound across Helen's neck. It was superficial but Helen's look of apprehension, incomprehension and then terror were caught by the camera.

Treachery

The Colonel was standing to one side of the plain, unadorned, windowless, room into which Iftekhar was ushered.

"Hello, my boy, we meet again. Have a seat. I hope they haven't hurt you?" *The Colonel* was in a relaxed and loquacious mood. "The plan has run smoothly so far, despite an unexpected and disappointing outcome in Paris, but the international reaction that followed the abortive attack has had almost as much of an impact as if everything had gone to plan, which is satisfactory. And I congratulate you upon your contribution so far as we now have Helen Strachan, our biggest prize secreted away in a safe place. All is set as we move towards the critical stage, the success of which depends one last time upon your total commitment. You are indeed blessed to be the one chosen to make the ultimate sacrifice."

"I understand, sir, but was it necessary to drown me to ensure my participation? I thought my commitment was proven?"

"Ah, that was an overzealous patriot who went too far in search of authenticity, for which he is now truly repentant. I was distressed to hear of your awful experience, but it is not the time for us to dwell on mistakes as we approach the climax of our narrative, the culmination of so many years planning. I'm sure that I don't need to ask, but reassure me Ifty my boy that you are not having second thoughts about the final stage of our holy undertaking?"

"I am not, but I do now have a pre-condition."

A mixture of consternation and fury flashed across *The Colonel's* face. "I thought your commitment was unconditional," he snapped.

"It was until that brute you sanctioned nearly killed me. At the moment I thought was my last I realised there is someone I care for more than life itself. I want you to release Helen Strachan. Let me be specific, if Helen is not released then there is no pressure you can apply on me to ensure my compliance. Only if she is released will I fulfil my obligation."

"Are you in love with her?" *The Colonel* shot the question incredulously, anger and exasperation rising to the surface with the force of lava.

"I don't need to explain to you why I make this demand," replied Ifty furiously, but my involvement is contingent on your agreement. Moreover, I want to meet with her before she is released."

The Colonel struggled to control his ire but could see by Ifty's stiff demeanour and tense expression that he was unconditionally serious. It had never occurred to him that his protégé might exercise such independence, especially at such a critical stage, but he understood that much depended on his answer. Another unexpected complication.

"In which case, my boy," he said as emolliently as he could muster, "arrangements will be made for you to visit Miss Strachan and you will be taken to her, but I can only agree to a short visit after which she will be flown to a neutral destination where she can be collected by a family member. Now we must move on to other matters."

The Colonel turned his back and picked up the telephone to summon someone who had been waiting outside the door, which was the moment Ifty took to place a pen innocuously on the shelf beside where he was standing. As *The Colonel* turned back a military attaché entered holding a roll of cloth under his arm which he proceeded to unfurl on the table.

"This," declared *The Colonel*, "is a work of art. A body vest so thin and undetectable that it will pass all but the most rigorous security checks. It gives off no trace of explosive and contains no metal, and it will fit you like a second skin, but when you detonate it against the aeroplane's fuselage it will cause a catastrophic explosion."

Ifty stared at the instrument of destruction with a horrified fascination. "I understand," he said. "This then is the burden I was born to carry."

Acceptance

Following the mock execution, time passed very slowly for Helen and the days ticked by with pendulum monotony, accreting into weeks that eventually became months, but however much she analysed the facts she could not make sense of her situation.

Apart from the horror of the quasi killing the only other extraordinary occurrence had been heralded by a flurry of activity followed by the arrival of a portly, expensively dressed man in a woven silk kurta-pajama. He was clearly a wealthy Indian, and possibly a person of power and influence and she saw an opportunity to question him, but he pre-empted her.

"I have come to visit a woman whose beauty is legendary. I am the Nawab of Patiala and you are my guest."

"Please, please," she entreated, "explain to me why I am here and for how long. My parents are rich and influential and will pay anything you ask for my release."

"I am aware of who you are and your family, but as to why you are here you will have to be patient. In time all things are revealed."

With that he turned and departed before she could address him any further. Helen was left desolate and disconsolate with nothing other to do than sit on her mattress and watch motes of dust drift across a shaft of sunlight.

In the succeeding days she found it increasingly difficult to stave off the stupefaction of her inertia. She was determined to remain equable and was appreciative of the fact that she had never experienced the melancholic hopelessness of depression, but it was difficult to remain positive and she was not immune to the mood swings that accompany circadian and biological rhythms.

At first she managed to counter the dull repetition and inactivity by constructing mental games to offset the corrosive effect of ennui, but as time passed she found herself increasingly submitting to lethargy and her mind drifted aimlessly.

Thoughts of *Swan's Nest* brought fond memories and she recalled days when she and Clemmie would roam the grounds inventing games to pass the days they considered boring.

She tried to be philosophical and understand the cruelty of her captors, at which moment she immediately thought of Ifty and imagined she could hear him saying sardonically, "Aha the perennial nature/nurture debate, which is of course to philosophy what constipation is to rectal health!"

Ifty. Thoughts of the dashing young man and his devotion made her sad. '*Where is he now? Such a lovely, caring, joyous boy. I wonder if he knows that I was taken'*?

And, of course, recurring as regularly as a leitmotif, was William. When she analysed what it was that had drawn her to him, she concluded it was a combination of physical and moral strength.

'*He manages his world without the desire to rule it and he values the responsibility human beings share for one another; it is in his nature to protect. He is a good man who understands that we must love one another or die, as Auden once wrote.'*

"Where is he now?" she kept wondering. "What is he thinking? Does he even know of my predicament?"

Insurgency

The Colonel was not an emotional or sentimental man, but he was angered by insubordination and therefore incensed by Iftekhar's defiance, especially at such a crucial moment. He was still brimming with resentment when he began his next meeting with two senior officers of the Pakistani army.

Lieutenant General Siddiqui, presently serving as Commander in Chief of the III Corps, and Major General Patel, recently promoted to General Officer Commanding 5th Armoured Division, had both risen to military prominence at a relatively young age. They were prime movers in *The Colonel's* cause, which would see the return of Punjab to a unified state under the aegis of Pakistan. Other senior officers had vowed commitment although not all had, as yet, declared allegiance.

Generals Patel and Siddiqui were charismatic patriots, popular with those who served alongside them. They had garnered recruits to the cause and fostered commitment by stirring resentment at the slights and offences inflicted against their country by its arrogant and colonial minded neighbour, as well as by exploiting the continuing Islamophobia of western nations.

"How quickly can you mobilise the army once control has been seized?" enquired *The Colonel.*

"It will take a month to ensure order and suppress military and civil resistance," replied Siddiqui. "Dissidents and dissenters will be rounded up and the media controlled, including the internet. Specialist groups will filter out opposition and launch a programme of propaganda that supports our actions. The first of December is therefore *Day One* when the regiments held in readiness will sweep south through Punjab and join the battalion circling from the north. A new border will be created and the reunification of Punjab as one entity belonging to Pakistan will be announced."

"The Indians will respond in force," commented *The Colonel.*

"Their army will be confused and slow to counter with military action," replied Siddiqui. "The international reaction to our invasion will be muted as the UN will consider us provoked, especially as our President and some of the Cabinet have been assassinated by a suicide bomber on a flight to attend a climate conference, blamed on the *PSM.* All the evidence for this outrage will lead to the *PSM,* and by implication the Indian government, added to which the callous execution of the English girl at the hand of the brutal Indian separatists will give moral authority to justify our invasion of Punjab and the annihilation of the *PSM.* The economic situation of the Pakistani people suffering from a banking crisis instigated by India will give further legitimacy to the call for military action. Before the rest of the world reacts and the United Nations can interfere our annexation will be achieved."

The Colonel nodded, "But," he commented, "we may have run into a problem. I have been put under pressure by our assassin to release the girl whose bloody and brutal execution is meant to trigger western outrage."

"Well that's impossible," said General Patel. "To meet our schedule, you have to ensure authentic evidence of her beheading is released on the thirty-first of October. The President flies to the climate convention in Washington on the next day, accompanied by his son, miraculously returned to his parents by intrepid members of the Pakistani special forces. No one will ever suspect the Diaz boy's complicity in the assassination of his father. Within hours of the fatal air crash a new government of Pakistan will be formed and the incoming President, you Siddiqui, will issue the secret orders to prepare for military action. We cannot deviate now."

Siddiqui continued, "The day before the girl's killing the economy of west Punjab will falter when the banks foreclose, resulting in massive civil unrest. Also, evidence will be unearthed of an India inspired banking fraud against Pakistan, all of which will justify the army taking control. India's involvement in the economic damage to Pakistan will be exposed, as will their role in the attack on Paris."

"In conclusion," said General Patel, "we are poised. Following the air accident those close and loyal to us will cauterise the opposition and call for a new President to take control of the army. There will be no organised resistance; indeed, we anticipate the news of our action will be met with an outpouring of popular support. The invasion should be complete by the second week of December, after which, in our own time, we shall return to the issue of Kashmir. So, sort out your problem, Colonel. We can't falter now. She dies on the last day of October."

Iftekhar waited in an adjacent room peeping through a closed venetian blind until he saw all three men depart, which was when he returned and recovered the pen he had placed on the shelf. Once safely out of the building and back at his lodgings he established a bluetooth connection between the pen recorder and his phone and replayed the conversation.

Next he typed an end-to-end encrypted message and pressed send, transmitting the recording through a myriad of redirections. It was from, *The Nephew*.

Ayesha

Sometime after the Nawab's visit, and unexpectedly, Helen encountered kindness in her hostile world. She was sent a local woman to be her maid, whose name Helen established was Ayesha; Ayesha visited every day bringing water and soap for Helen to wash and a luxury, toothpaste. Ayesha undertook simple tasks and after a few days offered to comb Helen's hair. Responding to the captive's obvious gratitude Ayesha went further, smuggling in a mirror so that Helen could at least gain some dignity by ensuring a neat appearance. One day Ayesha brought her a sari to wear and gradually Helen began to receive better food in response to Ayesha's intercessions. Over the weeks that followed an emotional connection started to form between the two women, who would otherwise never have entered each other's orbit: one from the pampered and privileged elite of the west, and the other drawn from the ignored, downtrodden, subjugated and oppressed underclass of the Indian continent.

As the days passed Ayesha taught Helen a few words in her own language and then some simple syntax. Helen had a good ear for languages and in the absence of any other activity the two women took every opportunity to converse. It was not long before Helen started to develop a rudimentary understanding of Punjabi. As her fluency developed, Helen expressed interest in Ayesha's life, asking endless questions that were answered simply and patiently. She wanted to know about Ayesha's home and when she probed deeply, she came to perceive the meagreness of the woman's life. When Helen contemplated the gulf that separated them, she came to realise that her warder had an inbred resilience that made life bearable, a quality Helen recognised she would do well to emulate. Ayesha was invisible in her society, a childless middle-aged woman treated with utter indifference, even contempt, but she had developed the strength to cope in an ill-disposed world while retaining an innate kindness that was beyond value to her prisoner. While the eyes of the male gaoler remained implacable, Ayesha gave Helen the strength and determination to preserve a belief in a better future.

One morning there was a flurry of activity. Ayesha appeared nervous and escorted Helen to the shower instructing her that she must look her best. For the first time Ayesha used scissors to cut, tame and shape Helen's hair, which she then washed, drying it with a soft towel before applying perfumed cream to her skin. The cuff was removed, and Ayesha rubbed an unguent where the manacle had abraded her wrists and also to her neck where the scab had fallen away leaving a thin white trace. Then she patiently manicured and painted Helen's broken nails. It was not at all clear to Helen why this unusual activity was taking place.

Ayesha had brought with her a new sari for Helen to wear woven from silk in golds, reds, jasmine yellow and sapphire blues; it fitted like a kid-leather glove emphasising every curve of Helen's figure, which had been enhanced by her deprivation and exercise regime. Ayesha told Helen to sit on the stool while she applied make up. For a woman who never used cosmetics herself Ayesha exhibited an artistic flair highlighting the soft tones of

Helen's skin and rouging her cheekbones to enhance the contours of her perfect face. At last Ayesha was satisfied and put her head to one side assessing her efforts, glorying in the knowledge that she was gaoler to a goddess, the loveliest person she had ever seen.

There was a noise from the guard room below and before Helen could make sense of what was happening Ifty was ushered into the room. Ayesha crept away. At first Helen was utterly bewildered, but then relief and such a multitude of emotions overwhelmed her that she rushed into his arms clinging to him as if he had swum out to save her from drowning. Her tears flowed unchecked and they stood for an age as if locked together. He held her, stroking her hair, absorbing her very essence until at last her sobbing ceased, replaced by an onslaught of questions.

"What happened to you? Where are they holding you? Are you hurt? Do you know why we're here? Are we going to be released?" Words tumbled from her.

Bandargarh Fort

October 30th

At 08.59 a perfectly polished, gleaming, Mercedes S-Class Saloon glided to a halt outside the massive wooden gate that is the entrance to Bandargarh Fort. Protruding from the reinforced, fortified barrier were conical iron spikes nearly a metre long, designed as a defence against a charge by elephants.

The chauffeur was immediately out of his seat and around the bonnet to open the passenger door for Henry who was dressed impeccably, his expensive sartorial neatness understated but sharpened by heavy framed Chanel dark glasses and a Patek Philippe watch, all ostentatiously contributing to the impression of a powerful and influential man.

From the rear seat of the car emerged William, Henry's putative personal assistant, and two other men; one ostensibly a subordinate from the bank and the other a legal advisor, each carrying a sturdy rectangular briefcase. The team were greeted by Radjit Kapoor, responsible for the Nawab of Patiala's security.

As the banking team were ushered through a small pedestrian gate to the side of the imposing entrance, Radjit Kapoor apologised for the fact that their briefcases would be required to be opened and passed through an x-ray scanner, while they would have to step through a body scanner.

He addressed Henry. "Regretful Sahib, but at all times it is my job to ensure the Nawab's safety. We live in uncertain times and there have been grievous threats made against the life of my master, so let me apologise for these intrusions."

"We quite understand and commend you for observing such strict security," said Henry. "We find it reassuring."

Having cleared the checkpoint they were escorted along a passage that curved inside the high outer wall before arriving at an electronically operated gate that opened upon another concentrically curved passageway that reversed their direction of travel. William's military eye confirmed that the first line of defence was a series of easily protected corridors, exactly as described in Major Rasheed's report.

Radjit Kapoor signalled to a guard who opened a postern gate carved from strong hardwood timbers and reinforced with iron studs. As they passed through William could make out the formidable towers that flanked the main gates at the rear of the barbican. An invader would have to overcome daunting defences even before facing the troops garrisoned within the walls.

They emerged into an enormous courtyard, a parade ground, dominated at one end by a round tower three storeys in height with iron grills across the windows. Guards patrolled between stations armed with pistols attached to one hip and viciously sharp, curved Talwar sabres on the other. Gaining access was one thing, attempting to leave without sanction would be folly, and probably short-lived folly. Parked near the great gates, William noted, were five American *Willys* jeeps well maintained and adapted to carry impressive firepower should the need arise. They were ready to be deployed at short notice. A little further beyond sat a Mil Mi-17 Russian helicopter.

Their route led to an archway situated to the left of the tower and as they approached William could not help an involuntary glance upwards where, thankfully, there was no sign of Helen. Had she seen him she might well have called out, ending the mission before it started.

Following Kapoor, they passed along a short passage emerging into a quadrangle of completely different character, clearly designed to be restful and pleasing to the senses. It was a very large scented formal garden surrounded on three sides by high walls, and filled with an overflowing profusion of hibiscus, frangipani, lotus, jasmine and Ganges primroses, all laid out between small pools that contained ornamental fish. Shady trellised avenues covered with ancient vines concealed seated areas, while terracotta channels fed by some hidden source carried flowing water through ducts above and below ground traversing the garden and cooling the air. In the centre stood a large fountain surrounded by water lilies and flanked by four ancient broad-leafed magnolia trees bearing flowers of white and magenta. Beyond was a princely and perfectly proportioned bright white building, designed to be opulent, peaceful and secure; the retreat of a powerful and influential Moghul. It had been home to the Nawabs of Patiala for generations.

Kapoor ushered the guests into the palace where the air was cool, and the sumptuous décor was in stark contrast to the inhospitable surroundings through which they had first entered. There was a mellow stillness in the air as they followed Kapoor up a long flight of stairs, wide enough for three men to walk abreast. The only discordant note was the sound of their shoes clattering harshly on the stone, *'Like harbingers,'* thought William. They passed enormous pictures hung from high ceilings depicting ancient battles and triumphal hunting scenes featuring men on elephants in pursuit of tigers.

The stairs led to a large open landing area carpeted with an enormous Persian rug where a secretary sat behind an intricately carved teak desk. He rose to greet them and introduced himself. Ahead were two tall, solid mahogany doors, on each side of which stood a turbaned armed guard. The assistant was clearly expecting them and indicated they should follow him. At his command the doors were opened to reveal the secure inner sanctum where, waiting to greet them, was the Nawab himself in expansive mood.

"Ah, Henry," greeted the Nawab jovially blinking behind his spectacles, "My dear fellow, I am delighted that you have arrived safely and that you managed to iron out the wrinkles in London. Meet Godbar, my legal advisor of many years standing. He will examine the documents you have brought and witness the transactions. He will then authorise the transfers from our side."

Godbar was a short, dapperly dressed, overweight middle-aged Indian wearing a wide striped suit who blinked regularly and seemed myopic. His over-long hair was brilliantined and swept back making it seem rather thin. His greeting was unctuous and his demeanour not that of a soldier, unlike Kapoor who was tall, turbaned, wonderfully moustached and displayed the muscular bearing of a military man.

"Mr Godbar, good morning," responded Henry.

Turning to the Nawab, Henry repeated, "Indeed it is a good morning old chum, after today's business is concluded you will have to squeeze even more coffers into those vaults of yours. Once we have completed our transactions your rupees will be flowing like the Ganges in flood."

Pointing to Hector and Ray, Henry said, "Meet my team. Hector

Edwards is assisting us with compliance matters to ensure we are not deemed by the Regulator to have played foul, squeaky clean is the order of the day. Edwards is ably supported by Mr Raymond Jones who will arrange our online transactions. And, lastly, meet William Roberts, my Personal Assistant who flew from England yesterday with the codes we require for today's operation. I assume you have organised the necessary transfer arrangements for signature and authorisation?"

"Indeed," replied the Nawab, "Godbar only has to send our permissions to a bank account in Switzerland and you will receive confirmation almost immediately that the purchases are ready to be made."

Looking around William saw the decor was both functional and affluent. A large ebony meeting-table was circled by eight comfortable, high-backed, white-leather office chairs. Around the room stood tallboy bureaus crafted from mahogany that shone with a deep glossy patina, each inlaid with exquisite ivory, mother of pearl and silver filigree, while from the walls hung a mixture of classical and contemporary Indian art bringing depth and colour to the sumptuous room.

On the far side a large single window offered a panoramic view of the dusty and chaotic city beyond and William wandered over to look down upon the street below. A city always on the move, he thought, hot and grimy, its people generating and regenerating, propelled by the ceaseless struggle for survival and far removed from the luxury of their overlord, a man utterly indifferent to them or their plight.

William turned back seeking reassurance that, so far at least, events were going to plan.

He heard Henry asking the Nawab a string of technical

questions and he tuned into their conversation, now applying clinical detail to the task in hand as he began the countdown.

Ray sneezed twice in close succession, which was the signal for Henry to issue a series of instructions requiring the attention of the Nawab, Kapoor and Godbar at the table. As if synchronised, the three businessmen placed their briefcases on the table and snapped open the clasps creating a small fusillade of clicks. Unnoticed, a small spring triggered the ejection of an object in the lower right-hand corner of each attaché case, and it took only a thumb nail to ease out a deadly weapon. While the attention of the Nawab and his attendants focused on Henry, Hector and Ray slid graphene plated stilettos into a sheath sewn in the lining of their jacket sleeves.

Looking around the room William noted the lavish cushions, comfortable chairs and low tables delicately arranged between sculptures and Indian objet d'art, but what he was looking for was the curtain behind which a door opened into a bathroom for the use of the Nawab and the comfort of his most important guests.

From his briefcase William removed a small glass bottle, ostensibly drinking water, and placed it to the right of the notepad on the table in front of him. The Nawab was seated at the opposite end of the table with Godbar to his left, while Kapoor stood slightly to one side, out of the way, constantly alert. Godbar had a laptop open in front of him connected to a bank in Switzerland and was preparing to input the complicated instructions required to move large amounts of money. William took from his breast pocket two pens and unscrewed the top of the one with a gold ring, then placed both on the table.

As they waited Kapoor began dispensing tea from a silver urn while Henry and the Nawab swapped anecdotes about their time at school. There was a relaxed mood in the room, noisily interrupted by Mr Jones, who suddenly doubled up in pain and looked as though he would throw up. All eyes turned to look at him and, apologetically, he explained to the Nawab that he had an acute and urgent need to use the nearest convenience, explaining that he must have eaten something which was having the most dire and violent effect upon his insides.

Kapoor looked at the Nawab who nodded, and Ray was shown to the private bathroom. As soon as he had locked the door, he took only a second to admire the decor; porcelain decorated with an intricate maroon floral pattern depicting a tiger hidden in the jungle, although what really caught his attention was the solid gold taps of the basin.

Moving silently, he crossed the room and drew back the muslin curtain that covered the tall window opening onto a small Juliet balcony. The clasp was complicated, but in his pocket was a device with which Ray released the lock. He glanced briefly down upon the noisy bustling street, some twenty feet below from where heat and smells rose in waves of dusty confusion. He closed but did not lock the window. Pulling the chain, he washed his hands noisily and re-emerged to hear Henry outlining the process to initiate the transaction.

The atmosphere was still relaxed although a touch more tense as the moment approached to commit to the purchase. Ray pulled the door almost closed behind him and shook his sleeve sliding the concealed weapon into his palm. It was twenty-two centimetres long and two wide at the handle with a razor-sharp double blade that tapered to a pinpoint. Fashioned from compressed plastic and fused with flakes of graphene, it was stronger than steel.

As he passed behind Kapoor, Ray readied the weapon and with exactly judged force slid the blade between cervical vertebrae, C3 and C4, severing the spinal column in one fluid movement. Kapoor died in an instant, not even making a sound, and Ray, holding his collar, lowered his lifeless body to the floor.

The Nawab and Godbar were entirely focused upon the computer screen and were both surprised and irritated when William interrupted them at a critical moment.

"We are short of time," William announced loudly, and as the two men looked up Hector and Ray stepped up behind them and forced their heads down on to the table. In that moment of surprise, and before they could react, gags were placed over their mouths and cable ties slipped over their arms pinning them to the chairs on which they sat. Godbar was the first to respond attempting to push back his chair and stand, but he couldn't. At the same moment Hector slipped a rope garrotte over his head. The Nawab looked on in horror as, with only a few turns of the wooden handle Godbar turned puce and his face bloated like a bullfrog. He wanted desperately to insert his fingers beneath the cord but with only a few more turns there was an audible crack and his spine snapped. He fell forward limp.

William stood over the Nawab, who looked up at him in horror, and addressed him calmly. "Please don't make any futile gesture, because to do so will result in your instant death. Nod your head if you understand what I have just said."

Bewilderment lasted a few moments more as the Nawab assimilated the gravity of his situation and shook his head vigorously to indicate compliance. William reached down and ripped the sleeve of the Nawab's exquisite kurta, tearing it to the elbow on the left arm. The Nawab understood that these men were intent on causing him grievous harm and he was frightened.

William sat facing the Nawab and looked him directly in the eye. "So that you understand the gravity of your situation,"

William continued, "let me explain. These two pens are in fact syringes." He held up the one with the gold band. "This one I am about to inject into your arm contains a highly concentrated, very fast acting and lethal dose of cholera. The other holds the antidote, which must be injected within two hours if your life is to be saved. Should you choose not to comply with my instructions, exactly as I tell you, then you will die in excruciating pain wallowing in your own vomit and shit.

"For the sake of authenticity, and so that you can monitor your progress, let me describe what you will experience. Very soon you will begin to sweat and then start to vomit copiously. You will experience violent convulsions in your bowels which will void themselves involuntarily. Your watery excretions will have a fishy odour and your skin will feel cold, moreover, it will turn a bluish colour. As you become rapidly dehydrated your blood pressure will drop and without the antidote your heart will stop."

William pumped a lever on the side of the pen casing causing a thin needle to emerge from under the nib where a small droplet of liquid formed. As the Nawab watched in abject fascination William inserted the syringe into a vein in the hollow of his left elbow and injected liquid.

"Please observe. I am injecting intravenously into the brachial artery which will carry the bacterium at a rate of eighty-three gallons an hour around your body. To be exact once every minute your blood will pass through your heart accelerating the fatal consequences."

As the toxin flowed into the Nawab's arm he tried to speak. Hector loosened the gag slightly to hear what he wanted to say.

"I don't understand, why are you doing this to me?"

"Then let me explain," said William. "I know for a fact that in the tower of this fortress you are holding a prisoner, Helen Strachan. Moreover, under your orders she is due to be killed as required by your paymasters in Pakistan. Her decapitated body will be discovered with documents indicating complicity by the Indian government in her abduction and execution. This I know. Remember we do not have much time. Would you like me to continue explaining how we know these things?"

"No," said the Nawab as he felt a cramp in his abdomen.

"Then let me repeat, if you want me to inject the serum to save your life we need to act quickly before the poison becomes irreversible." Hector placed a telephone handset in front of the Nawab.

"You will issue an instruction to the guard that Miss Strachan is to be escorted to this room immediately. If you attempt to issue a coded warning, or if I think you do, then you will die immediately, and that is a promise." William nodded to Hector who placed the garrotte he had removed from Godbar around the Nawab's neck and tightened it a couple of turns. "However, if she is brought here immediately and safely then we will all leave this room together and you will accompany us to ensure our safe departure. Once we are safely out of the fort, I will administer the antidote and you will live. Do you understand?"

"Yes," gasped the Nawab as William peered deeply into the Indian's eyes looking for any sign of treachery. He held the telephone earpiece to the Nawab's ear and told him to dial.

"Speak slowly," growled Hector into his other ear, "or you will be spared a slow, painful death as I'll throttle you here and now," and he gave the cord a warning twist. The Nawab nodded vigorously as the ligature was loosened to let him speak.

The moment the telephone was answered the Nawab issued a

series of instructions curtly and as he replaced the handset he experienced another, stronger convulsion. Ray and Hector picked up the Nawab in his chair and moved him to the far side of the table arranging it so that his hands were hidden.

They then dragged the two corpses to the bathroom and took up positions against the back wall where they would be hidden when the doors opened. William removed the garrotte, handed the second pen to Henry and once again placed himself directly in front of the Nawab looking at him directly. "Remember," he said with a fierce look, "if you attempt to alert your men when they arrive Henry will immediately empty this pen with the antidote. In which case nothing will save you."

As the minutes passed the Nawab became increasingly distressed, and it was approaching a quarter of an hour before there was a knock at the door. The Nawab called out a command and Helen was escorted into the room surrounded by a phalanx of four muscular and heavily armed men.

Avowal

When Ifty first entered the cell, Helen's confusion was rapidly succeeded by elation. The warmth of his embrace and the human contact that flowed from him infused her with a buoyant sense of happiness, although she could not initially formulate words to express her emotion and so she just clung to him while tears welled up from somewhere deep within her. After a time, her sobbing quietened to be replaced by a torrent of questions, most of which remained unanswered. He told her that they only had a short time, no more than two hours. He was ignorant, he said, as to why they had been kidnapped in Paris, but he had been insistent with his captors that he be allowed to see her and eventually they agreed. She told him of her mock execution, and he described his experience in the cage where, in the moment he believed he would die, it was her image that filled his mind. He needed her to know that whatever happened to him his feelings had always been sincere.

"My life," he said, "would be empty without you, but I have no future. When you know the whole story, you will consider my actions unforgivable."

The only place to sit was on the bed and they lay side by side, she cradling his head to her breast as if he were an infant. They did not speak of, or discuss, their situation any further, but he told her he had come to give her hope. When she tried to reciprocate his reassurances, he looked at her as if puzzled and there was a sad wistfulness in his expression. Aware of time slipping away they were overwhelmed by a desperate need to cling to each other, and when the tread of boots signalled the return of the soldiers, he kissed her, as if he might draw upon her decency and sanctify his soul. She did not draw away.

As he was about to be taken from the cell, he turned and looked at her with an intensity she would never forget.

"Please remember me with love in your heart, the one who adored you more than life itself."

"I will," she said, "and know, dearest Ifty, that I shall always love you also."

These were her last words to him, and she knew in her heart that she would never see him again.

Listless in the days after Ifty's visit the despondency Helen had experienced before seemed amplified, and for the first time she felt herself descending into a depression that sapped her resilience to the point where she ceased to care about her appearance. Despite the encouragement and imploring of Ayesha who wanted to attend to her hair, nails and makeup she became increasingly convinced that her death was imminent and so all happy thoughts were pointless.

It was when she heard a party of soldiers forming up outside the tower that she knew the end had arrived. The barking of orders and scraping of iron shod boots indicated that an armed guard were assembling and if that were the case then they could have no other purpose than to have come to escort her to the place of her death. A surge of adrenaline inclined her to struggle, but as she heard the key inserted into the lock a surprising calmness descended and she resolved to go to her death with dignity and self-possession. Ayesha jumped to her feet as if to resist the guard, a loyal puppy yapping futilely to defend its mistress.

Helen turned to Ayesha whose devotion shone through her tears. "Little mother, be calm, it is my destiny." She hugged the older woman who started to shake and cry inconsolably as Helen rose to greet the soldiers with all the dignity she could muster. A troop of four had arrived to take her to the place of execution, the moment she had long known was inevitable. She trembled and her knees nearly gave way, but she called upon all her strength of self-possession, determined not to show her fear. William would be proud of her at the end.

She had expected to be taken to the parade ground and tied to the post once again, but instead was marched through an ornamental garden and into a palatial building. At the top of a grand stairway the senior NCO knocked on the large double doors which opened immediately. As she entered, she saw the Nawab sitting on the far side of a table beside which, incongruously, sat someone resembling Henry. A man in a suit stood with his back to her.

Escape

Her bearing upright, Helen was escorted into the room and she heard the heavy doors close behind. A tall man unscrewing the lid of a bottle turned to face her. She lifted her head to look at him directly and disdainfully, determined that she would not waver, and found herself staring at William, who shook his head minutely to communicate that she should not react. With an act of enormous self-control, she did not utter a sound although her eyes lit up. At the same moment the two soldiers at the rear were felled with practised ease by Hector and Ray before the door was locked from the inside.

As the guard in charge sensed danger William shook the contents of the bottle in his face, immediately causing his skin to bubble as acid burned into his skin. He reacted automatically and raised his hands to his eyes which was when William drove the bottle into his nose smashing the cartilage.

The other guard reached for his pistol, but Hector was standing behind him and drove his dagger through the man's back with such ferocity that the tip emerged between his ribs having passed through his heart. Impaled, the man died on the spot and slid forward while Hector held on to the hilt. The guard, whose face was now dissolving, began a scream that welled deep within him, but it never reached his lips because Ray reached from behind, stretched his neck and severed his windpipe. Twelve seconds had elapsed, and Helen found herself standing in the middle of the room utterly bemused by the mayhem unleashed around her.

William crossed the floor and took hold of her hand, "Now is not the time for explanations, that can come later. You must do exactly as I tell you and trust me without hesitation."

"The antidote. The antidote," squealed the Nawab. "You promised. Give it to me now."

Helen turned and approached the man who was the cause of all her suffering and her long-suppressed rage boiled over.

"You inhuman despot. You turd. You dung heap. You evil bastard. You have held me here in disgusting conditions for months, had my throat cut and waited until it suits you to kill me in cold blood. May you rot in hell."

"My my, what unladylike language," observed William. "Nawab you have offended the woman I love and that, old man, is your worst mistake." He leaned over and replaced the gag ensuring that the Nawab could not call out, entirely unmoved at the possibility that his adversary might choke on his own vomit, at which moment Hector appeared from the bathroom and said, "All's ready. Come now and come quickly."

William walked Helen into the small room just as Henry, Ray and Hector were lining up in front of the window. One after another, and in rapid succession, they stepped onto the windowsill and then the rail of the balcony and launched themselves, seemingly into thin air. Helen noticed that just before each jumped, they placed their arms across their chests like paratroopers. William lifted her into position in the window and said, "Don't worry. Step onto the rail and then take a small jump and try to fall horizontally onto your back with your arms crossed at the front."

All she could see below was a truck, and before she had time to question what was happening William yelled, "Jump," giving her a firm push that propelled her into space.

She had no time to think before she felt herself suspended, enmeshed in something like a cobweb that had absorbed the impact of her fall. A voice was yelling, "Roll right. Roll right." She obeyed and slid down a chute where hands grabbed her and pulled her on to the floor at just the moment William landed above her. He had delayed momentarily to ensure that she was safely out of the way before he too exited the window.

"Go," yelled William as the driver released the clutch and the three-ton truck started to move ponderously, grinding into second gear and gaining speed slowly. As it approached the great gates, it slowed and drew to a halt. Telescopic extensions in the four corners of the flatbed were collapsed by Hector with the flick of a lever, while at the same time, and in a well-practised move, the three soldiers released the apparently flimsy net from its fixings, gathered it up and carried it to the gate where the graphene mesh was spread across the ancient wooden entrance and nailed in place with six-inch staples fired from pneumatic guns. The net would not be removed easily or quickly, and valuable time would be gained. The large vehicle jerked forward again forcing its way through the cloying mass of pedestrians and dense traffic.

*

As it forged a path through the melee, other drivers hooted in a cacophony and those on foot or riding bicycles swore and shouted and refused to be hurried. Progress was achingly slow as William silently urged the driver to increase speed knowing that the response of the enemy, once the plot was discovered, would be rapid and overwhelming. It was a relief when the throng gradually thinned, and the truck started to gain speed. Once beyond the town centre, progress became more rapid and when they reached the outskirts the driver made no attempt to observe restrictions or reduce speed. After what seemed an agonising age, they joined an evenly cambered highway with storm ditches on both sides and fields beyond where labourers stooped and baked and suffocated in the unrelenting dust and heat of the day, unaware and uncaring of the predicament of those passing in such haste. The traffic reduced to an occasional overcrowded bus or wooden cart filled with maize, pulled by oxen unperturbed by a large vehicle hurtling past. Speed was of the essence and the truck driver kept his hand on the horn to clear the way.

The men in the back were well drilled and armed themselves with Heckler & Koch MP5 submachine guns retrieved from a metal box behind the driver's cabin. The canvas sides of the truck remained up, but Henry was under instruction to pull a handle that would release them should it be necessary

"Did ya-gi him the anti-do-at, asked Ray?" Henry fumbled in his pocket and retrieved the pen-syringe containing the remedy.

"It seems we didn't," said William. "But I don't think we'll go back." At that moment Helen, overwhelmed by a combination of relief, fear and adrenaline, grasped him around the neck and hugged him.

Pursuit

The heavy wooden doors muted any sounds from the interior and so initially there was nothing to alert the Nawab's secretary to danger, but he was becoming increasingly anxious when the soldiers did not reappear. He hovered outside the door sensing that something was amiss but not daring to knock. As his perturbation grew, he made the decision to summon the Captain of the guard, to whom he expressed his concern, although neither man wanted to ignore the strict instruction not to interrupt. The secretary telephoned the Nawab's sanctum repeatedly without answer, which raised the level of disquiet further.

At last the two men exchanged a look of agreement, torn between the conflicting duties of ensuring the Nawab's safety and protecting his privacy. By the time the Captain decided to act, ten minutes had elapsed since the escape. The officer abandoned timorous knocking and pushed against the door, but it was locked on the inside. He thumped loudly with a paper weight and when this elicited no response ordered the two burly soldiers on duty to use force. It took a couple of minutes before the lock gave way and then it was immediately obvious that something bulky was obstructing the door. The two brawny guards used their combined weight to shunt it open revealing the inert form of a uniformed leg. Pushing the obstruction out of the way they entered warily to be faced with a scene of carnage, but no sign of any perpetrator. At first glance they did not recognise the Nawab who was grunting at them, tied to a chair and surrounded by his own mess, but still alive. They tried not to let their disgust show as they hastened forward to release him.

As soon as they removed the gag he snarled, "Catch them alive. They have the antidote. Find them quickly and bring them to me immediately."

The ex-Russian, Mil Mi-17 twin turbine helicopter stationed on the parade ground was adapted for civilian use, most frequently to transport the Nawab and his retinue to the local airport or to other destinations within its range, indeed it was the means by which Helen's inert body had been smuggled into the fort. There was no reason for it to carry ordnance and so it was not fitted with weapons. Within seven minutes of the discovery of the escape the rotor was being started and a cohort of twelve heavily armed men were embarking to intercept the truck, which it had been rapidly established was transporting the renegades. It was reasonable to assume that the insurgents were making for the airfield where a large unmarked transport plane had been reported parked for the last two days. As the helicopter's blades picked up speed the pilot calculated his interception time and was confident that he would be able to overtake the vehicle.

Nearby heavily armed jeeps were lining up ready to stream from the gates in pursuit, but to the surprise, anger and disgust of the officer in charge however hard the gates were pushed they would not open. On investigation it was discovered that a net was holding the gates closed, a lattice so strong that it was resisting everything employed to cut it.

The helicopter pilot's estimate was that the escape vehicle must still be at least thirty minutes short of the airfield and in this he was almost correct.

Having received William's signal, the pilots of the Globetrotter were preparing for immediate evacuation, but William knew that his head start might not be enough if the Nawab's helicopter was called into action. Much depended on how long it had taken to find the Nawab and mobilise. William was very aware that while they may have progressed beyond the treacly traffic, they were by no means home and dry and any posse despatched to pursue them would travel far faster than they could.

The moment the rotors reached optimal revs the Mil Mi-17 rose vertically. It cleared the battlements and rotated through a hundred and sixty-eight degrees before heading off on a direct course to intercept the escape party.

In the back of the truck Henry was prematurely ecstatic at their success. For hours his nerves had been coiled as tightly as a fully wound clock, but as they placed greater distance between themselves and the enemy, he felt triumphant. The tension had begun to leach away to be replaced by a euphoric adrenaline rush.

"We did it, we bloody did it. William you are a bleeding marvel and you lads are the heroes of the day. We snatched Helen from inside the dragon's lair. We outwitted them. We achieved the bloody impossible and escaped intact from that fucking fortress."

"Yes," said William, "but unfortunately, it's not over yet, hold on to your backside Henry because there is still time for a serious problem in the shape of a helicopter. Sit here, keep your eyes on the horizon and if we run into trouble and I give you the command then release this handle."

Using high definition binoculars William scoured both the road and sky behind them for any indication of danger. Nine minutes now separated them from the airfield and William knew that each would count.

Raising his glasses again he made out a speck on the horizon that was growing by the second. He knew what it was and that it would intercept them before they could reach the airfield, also that it was highly unlikely they would be able to outgun an incoming force as they were only lightly armed and extremely vulnerable to overwhelming firepower. His overriding concern was for Helen who sat curled up beside him and had not yet recognised the danger. Remaining close to the ground the helicopter was approaching directly and despite the truck driver pushing his vehicle to its absolute limit William knew they would have to fight. He ordered Helen to climb into a large reinforced steel toolbox behind the driver's cabin that had air holes drilled in its base. At the same time, he ordered Henry to lower the canvas sides to allow a clear line of fire.

The officer in the helicopter issued his orders. The two best marksmen were instructed to crouch in the open door on either side and fire at the vehicle aiming to take out its rear tyres, "But, on the life of the Nawab, you must not hit any of the occupants."

Once the truck was disabled the pilot's intention was to overfly, turn and land on the road to block any further progress. The moment the soldiers were on the ground they would deploy left and right to encircle the stationary vehicle before securing the insurgents and bundling them into the helicopter with maximum haste.

As the helicopter began to overhaul the truck the two snipers opened fire. One was accurate, the other erratic and the officer saw a shot strike one of the rebels. In his fury, and in the knowledge of the retribution that awaited him, he kicked the man out of the fuselage and watched dispassionately as he fell, flailing wildly, until he struck the ground.

William recognised the sound of a bullet striking flesh and turned in dread to see who had taken the hit and how badly injured he was. It was Ray. William could see immediately that his ankle was mangled, a tangle of bone, muscle and sinew. He needed surgery and quickly if he was not to bleed to death. William tossed Hector a medical pack that included a tourniquet and morphine, the best he could do for the moment.

When the tyre exploded the driver controlled the skid but had no other option than to brake and draw to a halt as the helicopter rushed overhead low enough for the downdraft of the rotors to cause the men below to stagger. William fired into its underbelly but without hope of causing debilitating damage. He could see the gates of the airfield in the distance, but they were not going to be reached in the truck.

Having overshot, the helicopter pilot swivelled through a hundred and eighty degrees and landed facing the lorry driver, just out of shooting range. He kept the rotors turning in the expectation of a rapid departure.

William watched as heavily armed men jumped from the sliding doors on each side of the helicopter and began to circle left and right. He called to his men to hold their fire because in a straight firefight they would be killed, and he could not risk sacrificing Helen.

William instructed his men to lay down their weapons and raise their arms.

The helicopter pilot was watching the soldiers closely as they approached the disabled vehicle and was beginning to revel in an easy success when he became aware of another presence. Glancing up, to his horror, he saw an Apache helicopter hovering just above, and it was facing him directly with its piggy-backed crew pointing Sidewinder air-to-air missiles down his throat. At the same moment the Apache's 30mm chain gun rattled out a tattoo that scattered the soldiers on the ground.

The Nawab's pilot was a civilian and had never been so frightened in his life. Facing imminent immolation, he looked up at the pilot of the military helicopter who returned his stare implacably through his darkened visor, like an insect. All the helicopter pilot could think to do was turn off the engine, open the door, and walk away hoping that he would not draw fire, which is what he did and in so doing saved his life. The soldiers who had set out to capture the men in the truck placed their weapons on the ground and capitulated as they also walked, herded away from the truck by the Apache and watched by the three British soldiers who covered them with their weapons to ensure no rear action strike.

William felt profound relief as the soldiers trooped away. He turned to check that his men were safe and received a thumbs up from Hector, but it was increasingly obvious Ray required urgent medical assistance and they were stranded still some distance from the airfield and safety.

He turned his attention back to the road behind them and in the distance made out a dust cloud that must be a column of vehicles brimming with armed men approaching fast. The pilot of the Apache had seen the danger and was already banking to speed down the road and protect their rear. Having been instructed to limit his firepower to a minimum the pilot resisted firing a missile but strafed the column inflicting enough casualties to take the fight out of the troops and halt their charge.

From the airfield Ben Francis, one of two technicians, had been watching events unfold and when he realised that assistance was required, he reacted quickly driving a jeep out of the main gates to assist the men on the truck. With his foot flat on the accelerator it took him just under four minutes to reach the immobilised truck, where he was astonished to see the most beautiful woman he had ever beheld emerge from the back. He very nearly lost all concentration as he reached up and placed his hands around her waist to lift her down onto the seat beside him. William and Hector formed a chair with their arms and carried Ray to the rear of the jeep and alongside Henry scrambled into the back. They made room for their driver who could not be abandoned.

Immediately Ben spun the jeep and sped back to the airfield shooting through the gates as the Apache passed noisily overhead. Without stopping Ben drove to the rear of the transport and up the ramp into the relative safety of the Globetrotter. William and Hector rushed back out and deployed, ready to give a covering field of fire should it be required while the Apache's blades were folded, and it was winched into the hold.

With the departure of the threat from the air the Nawab's men rallied and a cavalcade rushed towards the airfield's meagre fencing convinced they could still apprehend the enemy. Knowing how long it would take to become airborne William's concern deepened, but then, as if from nowhere, a troop of heavily armed Indian army soldiers appeared to form a barrier and offer protection. An enfilade of rifle fire stopped the Nawab's men in their tracks.

Once safely onboard Ray was sedated and taken straight to the small operating theatre where the military trauma doctor and nurse were waiting. An amputation of his foot would begin as soon as they were in the air.

As the ramp started to lift and close the Captain of the Globemaster opened the throttle allowing the four Pratt & Whitney F117-PW-100 turbofan engines to increase to maximum thrust. The pilot kept the brake engaged until utmost propulsion was reached, at which point the large, graceless machine began its lumbering advance down the runway. With the standard measure of temperature set at fifteen degrees and flaps at 20, the pilots applied their full concentration to get her off the ground, calling on every ounce of power they could muster. Leaving it until he judged the last moment the Captain finally pulled back on the joystick, by which time the end of the runway was rushing to meet them, and all the two pilots could do was resort to prayer.

Like an ungainly swan stepping across water the clumsy machine gained air speed and just as the tarmac disappeared under its wheels the cumbersome land animal became a beast of the air rising rapidly and making a two hundred and seventy degree turn north to begin its long migration back to Europe. An Indian Air Force jet materialised as if from nowhere to fly on their wing greeting them with a victory roll. The fighter stayed with them until they departed Indian air space, which was when the pilot of *Cygnet* sent the call sign, '*Odette*', to indicate they were safely on their way home.

Sometime later, and somewhere over eastern Europe, Helen took William's hand and led him to a private nook at the rear of the fuselage.

"I always said you were my hero," she whispered, "I had given up hope that anyone would ever rescue me. They had told me to prepare for my end and to make peace with my maker, and then you arrived, like a god, to whisk me away. I love you William Edward Montgomery."

The gates to the fort were open when a troop of constabulary arrived. They met no resistance because the palace was almost deserted. They found the dehydrated body of the Nawab in his personal quarters where his venal Excellency had expired.

The soldiers, servants and personal staff of the Nawab had melted away and little remained to be tidied up by the team sent from the Ministry of Internal Security. Nevertheless, a very thorough search was undertaken, especially of all the Nawab's finances, personal records and papers, as well as those of his advisors and business acquaintances. Before the investigators departed a few weeks later a thick dossier was handed to Dr Aziz who had been present throughout trying to make sense of the events that had transpired that day when her team had responded to a code red request for assistance.

*

Brian Andrews, the Head of Cybersecurity at GCHQ, Cheltenham, England sat in front of his computer monitor in a semi-darkened room surrounded by screens that glowed with an ethereal light. An observer might have thought man and machine had merged into a single entity as he typed, and computer code flowed like words, across the page.

"God, I pray this works," he muttered to himself, "because if it doesn't, I dread to think what the consequences will be."

Across the globe in Pakistan a small piece of code was activated and began to attack a destructive 'bug' lurking in the intestines of the country's banking infrastructure waiting for the instruction to propagate. As an antibiotic does battle with injurious bacteria so Brian's remedy went on the offensive and combat started in a realm unseen and mostly unknown.

Judas Kiss

A few hours after Helen returned to Europe a Falcon 20 private jet stood on the tarmac at Lahore airport and the crew bustled around preparing for the arrival of their exalted passengers. The Falcon 20 is a fast and luxurious choice of aircraft and as the name suggests, seats twenty passengers.

Everything about this trip was top secret, and the reason became obvious to the crew when an autocade drew up at the steps accompanied by motorcycle outriders. The manifest handed to the senior steward stated a passenger list comprising sixteen adults, including three Cabinet ministers, the President and one other. The flight plan was handed to the Captain by an aide-de-camp.

Iftekhar had been brought to the airport separately from a secret location and greeted his father with humble respect clasping his palms in deference and kissing him once on each cheek. Ibrahim Diaz was overjoyed and kissed his son's forehead in return, delighted that following his terrible ordeal Iftekhar was to accompany him on this journey. Father and son would have time together as Ifty began his recuperation following his appalling incarceration and torture.

When the first video suggesting Iftekhar had been beheaded was first released his father experienced emotional panic the like of which he had never known before but was assured that without definitive proof there was hope. Not so everyone thought with the film of Ifty drowning, published on YouTube only a few days earlier, although it seemed now that this had been yet another cruel deception. For reasons they did not understand Ibrahim and his wife had been toyed with.

The patriotic choice to gift their child Iftekhar to the cause of their country had been a matter of constant regret to both Ibrahim and his wife, and as the years passed and they remained childless they could only watch over their son from afar. Ibrahim came to understand that in forsaking the most important of all relationships he had inflicted on himself and the boy's mother loss beyond compare. But now, completely unexpectedly, here was Ifty, returned to them and there was a chance to talk to him of their love. Ibrahim had determined he would open his heart to his only child for, while ambition had brought him many rewards, none could equal the love of a father for his son. They now had a few days together in which there would be time for openness, honesty and forgiveness.

Iftekhar had asked to accompany his father on this diplomatic mission to America and Ibrahim had acceded with alacrity secretly harbouring the dream that their time together would be the first step towards preparing his son for the greatness he would be bequeathed when the time was right. If Iftekhar grew to be the man his father believed he would be, then in time, the reins of power would pass to him. A son who would build a dynasty upon his father's legacy.

But sitting opposite one another in the large, comfortable chairs Ibrahim was concerned that his son was unwell for he was sweating and highly agitated. He assumed it was a reaction to recent events, but in this he was wrong. It was the combination of knowing Helen was still not safe, and the thought that the vest he was wearing was about to trigger a revolution resulting in untold suffering were images that burned his psyche like napalm.

As the crew started to make final preparations for take-off the moment of no return arrived. Iftekhar excused himself to make a call on his mobile phone and returned almost immediately announcing to Ibrahim that he could not now accompany him. He was deeply apologetic but adamant and, offering no explanation, left the cabin assuring his father of his enduring respect and love.

Iftekhar watched as the Falcon roared down the runway and soared gracefully into the sky disappearing rapidly through the cloud to its ceiling of 42,000 feet. He turned slowly and walked to one of the official cars explaining to the chauffeur that he needed transport to undertake a task for his father. He gave the address and sank into the upholstered seat saddened that he and Ibrahim had never had the opportunity to know one another properly.

Looking out of the limousine's window, but unseeing, Ifty was tense and brooding. He admired Ibrahim for his achievements, for his intellect and political adroitness, and occasionally he had felt the tug of an emotional connection, but there was no binding link or bond. Had Ifty not been separated from his father and quarantined by *The Colonel* then father and son would probably have developed a strong attachment for, as a family, they would have had a bedrock of shared experiences, activities and memories. 'But, do I love my parents?' Ifty wondered. He had no doubt that they loved him and were proud of his achievements, testaments to which were displayed all around the family home, but in the final analysis their relationship was superficial. *The Colonel* had stolen his childhood and groomed him for a martyrdom that required the most heinous crime, patricide.

As Ifty's introspection deepened and the car cruised through the suburbs Ifty posed himself another question. 'What about the love I have for the land of my birth?' He had always considered himself a radical patriot who could not quell the wrath he felt at the way Pakistan had been abused at and since its inception. A subcontinent arbitrarily apportioned in a scheme fashioned by a British government plotting to flee its imperial past irrespective of the human cost. The plan for Partition had been deliberately announced two days after Independence so as to deflect any responsibility for what might follow away from the British. His father argued that the British even gained satisfaction from the chaos that ensued for it demonstrated that the continent would fall apart without them and their Empire, moral abdication on a grand scale.

It was an iniquity that the two-nation border had been drawn up by a British lawyer sent from London, and the fact that Radcliffe had split Punjab, the wealthiest state, in favour of India was an affront. The British divided a nation and precipitated a religious civil war between peoples who had previously coexisted peacefully.

But, despite its violent birth, Ifty was proud that the new Muslim country of Pakistan had emerged with belief in itself and the determination to build upon its past and create a future at the centre of the Islamic world. It had the potential to develop a first world economy for it had vision, military might and industrial competitiveness, but it needed wealth, which was why, decades earlier, a cadre of zealous men had determined to annex Indian Punjab when the time was right. 'But,' thought Ifty as the car passed through the outskirts of the city, 'the dreams of war by old men only perpetuates revenge. If I truly love my people, then my greatest gift to them is peace and the prosperity that follows.'

And as the car made its way towards the centre Ifty questioned his love for God. Ali ibn Musa had helped him navigate the theological maze that so troubled him, and now he was at peace having found the certainty he sought. Jihad might justify punishing the perpetrators of a wrong against Islam, an avenging sword, but a true Muslim's first duty he concluded is to protect the innocent, Allah's children.

"A Muslim can be self-determining and is so when he follows his conscience," had been Ifty's parting words to his spiritual guide who smiled in benediction.

As the car arrived in the heart of the city and approached its destination Ifty could not help but think of Helen and his love for her. When he had first been told the news of Helen's rescue the day before, he rejoiced. But then he learned that *The Colonel*, incandescent with anger at her rescue, had initiated a fatwa. In an act of unadulterated rage and revenge he ordered Helen's assassination in England.

As the car drew up at the centre of the web that had taken half a century to weave Ifty was calm and at peace.

The driver left him outside the building where final plans were being laid for a new government and subsequent invasion of East Punjab. The men in conclave were assembled awaiting the news of the fatal air crash that would usher in their regime. They were, therefore, astonished when a junior officer showed Iftekhar into the room in which the *coup d'état* was being finalised.

Ifty explained the flight had been postponed for a few hours because of a technical hitch. An aide was despatched to confirm this change of plan. The atmosphere was intensely charged and hostile, and the members of the self-proclaimed junta fired questions at him aggressively, demanding to know why he had not stayed alongside his father. As he faced the frustrated and furious conspirators Ifty slipped his watch off his wrist, at which moment *The Colonel* quietly left the room.

Surrounded by those who sought his sacrifice and wanted to bring war, death and destruction upon his country Ifty started to wind his watch. It was time. Oblivious to the tirade directed at him he turned the button anticlockwise three times before inserting his thumb nail below the knob and clicking it out two notches.

As the aide returned, loudly announcing that Iftekhar had lied and the flight was airborne, Ifty took one last look at the faces around him and waited a brief moment before depressing the winder.

*

The people of Pakistan were confused and angry when they heard the news of an explosion that resulted in the slaughter of so many of the army's top ranked officers, undertaken by a lone suicide bomber whose identity would remain a mystery despite years of subsequent investigation. Very few could have imagined that their country had teetered on the precipice of war, and within days any talk of a political crisis receded, the language of military belligerence replaced with that of diplomacy. Concern over economic uncertainty began to ebb, and the populace never knew how close they had come to the brink of an economic and military cliff edge. Arrests were made quietly in both Pakistan and India and any whispers concerning a plot to annex Punjab were stifled. Remarkably quickly the status quo returned and a dark curtain that had gathered on the borders of two powerful countries rolled back into an uneasy armistice. Nothing was ever heard again of the *PSM.*

Once order and regularity returned the President of Pakistan resigned, citing ill health, and with his wife retreated to the country where they never came to terms with their loss, a loss that had begun decades earlier when they sacrificed their son to a cause that would prove futile.

ACT FIVE

Reckoning

"What shall I wear?" called Cassie through the open door from the en-suite bathroom.

"Well, given the size of the bump I don't think you have too much choice," Henry replied listening to her wallowing in the bath. "What about that lovely black velvet frock with the diamond choker that I gave you for your birthday? I love that outfit and it does stretch. Wear your hair down, and keep your legs crossed because tonight will be our last before we become parents."

He heard her emerging from the water, dripping, as she called back.

"OK, I can just about squeeze into that one, but I can't guarantee holding on much longer. She is definitely knocking at the door and wants to be let out to play. Where are we dining and what time are we due?"

"Seven-thirty at Rowley's in Jermyn Street, I've ordered a taxi for six-fifty."

Henry was relaxing on the bed with a gin and tonic in hand reflecting on the seismic changes that had taken place in his life over the last few months. In his wildest dreams he would never have imagined taking a leading role at the centre of a covert, military operation, being chased by bandits and escaping in the nick of time – "Henry de Quincy Adams, the Indiana Jones of our times," he chuckled to himself.

And he recognised that since his return he was content with life. Cassie might be indecisive and flighty, but she loved him for who and what he was with a simple, undemanding devotion that meant their life together had settled into a pattern that suppressed the wilder aspects of his nature. He had not been tempted into infidelity and was enjoying domesticity, he was actually looking forward to the birth of their daughter, his little princess.

Thank God he had escaped the clutches of that witch Clemmie, or at least he was hopeful he had. He could not have realised what he was letting himself in for when they married. Blinded by her family name and connections he had not seen the manipulative, vindictive bitch below the surface. His grief at Iphy's death had equalled hers and was actually greater, exacerbated by a guilt he could never admit to or expiate, but Clemmie would never let go, she seemed determined to exact some sort of twisted revenge. He shivered at the memory of the man emerging from the river with the little, limp, bedraggled body in his arms.

Good heavens, how he regretted that incident in the office at Canary Wharf. For a while afterwards he had lived in dread, made worse when a week later Clemmie informed him that she had syphilis and he must in all conscience tell Cassie. He had visited a sordid clinic for a test and thank heavens, she had lied, but then she demanded a paternity test, claiming she was pregnant with his child. He would, she informed him by solicitor's letter, be named as father on the birth certificate. God, she knew how to turn the screw. He had considered conceding to the paternity test but then was frightened it would prove conclusively that he was indeed the father and a copy be sent to Cassie. Better to play her game for now.

His response was to agree to sign the divorce papers if she agreed to drop the paternity claim. Two weeks had passed, and he hadn't heard anything more, so he was beginning to relax, but he still shuddered when he thought of her bitterness and what she might do to humiliate him publicly. To his surprise her alimony demand was not excessive, so perhaps when the decree nisi came through he could look forward to a future as father and family man without his past undermining future happiness.

They were meeting William and Helen for dinner that evening and it would be fun. The three of them had agreed not to talk about the events in India in front of Cassie, which was one of the reasons they had chosen a favourite 'public' restaurant rather than a private club.

The taxi dropped Henry and Cassie outside Rowley's, at 113 Jermyn Street, St James's where they met William and Helen who happened to be arriving at the same moment. The girls had always liked one another and enjoyed each other's company sharing similar interests, sense of humour and a delight in the exchange of gossip. Seated at the back of the room and tucked under the spiral staircase for some privacy they ordered their meal. Henry asked the sommelier to choose two bottles of very fine and expensive wine, declaring that it was a night for celebration.

"No expense spared on this auspicious occasion," Henry declared expansively ignoring the fact that Cassie was off alcohol and Helen had stated she would only manage a glass or two of wine. Henry was determined the evening would be special, it being the eve of his daughter's birth, alongside which Helen and William had recently announced the date they were to marry. He didn't mention it, but he was also celebrating the fact that three of them had avoided a very early introduction to the Almighty.

Cassie noticed that Helen was wearing a scarf loosely drawn around her neck but did not pay particular attention until it slipped to reveal a thin pale pink line, reminding her of the online video and the horrors that Helen must have experienced in captivity. She wanted to ask her about her time as a prisoner but had promised Henry not to mention the subject and so they stuck to light-hearted topics.

The evening passed very pleasantly, a thoroughly congenial and jovial affair that further secured the affection and bond that existed between the couples. Cassie wanted to know all about the wedding plans and Henry was elated when William asked him if he would reciprocate the honour by being his best man. Talk thereafter was almost exclusively of the wedding which was to be held at *Swan's Nest*. Cassie began to flag and so Henry ordered a taxi to return them to Belgravia.

As they opened the front door Cassie stumbled and Henry caught her. When he looked at her, she was white and shivering.

"Oh my God are you alright?" he asked.

"Forgive me," she replied. "I just experienced a moment of awful foreboding and it made me feel faint."

"Don't be silly old thing," said Henry. "Giving birth in the modern world is perfectly safe and we will soon be welcoming our gorgeous daughter into our lives and home. She will be one of the most loved little girls ever."

"Oh, I know my darling. I'm sorry for being so melodramatic, but for a moment it felt as if some terrible calamity is about to befall us and I couldn't bear the thought because we are so happy."

With the help of a strong cup of tea Cassie soon recovered her equilibrium and they decided it was time for bed. Henry was feeling soporific and was considering whether to have a bath when Cassie returned from cleaning her teeth in an excited state to tell him that she had had 'a show'. He was immediately energised and on the phone to the private Lindo Wing of St Mary's Hospital, Paddington, not far away. The doctor he spoke to was very reassuring and said that it was too early for Cassie to be admitted, they should wait until the contractions were four minutes apart and lasting a minute.

Henry decided there was time for a bath and Cassie salaciously promised that afterwards, and to pass the time before hospital, she would give her old friend a kiss as long as the private on parade could stand to attention after so much wine. With burgeoning arousal Henry walked into the en-suite and turned the taps on full.

As he relaxed in the steaming bath his mind drifted back to the events of the last few weeks and he tried to analyse what had changed in his life. Since his return he had certainly felt more at peace with himself, no longer pursued by the doubts, uncertainties and insecurities that had haunted him since childhood. He would, he promised himself, now fulfil his responsibilities and avoid any temptation to satisfy his sybaritic proclivities. He had proved to himself that he was not a coward for he had taken part in something where real danger and fear tested his resolve and he had not been found wanting; if seen romantically then he had assumed manhood and matched the bravery of those he most admired. To his great relief he had shown himself able to remain steadfast in the face of danger and he was resolved that he would no longer drift through life. Henceforth he would devote himself to his family with honesty and devotion.

Outside, in an unlit alleyway at the rear of the house, two men checked that no one was watching. Then, under the shadow of a large horse chestnut tree, they scaled with ease the two-metre brick wall that marked the boundary. Flitting silently from shadow to shadow in close-fitting black outfits and wearing balaclavas they crossed to the patio unseen, whereupon they placed a small electronic device against the pane of the sliding patio door. Having established that an alarm had not been set one of the men slid a jemmy under the sill of the sliding door and raised it until it could be manipulated out of its runner. Sharing the weight, they lifted the heavy glass door silently from its frame and having gained access to the dining room drew upon their knowledge of the house, gleaned from a planning application downloaded from the internet, and then they made their way to the staircase, rubber-soled shoes silent on the carpet.

They would leave no evidence of their identity having taken professional care to ensure no forensic evidence would remain after their departure. They crept up the stairs and paused outside the bedroom door until they heard the taps of the bath being turned off. With economy of movement one man pushed the door open and entered fractionally ahead of the other.

Cassie had changed into her white flannel nightie and pink dressing gown, ready for the journey to hospital and was lying under the duvet with her hands resting on her bump as she traced the movements taking place within her. She was concentrating on a tiny foot and was slow to react when two men materialised in her bedroom. Shocked, she did not at first respond in any coherent fashion, other than to look at them in incomprehension, and when she did focus, all she saw was the barrel of a pistol pointing down at her. In a state of heightened disbelief everything that followed seemed to take place in slow motion.

She took a deep breath to scream but in the same moment the intruder pulled the trigger. There was no discernible sound, but she watched a wisp of burning oil curl from the end of the barrel, unaware of the wound made by the soft tipped bullet that tore through her womb, its enormous kinetic energy causing massive damage before impacting upon her lower spine which shattered. She slumped forward without uttering a sound.

In unison the two men pushed their way into the bathroom. Henry reacted much more quickly than Cassie, but they were burly and muscular. With ease, they grasped a shoulder each and pushed his head under the water where he thrashed and struggled, but to little effect. As he began to weaken one of the men, using his free hand, slid a small curved surgical knife from a disguised bag on his belt and with medical precision placed it against the soft skin of Henry's inside thigh. With one upward movement he cut into the soft flesh and muscle before severing the femoral artery. As the bath water turned crimson Henry's heartbeat dwindled. The men waited, watching dispassionately until life faded from his eyes, at which point they released their hold and returned to the bedroom.

As they passed through, they could see that Cassie was still alive, large tears of pain and despair rolling silently down her cheeks. Her eyes followed their movements and she watched as one of the two withdrew a polythene kitchen bag from his pocket. He stood at the side of the bed and when she looked up at him, he pulled the bag over her head before ratcheting a cable tie tightly around her neck. She tried to take a breath, but this caused the plastic to be sucked against her features as if a vacuum former had been turned on. The man went to draw the cable tie tighter, but the precaution was unnecessary. She did not see the men exit, one turning off the overhead light before gently closing the door.

The next morning the twice weekly British Airways flight bound for Tirana left Heathrow on time. Included on the passenger list were two anonymous men travelling in separate parts of the cabin on counterfeit passports. They left no tangible evidence of their visit to London and the investigation into the case of the *'Mayfair Murders'* was 'cold' even as it began, notable only in a comment on a police file that observed: *'The killings had all the hallmarks of an execution or assassination.'* But no motive was ever attributed to the case and it was eventually closed, unsolved.

Leda was contacted by David who informed her of the double murder before the media got hold of the story. Leda had always been fond of Henry who she thought of as an affable rogue but harmless; he certainly wasn't the type to be involved in underworld activities and revenge killings, which is what David said would be the angle taken by the tabloids desperately hoping to spin a sensational story. The fact that Cassie had been in the early stage of labour would whip public interest into a frenzy.

Leda called Clemmie to give her advance notice of the terrible events that had befallen her erstwhile husband. She mentioned that David had said the press would probably greet the news with media glee and camp on her doorstep for a while and that there was little doubt that the events around Iphy's death would be raked over once again.

Leda thought Clemmie's reaction to the news restrained, she thanked her mother for calling and enquired after her health but showed little emotion considering her recently divorced husband had just been horrifically murdered.

After Clemmie replaced the handset she walked upstairs silently followed by Aegisthus. From the ceiling in the second bedroom hung two large straps attached to rings on metal plates screwed to the ceiling.

At the moment Aegisthus thought she would reach up, she rounded on him and attacked his face raking at his eyes with her nails. "You bastard," she screamed, "I was about to complete his humiliation by announcing to the world that he is the father of my child, his legitimate heir. Cassie would have left him and any happiness they had looked forward to would have been ruined. My revenge would have been sweet, but you spoiled it."

Aegisthus held her arms easily as he gauged her mood. When she quietened, he said in his deeply accented voice, "I only did as you wanted." He held her until she was calm and then lifted her arms, powerfully, placing her hands through the hoops. From behind he ripped her shirt inflicting a little gouge with his nail that made her flinch. He tore off her bra and from a drawer at the side of the room withdrew a small flail of his own devising. He heard her gasp as she received the first stroke and he knew that for her the pain was exquisite.

When at last her anger abated, she recognised that her bitterness was now assuaged. It was as if a curtain had been drawn back allowing light to return to a darkened room. From the moment she had first heard the news of Iphy's death a knot of gall had grown in her embittered spleen which festered and corrupted every element of her existence, but at last, it was beginning to melt and she could breathe again without the acrid bile of vengeance burning her soul.

Aegisthus was greatly aroused and as they came together her final yell of climax and triumph caused the twins within her to kick as if applauding.

Espousal

The wedding between Mr William Edward Montgomery and Miss Helen Johanna Strachan was much reported by the media as one of the social events of the year, covered in multiple pages of magazine print as well as on numerous social media websites. The glare of media scrutiny generated plentiful articles, opinions and biographies with details that dissected the background of the protagonists, including frequent references to the events surrounding Helen's abduction, torture and mysterious return. The fact that William's best man and his heavily pregnant wife had been murdered in brutal circumstances only contributed to ever more lurid by-lines, including in the tabloids, salacious and mendacious, if oblique, references to events in Paris. Some of the press went so far as to speculate provocatively that Helen's father might have misused his position to negotiate his daughter's release, despite hostages remaining in captivity elsewhere in the world because the government refused to give way to terrorist demands.

The high level of security surrounding the event kept the press pack at bay, but the paparazzi and social columnists were inventive and seemed prepared to go to any lengths to acquire photographs of the wedding or claim a first-hand source to quote. By the time the hurly burly eventually died down Helen and William had become household names often recognised when they travelled, which was a cause of great annoyance to them both.

Swan's Nest was transformed. Leda's attention to detail was evident in every aspect and at Helen's suggestion she themed the wedding around swans, an emblem that appeared everywhere: on the invitations, in the order of service and amongst the flower and table decorations, as well as in leitmotif in the bridesmaids' dresses. The white of swan down and yellow of a swan's beak featured in Helen's dress which was a masterpiece of couture, striking in its simplicity. Cut from white silk lace it hugged her figure while yellow spring flowers were braided into both her hair and bouquet. She shone like a summer's day radiating beauty and happiness.

William in dress uniform, with sword at his side, created a dashing image that drew admiring looks from many of Helen's friends when he entered the church. Hector, acting as his close companion, accompanied him at every step and the two men waited at the altar fidgeting.

Helen arrived in an open carriage and there was a gasp of appreciation when she walked to the lychgate where she lowered her flimsy lace veil and waited a moment before being joined by her distinguished father. Together they proceeded up the aisle until Helen arrived at William's side where she took his arm as if docking.

The parish church of St Mary's in the village near to *Swan's Nest* was relatively small and limited the guest list to just over a hundred. Local well-wishers had been allowed into the grounds and supplied with yellow and white rose petals to throw as confetti when the married couple emerged after the service.

When the first hymn rang out Leda caught Helen's eye. There passed between mother and daughter a moment of mutual insight as the congregational voice swelled and rose to a resounding climax softening on the final line with the promise, '*I will ever give to thee'.* Leda smiled contentedly at David's side while secretly brushing Peter's hand.

The final hymn was gently suffused with special meaning for Helen and William, their voices joining melodically as they looked into each other's eyes and sang the words, *'O still small voice of calm',* seemingly encapsulating all their hope for the future.

As the final chord melted away William leaned towards her and their lips touched. In that moment it was as if their troubles had finally receded and they could look to the future with hope and confidence.

Then they were walking down the aisle smiling inanely, and the hustle and bustle of the occasion took over. It was many more hours before they finally managed to get to bed and curl up together as man and wife.

Martyrdom

In 1949 the boy Zuraib Nasir, who would later come to be known as *The Colonel*, was adopted by his uncle, and once the nightmares began to recede he found solace in his local mosque. In his teenage years he was deeply religious, although one of his teachers portentously noted, *'The intensity of his observance is not matched by a similar measure of spirituality'*. What he always kept hidden was the knowledge that his reverence for Allah and respect for the Quran was underpinned by a personal obligation to exact revenge for all that his family and his inchoate nation had suffered.

The intensity of that flame never diminished but now, with a lifetime of planning in ruins, he had returned to his retreat in Switzerland and was taking time to reflect on his failure. He had read in Iftekhar's eyes what he intended to do and managed to leave the room ahead of the explosion, thereby escaping great injury.

Cataloguing his failures, he was trying to identify by whom he had been betrayed. The detailed and scrupulously planned massacre in France had been anticipated and while the outrage had gained worldwide attention, it had been foiled. The banking crisis in Pakistan and the IT chaos so meticulously prepared had somehow been circumvented. Iftekhar had been turned against him and any chance of a military coup died with him. The whole edifice of a lifetime's planning had collapsed, and worse still India was now quietly briefing against Pakistan creating even more of a pariah state of his homeland.

The public killing of Helen Strachan would have had the world clamouring for revenge and given lasting legitimacy to Pakistan's military action, but her rescue foiled that central plank of his strategy.

The failures were a bitter defeat and deserved revenge, but he no longer possessed any of his previous resources and the revenge he could inflict had to be low on requirements while high on impact.

Muznah Rahim was twenty-two years old, born in Luton, England, and radicalised at a mosque in the town from the age of twelve. Her faith had always been central to her way of life and as she passed into womanhood, she adopted the burqa foregoing the hijab. The war against ISIS outraged her political sensibilities and for a time she contemplated travelling to the Middle East where she would join one of the female units. However, there were too many stories about the way women were abused by ISIS soldiers and the complexity involved escaping England persuaded her against this course of action. But she remained steadfast in her conviction that Allah had a purpose for her which would be revealed when He was ready.

After their return from honeymoon William and Helen fell into the routine of married life. He had a posting at the Ministry of Defence and so worked a five-day week, which meant that most evenings and weekends were spent together. There were moments of tension as they learned to adapt to one another and make the compromises expected of singles becoming a couple, but any differences were quickly resolved, and their disagreements cast no lasting shadow.

They had moved into a recently renovated mews apartment in Central London and one of the great pleasures they shared was furnishing the house to their taste. Regular weekend visits to markets, stores and boutique shops gave them enormous pleasure and as a result most Saturdays included a shopping expedition. The rule they established was that whatever either one of them wanted for the house must be necessary, desired by both, and would not clutter their lovely home. As a result, many a shopping trip resulted in a return home to discuss, consider and agree before making a purchase. Space was definitely an issue. What they would do when junior came along was a subject they agreed to avoid until such a time as it was relevant.

During the first weeks of March neither William or Helen were conscious of the fact that their movements were being logged in great detail. A team was tracking and recording all their comings and goings.

Muznah attended mosque every day as a matter of routine and in obedience to the teachings of the Prophet she observed all the practices expected of a woman, but at her core she yearned for the opportunity to make a noble sacrifice.

It came as a surprise to her when one day she was handed a note requesting she attend a small room at the back of the mosque. She was angry to find a man sitting alone at a small table, however he was very much older than her and asked that she listen to what he had to say.

He spoke to her of politics and religion. He explained that as a Muslim her family and her religion had been oppressed for decades by an elite of heretics. He spoke of the love Allah had for her and the future reserved in Paradise for those who earned His gratitude. Using her beliefs, the man wove a web and stoked her anger, giving oxygen to the flames of her resentments. He asked if they could meet and talk again.

In the days that followed, her mind was filled with the ideas and thoughts he initiated and as she stacked the shelves in the supermarket where she was employed, she began to rage at the injustices against Muslims described to her by the old man. When she thought about the profanity and sacrilege practised against the one true and loving God, her anger became almost visceral. An elder at her mosque, a Mufti, talked to her about a fatwa that had been secretly issued against an English woman who had blasphemed terribly and was a despicable enemy of Islam. One day the Iman and the old man met her together and suggested that she become a handmaiden of God, one who would live for eternity in his grace and love.

Helen had been longing for the weekend. She was unusually tired, and William had been away working all week. She had seen a lamp in the John Lewis catalogue that she thought would be lovely on the table by the door in the sitting room and when she told William on the phone, he heard the enchantment in her voice. They agreed to make a trip to Oxford Street on Saturday.

The watchers reported that the couple had taken the tube to Oxford Circus. This, they decided, was the moment to act, in a crowded street at peak shopping time. A bloody murder in full public view would gain the attention of the world, especially as the victim was the survivor of a previous assassination attempt and daughter of the second most important politician in the country.

The minivan was standing by and was directed where to drop off Muznah who was in a trance of political and religious fervour.

Helen hugged William when he agreed they should purchase the lamp. It was wildly expensive and far too extravagant but would look beautiful, with its muted light shining through a mosaic of stained glass, when placed next to the oak lined wall containing their books. She looked up at him and once again revelled in her good fortune. He smiled and his boyish dimples captivated her as always.

Muznah, both inconspicuous and obvious in her burqa, waited in the street at the corner of the building praying that Helen would exit into Oxford Street and turn left back towards the underground station, as indeed proved to be the case. What no observer could detect was the eight-inch kitchen knife hidden in Muznah's pocket. It was new and cruelly sharp.

As the couple emerged arm in arm, they seemed oblivious to their surroundings and the crowds milling around them. They approached Muznah without noticing the woman whose focus upon them was intense.

Muznah fixed her eyes on Helen's neck which filled her field of vision as she weighed up where to strike. As Helen came abreast of her all Muznah's suppressed rage and fanaticism reached a crescendo and she screamed her devotion, *"Allahu Akbar."*

Withdrawing the knife from the folds of her burqa, she raised it above her head and lunged. She saw the blade strike and blood spurt bright vermilion from the wound. As instructed, she prepared for a second strike, decapitation would be perfect.

Les Avants

The train left Geneva Airport at 17.00 precisely and arrived in Montreux exactly an hour and ten minutes later. The journey along the coastline of the lake was picturesque and Peter relaxed enjoying the view while considering how he was going to approach the meeting that lay ahead.

Disembarking at Montreux he took the stairs down from the station platform that lead into a concrete tunnel exiting at road level directly behind the Grand Hotel Suisse, a large, distinctive building that has welcomed guests since 1870.

Such was the popularity of Montreux in the late 19th and early 20th centuries that Maharajas, nobility and wealthy visitors from Europe, Africa and America visited or retired to 'Lac Léman' where the air is clear and invigorating. 'The Grand' as the hotel came to be known has occupied an important place in the cultural and literary history of successive eras and Peter was anticipating a pleasant night's stay.

Continuing down a further set of steep steps he rounded the corner to enter through the grand foyer on the lakeside and looking up at the majestic building and spent a few moments appreciating the striking architecture; sweeping rectangular sections rising eight floors with spectacular views of the lake.

He observed that the windows narrowed slightly on each ascending floor, creating a pleasing sense of grandeur and bestowing refinement and proportion upon a building of such bulk. Swiss town buildings are distinct and imposing, he concluded, so different from the pitched roofs and wooden clad chalets of the Alpine villages, such as the one he would visit in the morning.

Peter awoke refreshed and after a relaxed continental breakfast the impressive man, in a light-green three-piece tweed suit from Gieves & Hawkes of Savile Row, sporting a brown fedora, made his way back to the station where he purchased a ticket for the 'Golden Pass Train' that winds its way up the mountain on its journey to Gstaad and beyond. The weather was perfect.

With a jerk that rattled the carriages the engine pulled out of the terminal and almost instantly snaked into a long tunnel, fitting as tightly as an arm into a sleeve. The rapidly rising gradient was immediately noticeable and when the rickety train emerged back into the sun it seemed perched on the side of the mountain. The view down to the lakeside was vertiginous with the town and vibrant green fields below, beyond which was the blue lake set against a backdrop of mountains on the far side. Like polished silver, the morning sun reflected off pockets of snow that remained cradled amongst the peaks.

The wooden carriages were considerably more basic than the previous day's train and on the steepest sections cogs beneath the locomotive engaged to give greater traction as it zigzagged its way upwards. Peter was absorbed by the view and could not escape a feeling of precariousness, rather as he felt about the day's mission.

The train turned away from the lake and headed inland, halting at various doll's house stations, all brightly painted and lovingly adorned with colourful flower boxes where locals boarded and departed, greeted friends and chattered away inconsequentially.

Then the character of the view changed again as they passed along the dark shoulder of the Gorge du Chauderon with its numerous waterfalls cascading into the ravine far below where Peter was fascinated by the tall pine trees growing uniformly pencil-straight, perpendicular to the steep side of the ghyll. Then the scene changed again as the train passed into dappled, deciduous woodland before emerging into the light lushness of an alpine valley in spring. He glanced up and could make out the *Dent de Jaman,* the enormous fang shaped rock feature that broods over Les Avants, his destination.

They drew into a sleepy little station and, without hurrying, Peter disembarked and watched as the carriages clattered into the distance. He wandered along the small platform and glanced up to his left where the ladybird sized red cars of the funicular passed each other on their impossibly steep journey to and from the hotel perched far above the town. Les Avants itself lay huddled, surrounded by steep fields and secluded, tall fir trees contributing to a pervasive sense of calm and inactivity.

The sky that morning was a deep, azure blue and he paused inhaling the cold air and the scene: the Toblerone-shaped wooden chalets tucked between the acutely angled fields, the ponderous cattle grazing the richly green pasture, and everywhere, across all the fields, a silk tapestry of pungent narcissi giving off an aroma of hyacinth with hints of jasmine.

Peter ambled past the doll's house sized station and crossed the road heading towards a large Swiss house that dominated the village, which he recalled had been built in the early twentieth century as an elite school for daughters of the English upper middle classes, an academy that offered a healthy alternative to the restrictive education experienced by so many girls in English establishments at that time. He knew that after the school closed it had been occupied by a number of organisations before being bought by the enigmatic and elusive owner who now made it his home in Europe.

Peter had to lean back to appreciate the scale of its three storeys and the intricacy of its wooden design. It put him in mind, ridiculously he thought, of a cuckoo clock on a grand scale. He checked his watch and approached the main entrance where he knocked and waited patiently. The door was opened, not by an automated bird, but by an English-speaking butler who enquired after his business.

"Is *The Colonel* at home? I have had a long journey."

"He is Sir. If you will follow me, I shall enquire if he wishes to meet with you, who should I say is calling?"

"Tell him, please, that I bring greetings from the government of Her Britannic Majesty."

*

Peter was shown into the study, a large comfortable room with an oak bureau desk situated under the main window that gave a splendid view across the valley. Seated, with his back to him, was a slight, narrow shouldered man writing a letter by hand. From behind, his hair was silver, thin, strictly combed and pomaded. The person Peter had travelled so far to meet screwed on the top of his fountain pen before placing it on the desk with movements that were precise and deliberate. He turned and rose from the captain's chair, a little arthritically, to greet Peter.

He was small, probably no more than five foot six. A dapper man expensively turned out, neat in every respect, impeccably dressed with a manicured moustache and folded silk handkerchief in the top pocket of his jacket. A lightweight suit, highly polished brown loafers and a perfectly tied Windsor knot put Peter in mind of a certain Belgian detective. Certainly, he was someone who took pride in his appearance and everything about him suggested orderliness, although with a hint of narcissism. His manner when he spoke was polite, although clipped and authoritative. He indicated that Peter should take a seat in one of the two wingbacked Chesterfields situated towards the centre of the room and he moved to occupy the other.

"The Marquis of Northumbria. Your reputation precedes you and as a senior member of the British establishment I wonder what interest you could possibly have in me. I am intrigued to know to what honour I owe this visit?"

Peter removed his hat and placed it on what looked like a Chippendale chair at the side of the room, its ungainly legs widely spaced putting him in mind, incongruously, of an old woman who no longer sits decorously. Peter turned and faced the man who had been his adversary for so long and for a few moments they sat in silence, opposite one another as if gauging their opponent before making the opening gambit in a game of chess.

Peter made the first move.

"We meet at last, Colonel. I have spent a long time following your spoor. It began with a trace, a faint trail that grew stronger over the years, and now, at last, I have tracked you to your retreat, where I meet the man whose devious ambition has threatened all I hold dear. I find you in immensely civilised surroundings far from the land that bore you and the horror you would have inflicted upon the world."

In a tone implying nothing more than mild curiosity *The Colonel* replied, "I am interested to know how you found me as I thought my identity, to adopt your metaphor, had been no more than a mere fragrance."

Peter scratched his head. "Over a long time I have garnered scraps and gradually, a faint odour began to emerge, but your most serious mistake was to involve my daughter."

"I didn't know you had a daughter."

"It's often the unknowns that catch us out. Yes, Helen Strachan is my daughter and like any father I will exercise all my powers to protect her."

"Ah," commented *The Colonel*. "So a little key opened a door behind which stood a giant."

"It was you," said Peter, "who planned her murder in India and then when that failed you plotted her assassination in London. It was only because of the lightning reactions of her soldier husband, William, that her life was saved. He deflected the knife so that it entered her shoulder at the tip of the scapula where the bone deflected its trajectory inflicting only a relatively minor wound. By the way it was William, now her husband, who led the team that extracted her from the Nawab and foiled that conspiracy. You have much to answer for."

"I see," *The Colonel* observed. "Our paths have crossed without my knowing. I have suspected for some time that I faced an adversary of unusual perspicacity, but I never had any indication as to the identity of that antagonist."

"The purpose of my visit is to seek understanding," continued Peter, "I would like to know when you first conceived the plan. It must have been decades ago, which is partly the reason it took me so long to pick up your trail. You constructed a labyrinth in which all paths led to death, destruction and ruin, and at the centre of the maze was a monster, you. Your conspiracy was a devilish plot, a devious, multi-layered and complex design requiring extraordinary patience to construct. I can only assume that the linchpin, Iftekhar Diaz, was chosen and groomed from a very young age, which means that you have been consumed by a lifetime of hate."

"Ah Iftekhar, my protégé, my Trojan Horse who turned against me in the end, presumably at your behest?"

"No," said Peter. "In the end he was motivated by love and not hate."

"Hate," said *The Colonel* ruminatively. "Yes, certainly I recognise that emotion. In my case it began with events that destroyed my family in 1947. Since then I have sought reparation and amends for my country."

"And now you are hoping to maintain your anonymity," Peter observed, "So that the wrath of world power does not descend upon your head. I dread to think what the Indian government would do to you if you fell into their hands and those in Pakistan also, given that you failed your masters. This, I assume, is why I find you tucked away in a remote corner of Europe. I have sought you out because I now know all that happened, but not why and I am curious."

The Colonel leaned back in his chair and steepled his fingertips in the fashion adopted by another famous detective when faced with a complex enigma. "Indeed, mine has been the work of a lifetime," he sighed. "As to why, well I doubt we differ greatly in the love we hold for our country, but the West, and that Satan, India, continue to inflict great injustice upon my country, my people, my religion and our beliefs."

"That may be," responded Peter, "but it does not explain your inhuman disregard for human suffering, and, by the way you are wrong for we are very different. As a Muslim you serve a theocratic government, while I uphold the values of a democratic one. Your work is purportedly undertaken in the service of God while I serve only the people of my country. I concede that we are similar in terms of our vocation, but what I truly don't understand is that while I have always worked to uphold the rule of law in a secular world, where laws are fashioned for peaceful purposes, you have spent your life promoting violence, aggression and destruction in the name of patriotism and religion. You could have employed your talents constructing a better world for your people rather than seeking to destroy mine."

A look of anger flashed across *The Colonel's* face. "Your country behaves with moral ambivalence when it suits its political ambitions. Look at what happened following Partition. Where were the British then in defence of the rule of law?"

"I accept that my country has resorted to violence from time to time and, to its shame has looked away when it could have acted for good, but only when it has felt it necessary to protect the nation. You, on the other hand have promulgated violence in the pursuit of your convictions. You justify acts of national aggrandisement and revenge as the Will of God. You have contempt for my world while I am tolerant of yours. You live by a creed that espouses revenge, hatred and scorn, while my doctrine exhorts people to love and forgive. I am here to seek understanding as to why someone comes to hate so profoundly. Do you truly believe that the God of Islam desires the extermination of all other creeds, or that it is God's Will to kill the innocent? I am of the opinion that your devotion is in fact to war and that you hide behind religion to vindicate your actions."

The Colonel was silent for a while and Peter waited patiently. When he spoke, his tone was measured but intense. "Indeed, in Islam we live by the scriptures and we dedicate our lives to the highest authority, for Islamic religious law is the basis of our civil law. Islam is the one and only true religion and it is our beholden duty to spread the Holy word. In doing so we seek peace but understand this, as a people we do not tolerate those who blaspheme. Where we find blasphemy, we seek retribution and what happened to the believers of Islam in India during Partition was the greatest blasphemy ever to befall a nation. It happened because Britain walked away from its responsibilities and stood by as the cruelty it unleashed against the Muslim peoples consumed us like a wildfire in a forest.

"My country was not conceived happily; it grew from a violent rape by the British who ripped a nation apart when they forced Partition upon both Muslims and Hindus. Gandhi and the British isolated and disenfranchised the Muslims in the greatest act of political sequestration ever, greater even than the theft of Palestine for the Jews.

"Of course, Allah wants retributive justice and he chose me as his instrument; I am proud to be his disciple, to take back that which is rightfully ours, the golden fleece, which is Punjab, it has to be reunified under the flag of Islam. I knew that if my plan were to succeed the world must sympathise with our cause, and so I devised a set of narratives that were years in gestation. I so nearly succeeded and who knows, it might even have led to the overthrow of western governments and the acceptance of Islam worldwide had events transpired differently. I might have been instrumental in creating the Caliphate, which is Allah's true desire for his people."

The Colonel's tone became less strident and more reflective as he continued. "My favourite game is chess and in any battle on the board pieces are taken, there is a cost. You understand that. You and I are similar in so many ways, we just sit on opposite sides of the board."

Peter looked at *The Colonel* with an expression of interest and asked, "What will you choose to do now?"

The Colonel returned his look, quizzically. "I think you will lose interest in me as I am no longer a threat to anyone anywhere. I shall remain incognito and measure out my days in the mountains of Switzerland where the air is clear and invigorating."

"One final question," said Peter. "Tell me, do you have any regrets?"

This enquiry provoked *The Colonel* and the tone of his voice was, for the first time, bitter. "Oh yes I have regrets. Failure mainly. Your country, Great Britain, was responsible for an act of gross political expediency inflicted upon a nation that had served it faithfully for generations, that had even fought in its wars to defend its sovereignty. When the British Government made the decision to divide India along religious lines, it perpetrated one of the most egregious acts of national bloodletting ever known. As if that was not enough my young nation, a proud new Muslim country that sought to establish itself on the world stage, was impoverished from the outset when the British applied an arbitrary border that denied Pakistan its legitimate right to the wealthiest province, Punjab. You seek to understand my motive, well, at its root lay revenge."

"Revenge," said Peter quietly. "Revenge is an inhuman word," at least that's what Seneca the Younger wrote. You sought revenge and in so doing lost your humanity."

"It fell to me and other patriots to right an inequity. We knew it would take years, a generation even, but I planned patiently. I created the circumstances to legitimise our claim to reunite Punjab.

You should understand that everything that has happened followed as a consequence of Partition made more intense by the denigration of Islam that continues so virulently today. My purpose has been to redress an inhumane crime against my people, my nation and my God."

"Hmmm," commented Peter. "I suspect we could argue all day about the rights and wrongs and the political miscalculations and errors of historical decisions, but your justification that the end vindicates the means is not acceptable. Most people, wherever they live in the world, and I include the majority of Muslims, want to live their lives in peace, they do not share your outrage. But they do understand that it is the desire for revenge that leads to suffering and destruction.

"Your hatred and thirst for revenge could have brought a continent to the brink of war. Had your plan succeeded you would have released an inhuman monster; a creature that has no regard for civilisation or humanity, which corrupts and consumes moral codes and ensures the constraints of the rule of law and civil order are stripped away. Your ambition, had you been successful, would have resulted in death and destruction on an unimaginable scale and decades of suffering. Revenge only breeds revenge."

Peter looked deep into the eyes of *The Colonel* and addressed him directly; "The reason I lead my life as I do is because I am not playing a game of chess. I am the gatekeeper who devotes all his energy to protecting his people and guarding them against those like you who wish to create a world in which peace and order are subservient only to your will. I protect my people against those who justify violence and destruction in pursuit of their own ambitions in the guise of righteousness. I defend the innocent and uphold the rule of law. You claim to have acted in the name of patriotism and religion, but you did so with no regard to humanity. I have my answer."

He rose from his chair, reclaimed his hat and without further comment left the room while the old man remained seated staring at the door as it closed behind his visitor.

*

The Colonel sat for a long while deep in contemplation and then sighed aloud. He felt dejected. "Why," he asked himself, "Does such a rational man refuse to distinguish justice from injustice and right from wrong? A fairer world could have been created and the great blasphemy redressed."

He rose from his chair wanting some fresh air. Choosing a suitable coat, he left the grand house breathing in the alpine air in deep lungfuls. Victory had been stolen from him, but only narrowly, and when his story was eventually told then others would be inspired by his example. But for now, he was released from the obligations, danger and self-denial of those years, the constant struggle, the anxiety and relentless stress. All that had defined his existence since he was nine-years-old was over, and while the final outcome was bitterly disappointing he would live out what remained of his life in comfort and in peace.

Walking to the end of an adjacent field he looked across the meadows to a small chapel above which loomed the *Dent de Jaman,* the ragged wolf's tooth. He was unexpectedly filled with a sense of euphoria and serenity, so much so that he was not at first aware of a buzzing noise, as if from a swarm of bees or an electric razor. He turned, puzzled, and noticed something small flying towards him. He focused and looked more attentively, until, to his surprise, the flying machine stopped and hovered just above him. Fascinated he leaned upwards and looked more curiously; at which moment a vapour was discharged that he could not avoid inhaling. It was only when his chest was gripped by the aconite, as if by a belt that tightened when he tried to take a breath, that he realised what had happened. He never saw the drone bank to the left and disappear back down the mountain.

The smartly dressed man approached the station and mingled with a small group waiting for the train to make its return journey down the mountain. At first he was absorbed by his thoughts and only mildly conscious of the loud clanking coming from the alpine bells that hung around the necks of the cows that wandered slowly and contentedly across the field to his right. 'Bells,' he thought. 'Bells that enable the farmer to protect his herd and keep them safe.'

The jolting, shuddering journey down the mountain to Montreux was as spectacular as the ascent had been and he spent the time observing the other passengers in the carriage, watching them as they went about their innocent, ordinary, unremarkable lives.

When he emerged from the train, he looked back up the mountain and raised his hat, as if in farewell.

Delivery

Clemmie was in agony, rolling waves of clenching muscle spasms were overwhelming her, contractions so severe that they blotted out all coherence. In moments of cogency between convulsions she convinced herself the twins were fighting to be born first. It had been straightforward with Iphy who had slipped easily into the world, her arrival rapid and relatively pain free, but these two were determined to do battle with their mother and inflict as much damage as possible. Clemmie's labour had already lasted hours beyond what she thought she could endure, and despite summoning her most malevolent vocabulary to hurl at the obstetrician he had only just agreed to a caesarean.

As she was being prepped for theatre the midwife checked the foetal monitors again and noted that both babies were becoming distressed. She called the doctor who examined Clemmie once again, but what none of the medical team knew was that in their efforts to escape confinement, one of the twins had struggled so forcefully that the sac of their mother's uterus had developed a small tear which was allowing amniotic fluid to enter her bloodstream.

At the same time as the surgeon prepared to operate Clemmie's body was transporting fluid to her lungs that made the arteries constrict. In consequence her heart started to beat at an unusually fast rate and with an irregular rhythm.

As Clemmie arrived in the operating theatre she went into

cardiac arrest. The medical team gave CPR and attached a defibrillator. The consultant did not hesitate, injecting adrenaline immediately and making an incision through which to deliver both infants, knowing that the escape of amniotic fluid invariably results in the formation of a fatal embolism. In less than two minutes both babies entered the world safely and were breathing normally, at which point the doctor applied all his skill to saving the life of the mother, but to no avail. After twenty minutes the team agreed that no more could be done, and the doctor called the time of death. Two noisy, bonny little babies, the first wrapped in a pink blanket and the second in blue, gurgled away in a cot beside the inert body of their mother.

Aegisthus had been waiting near to the delivery room and it was here that John Summers, the consultant who had struggled to save Clemmie's life joined him. Mr Summers described the sequence of medical events resulting in Clemmie's sad death and went so far as to comment that, "The only brightness on this dark night is that your children have survived."

Sometime later as Aegisthus looked down upon the tiny infants in his arms he said aloud, "I claim the right to name these children. The first will be known as Electra and her brother, Orestes."

Northumberland

England

Peter invited William and Helen to join him for a couple of weeks shooting, golfing, rambling and recuperating on his estate in Northumberland.

The days passed pleasantly and were relaxed, just what Helen needed to recover from the emotional after effects of the recent attempt on her life and ten months of captivity. She was still convalescing and had yet to come to terms with the violent deaths of close friends Henry and Cassie, as well as the shocking sense of bereavement she experienced at the news of the death of her twin sister.

The golf had been rusty but invigorating, with both Helen and William pledging to spend more time reducing their handicaps.

The shooting had been therapeutic. Helen had brought with her the precious Holland & Holland Leda had passed on to her and it accompanied them when they wandered around the country estate. She had as good an eye as her mother and as each bird approached, she imagined the face of one of her captors. With every discharge she uttered a name and unerringly the bird was downed. One afternoon, to her great delight, she accounted for a bigger bag than her husband, a trained soldier, and she could not resist teasing him. He took her good-natured ribbing in his stride.

And so their time on the estate proved restorative. Uncle Peter was the most wonderful host; ubiquitously good-humoured and solicitous for Helen's well-being, and she began to relax and heal.

With William at her side she was happy for he brought her the contentment and security that allowed her emotional scars to mend, and as the days unfolded, she recognised that Uncle Peter was also gently assisting in her recovery. When she thought about it, he had always occupied a special niche in her life with his regular visits to *Swan's Nest* over the years of her childhood, accompanied by laughter and happiness. He had also brought warmth, generosity and love into their lives. *Swan's Nest* had felt like a family home when he was there. Now Peter and Leda seemed almost inseparable and Helen had hopes that following her parents' impending divorce the two would find happiness together.

One evening, when Helen and William were sitting in the drawing room after dinner, she asked her husband for a favour. "I have spoken to you of Ayesha, she was such a rock during my dark days, and I don't know how I would have coped without her kindness, she illuminated the path of hope for me. I would like to invite her to England where I can look after her, should she wish to leave India. You never know we might be in need of an ayah soon!"

"Of course, my darling," promised William. "Let's go and ask her together."

This was William and Helen's first visit to Peter's estate, and they were enchanted by Northumberland with its steep hills, tors, lanes, stone walls and richly green pastures. On some days they rose early in the mornings and greeted by the rising sun and mists of an early summer countryside, set about roaming local villages and byways, stopping for a ploughman's lunch somewhere in a local pub before returning home tired but not exhausted.

At Peter's request William never mentioned the older man's involvement in the rescue and as far as Helen was concerned it had been a military team that organised the raid and rescued her, a unit led by her saviour.

On their last evening, and following a relaxed and intimate dinner, Peter asked William and Helen to join him in his study where he had a legal document laid out on the large rosewood desk.

Helen had not visited the room before and was instantly captivated by the books, clocks, charts, and pipes - briars and Meerschaum - of different shapes and sizes. She had not known Peter to smoke, but noticed a humidifier, beside which was a personalised cigar cutter and a box of swan vesta matches. On the sideboard was a picture of Peter in his regalia as Knight of the Garter standing beside the monarch.

Captivated by the ambience she felt compelled to soak in the detail and wanted to absorb the atmosphere that so embodied Peter. Tucked away was a sound system with wireless speakers and as her finger passed idly across the iPod music started to play. The rich, deep, bass resonance of a cello, as if oak aged, floated around the room and for a few minutes all three listened intently while the rising and falling cadences of *Le Cygne* glided around them until the last note reverberated to silence. The mood was serene.

Her attention was drawn to a pen and ink drawing hanging on the wall to the right of the door, cleverly lit by a pencil spotlight. She recognised it immediately for her mother had been captivated by it when they first came across it at an exhibition in New York. Drawn with charcoal, pen and ink it depicted the mythological Leda lying naked in the intimate embrace of Zeus disguised as a swan. Her hair loosely coiled she is naked and there is rapture as she grips the swan tightly. His wing is wrapped around her protectively, tenderly.

Helen stared at the picture and William heard her quote, '*A shudder in the loins engenders there the broken wall, the burning roof and tower and Agamemnon dead.*'

She remembered what her mother had said at the time, "The relationship between Leda and the Swan is usually portrayed as one of violation, but I have always thought there would have been tenderness in their lovemaking. After all Zeus makes her immortal and their daughter, Helen, is so very beautiful, which is why you were named after her."

"Did my mother give you this?" Helen asked Peter.

"It was a birthday present and is one of my most precious possessions."

Scattered around the room on occasional tables and shelves were books covering a wide range of subjects reflecting a diverse mixture of interests and tastes. Rooms like this appeal to the senses, she thought, as she picked up a calf-leather covered volume and flicked through the pages before bending forward to inhale its distinctive smell. Moving further around the room she ran her fingers over the ancient walnut panelling, and paused beside an adjustable nineteenth century mahogany reading table with brass inlay. Glancing down she saw the book title, *A Tale of Two Cities*, open at the last page and she could not stop herself from reading aloud:

'*It is a far, far better thing that I do, than I have ever done; it is a far, far better rest that I go to than I have ever known*'. "Sydney Carton," she said in a whisper, "His love and sacrifice for Lucie was such an act of sacrifice and devotion."

William looked at her and noticed a tear trickling down her cheek. "Ifty's love was the same," she whispered. "There's been so much hurt and pain." William pulled her towards him and held her tight.

Peter coughed quietly and said, "Actually I have not brought you here tonight to discuss literature, I have in mind another matter altogether.

"The last few days have been delightful and have confirmed for me that you are both very special, the son and daughter I never quite had. I want to share with you the content of my Last Will and Testament, for, as you know, I have never married.

"William, I have nominated you as the sole beneficiary of my estates, lands and titles. It is my hope that when you are ready you will take up residence here with me to breathe life back into the old place, there is plenty of room, and it is my dearest wish that between you, you will oversee and manage the estate. On my death, William, you will become the Marquis of Northumbria. I know that my trust is not misplaced, and I am sure that together you will use the wealth and influence at your disposal wisely and responsibly and for the good of all those who depend upon you. After your death the title and lands will pass to your first-born child, and thus my familial line will continue unbroken."

Helen slipped her hand out of William's and walked around the side of the desk to where Peter stood, and she placed her arms around his neck. She reached up on tiptoe and whispered, "Thank you, Daddy."

EPILOGUE

On the evening of their wedding, Peter and Leda walked hand in hand from *Swan's Nest* down to the river and, as if waiting to bid them farewell, were two white swans preparing to take flight.

As the noble birds rose in intersecting circles they looked down and appeared to salute, perhaps in benediction, before ascending into the heavens.

CLASSICAL BACKGROUND

Zeus, the leader of the Immortals lusts after Leda and falls into her lap disguised as a swan. They make love. Leda is married to Tyndareus, with whom she has sex on the night of her union with Zeus to disguise the paternity of the child engendered during her adulterous lovemaking. Tyndareus is King of Sparta and becomes putative father to the twins Helen and Clytemnestra, the progeny of Zeus and Leda.

Helen grows to be the most beautiful woman in the world described by Phrygius as '*Beautiful, ingenuous, and charming. Her legs were the best; her mouth the cutest...*'

Her father requires her to marry Menelaus and so she becomes the Queen of Laconia a province of Sparta. Menelaus has won Helen's hand in a competition organised by her father when numerous suitors were invited to contend for her as the prize. Concerned that the competition might descend into conflict Tyndareus persuades all the competitors to sign an oath of mutual military assistance. Helen's sister, Clytemnestra, is married to Menelaus's brother, Agamemnon, and they have three children, Iphigenia, Electra, and a son Orestes.

Paris, a Trojan prince promised the most beautiful woman in the world by Aphrodite, visits Sparta and seduces Helen after her wedding. She either elopes with him, or is abducted, and is taken to Troy. Menelaus calls upon all the other suitors to fulfil their oath, and thus begin the Trojan wars that last for ten blood-soaked years.

The Trojans are finally defeated, by the device of an enormous horse sculpture presented by the Spartans, ostensibly as a gift, but which contains soldiers who, in the middle of the night, emerge to open the gates and allow the invaders to capture the city. Paris is killed and Helen returns to Menelaus. Many heroes fight in the wars, most notably, Hector and Achilles.

Clytemnestra's story is relevant to Helen's because Agamemnon has promised to assist his brother sailing a fleet to Troy, but the fleet is becalmed, and Agamemnon prays to the gods for assistance. Help is available but only if Agamemnon sacrifices his daughter, Iphigenia. The sacrifice takes place, a crime that Clytemnestra can never begin to forgive or forget.

While Agamemnon is away in Troy, Clytemnestra starts an affair with the brutal Aegisthus and they plot to revenge Iphigenia's killing.

Eventually Agamemnon returns from Troy with Cassandra, his paramour, and they are both murdered. In turn Clytemnestra is killed by her son, Orestes, encouraged by his sister Electra.

Revenge spirals onwards resulting in acts of vengeance that confirm the long-held assertion of a Greek stoic that revenge is an inhuman word.

ABOUT THE AUTHOR

As a seven-year-old boy I fell under the spell of an inspiring teacher who would tell tales from ancient Greece on Friday afternoons. I longed for those stories with a passion.

Often absent from school I spent many months in Great Ormond Street Hospital, where it was fiction that first opened the door to the world of my imagination. By sharing in the lives and worlds of my heroes their reality subsumed my own.

I graduated with a degree in English literature and became a teacher.

I didn't think I had a novel in me until one day, standing in the birthplace of Zeus in Crete, an idea began to tumble into place. I started to write, and a few months later completed my first novel, *Lifelonging*, based on the story of Theseus and the Minotaur.

The format of placing an ancient story in a modern context worked and so I chose the same model when I came to write *An Inhuman Word*. In the Iliad Homer explores how human nature falls prey to human weakness, a notion that fascinates me also.

When writing I try to be true to the experience that caught my imagination as a boy, to the thrill of adventure and the joy of reading. I aim to write books that gather up the reader and compel them to keep going to the end, while also leaving some food for thought.

Also by Michael Spinney:

Lifelonging

Printed in Great Britain
by Amazon

78773788R00190